What Readers Are Saying about Previous Books by

Ginny Aiken

"Captivating. I became a part of the story as it was unfolding."
   —Jean Klusmeier, Pennsylvania

"Couldn't put it down! Ginny Aiken can tell a good story."
   —Carole McAllaster, California

"Terrific. I laughed and I cried. But mostly, I just fell in love."
   —Kay Allen, Oklahoma

"Wonderful. A novel with heart and soul involved."
   —Shirene Broadwater

"Helped me through a bad time. I needed your wit and fun to help bring be out of it."
   —KG

"Great book—thoroughly enjoyed each page! Easy to read, never slow, great plot."
   —Cyndy Roggeman, Michigan

"Loved your characters. So much heart and emotion, not to mention an engaging story line."
   —MM

HEART
QUEST®

HeartQuest brings you romantic fiction
with a foundation of biblical truth.
Adventure, mystery, intrigue, and suspense
mingle in these heartwarming stories of
men and women of faith striving to build
a love that will last a lifetime.

May HeartQuest books sweep you
into the arms of God, who longs for you
and pursues you always.

Magnolia

GINNY AIKEN

HEART
QUEST®

Romance fiction from
Tyndale House Publishers, Inc.
WHEATON, ILLINOIS

To my sister,
Lou Schmitz, with whom, by the grace of God,
I have a wonderful relationship.

Acknowledgments

GRATITUDE AND THANKS TO:

My Lord Jesus	*—you are sufficient always.*
Claudia Cross	*the best agent on earth.*
Becky Nesbitt, Kathy Olson, and Jan Pigott	*editors extraordinaire.*
Ramona Cramer Tucker	*—you know why!*
Peggy Stoks	*for the years of sisterhood and her willlingness to read under fire.*
Karl Fieldhouse and Monica Doerfler	*for their constant support.*
Jeri Odell and Beth White	*for their friendship.*
George Ivan, Gregory, Geoffrey, and Grant Anikienko	*the four best sons a mother could want.*

And as always, to my husband, George,
who never bargained for a writer as a wife.

I will give you treasures hidden in the darkness—secret riches.
I will do this so you may know that I am the Lord,
the God of Israel, the one who calls you by name.

Isaiah 45:3

O N E

Bellamy, Loudon County, Virginia; Present Day

"I CAN'T BELIEVE I DID THAT," MAGNOLIA BELLAMY muttered, holding the telephone to her chest.

She'd just hired a carpetbagger—to restore a treasure of the Confederacy. Everything in Maggie told her she'd done nothing but rain an upset applecart of trouble down on her head.

Sighing, she cradled the receiver, then swiveled her office chair. Out the window behind her desk she saw early harbingers of spring: the warm-as-sunshine forsythia blossoms that rioted against the redbrick wall of the Bellamy Post Office across the street. Too bad she didn't feel half as perky as those flowers looked.

Her intercom buzzed. "Yes?"

"Miss Louella is here to see you," Ruby Fulkes, her stout, eagle-eyed, and efficient secretary at the Bellamy Fiduciary Trust, announced. "Since your office door is still closed, I didn't know if I should ask her to wait."

"Send her in."

She might as well get the unpleasantness over. Maggie doubted the born-south-of-the-Mason-Dixon-line Louella

1

Ashworth would relish a Yankee running the restoration of her family home and greatest treasure any more than Maggie did. But there wasn't much either truehearted Southern woman could do. Not after the phone call she'd just made.

"Mornin', honey," said the well-preserved sixty-eight-year-old as she entered Maggie's office. "I finished my hour of glowin' at the Fem Physique, and I thought I'd see what you'd decided."

Maggie gave her friend—and client—a weak smile and waved her into the leather wing chair across from her desk. "How was your workout?"

Miss Louella shrugged. "Same as always. Still and all, it doesn't do a girl any good to let herself go."

"You're a perfect illustration of your conviction. Why, you don't look a day over forty."

Narrowing her large gray eyes, Miss Louella cocked her chestnut-haired head. "Now, honey, I've known you all your near twenty-six years. And I know you're not particularly interested in my old five-foot-nine-inch bod. What are you mealymouthin' about?"

A blush heated Maggie's cheeks. After all, she'd only acted in Miss Louella's best interests—business interests, that is. Taking a deep breath, she plunged forward. "It's like this, Miss Louella. You know I was going to interview five architectural restorers, don't you?"

Miss Louella nodded.

"Well, three were Southerners, and two were Yankees. It turns out that . . . you see . . . this is somewhat hard to say . . ."

Miss Louella's lips pursed. "So, honey, just tell me you hired a Yankee and be done with it."

Maggie's jaw dropped. "How'd you know?"

"I'm no fool. If you hadn't had distasteful news, you'd never have waffled like that. What I want to know is why our Southern boys didn't win that bid."

It was Maggie's turn to shrug. "One Yankee was insuffer-able, so I discounted him right away. And each of our South-erners had something not quite right. One didn't have the experience I felt we needed. Another lacked the proper credentials. And the last had references I couldn't check. You know how important I consider this project."

Miss Louella responded solemnly, "Ours is an honorable cause."

"I know. And I tried—*really* tried—to hire someone born and bred in the South, someone who would respect the Ashworth Mansion as it deserves. Someone who would understand the importance of returning your home to its original splendor."

"You couldn't see fit to hire any of our boys? None of them?"

"Not a one, Miss Louella. Not in good conscience. Not when I had Mr. Clayton Marlowe's résumé right next to theirs." She extended the files to her client. "I hired the carpetbagger—against my better judgment."

Miss Louella's brow creased as she turned her attention to the files, running canny eyes over their contents.

Maggie's antique schoolhouse clock ticked loud enough to beat the band as she kept her peace, waiting for Louella's answer.

Finally Miss Louella slapped the files back on Maggie's desk. "Shameful, purely shameful. Why, we should be preparin' our boys here in the South better'n that. Imagine havin' to go north to find us a good candidate." After much dire shaking of her head, she pinned Maggie with a gimlet stare. "So, girl, what are you fixin' to do about it?"

Maggie felt the urge to squirm under the pointed perusal. But instead, she straightened, determined to prove herself more hardy than the fragile magnolia she'd been named after and most folks figured her to be.

3

"I mean to keep the sharpest buzzard eye on that man. Nothing is going to get past me."

Seeing Miss Louella's confused frown, Maggie rushed on. "As the officer in charge of your construction loan at Bellamy Fiduciary Trust, it's my job and duty to do so. As a loyal Daughter of the Confederacy, it's my honor to do so."

Miss Louella's gray gaze raked over Maggie's curls, then her face. "I have to wonder, girl, if a wily Yankee scalawag won't be too much for you to handle, as fragile as you are."

Stung to the core, Maggie gasped. "Why, Miss Louella, I never figured you thought so poorly of me." She rose to her full five-foot-one height. "You know perfectly well that looks can be mighty deceiving. Just you watch. I'm going to hound that man as if he were the last fox in town. No wily Yankee carpetbagger is going to steal you blind and leave you holding the wool over your own eyes."

Moments later, without a hint of an apology, Miss Louella left. Maggie again looked out the window and watched her friend march down Bellamy's busy Main Street.

Oh, yes, she was going to dog that Yankee. Just let him try and make a right-on-red at her no-turn corner. He'd learn mighty quick what Magnolia Bellamy's delicate Southern-belle features hid: steely determination.

🌿

"You look satisfied," Grant Smith said, taking a seat on the leather couch in Clay Marlowe's parlor.

Clay closed the front door. "And well I should," he said, crossing the small foyer of his one-hundred-fifty-year-old home with his usual long strides to join his attorney and friend. "I just got hired."

"Where are you going this time?"

"Not far. Small town in western Virginia. Up in the hills. Bellamy's the name."

"Beautiful country out that way."

After working closely with Grant for the past eight years, Clay had come to read him well. "That didn't sound like a rousing endorsement."

"Bellamy may be only a few miles away from us, but trust me, the distance between Gettysburg, Pennsylvania, and a small Virginia town is greater than what your odometer measures."

"What do you mean?"

The leather squeaked as Grant shifted and removed his steel-rimmed glasses. "Ever been down there?"

"No."

The lawyer said sagely, "That explains it. You need to know that too many of those folks are still fighting the Civil War. They don't look kindly on Northerners."

Clay snorted. "Give me a break. The war's nearly as old as my house. That's long enough for them to get over losing."

"Don't even think that, or you'll be sunk."

"Whatever," Clay said, shaking his head in disbelief. "Anyway, this is going to be a great job. Want to see the pictures?"

Grant took the proffered glossies. "Good grief, Clay!" he said at his first glimpse of the Ashworth Mansion. "Do you think you can salvage this mess?"

Clay chuckled. "Looks bad, doesn't she? But I'll tell you what. Even though she was abandoned years ago, she's a mess with a world of promise." He waved at his friend and counselor. "Go on. Look at the other pictures before you dismiss her."

He rose from his easy chair and sat by Grant, jabbing a blunt fingertip at the next snapshot. "Check the delft tiles around the fireplace. They're magnificent and irreplaceable. Worth saving."

At Grant's uncertain expression, Clay took the handful of photos, flipped through them, and chose another. "If only for these incredible stained-glass windows the house deserves to be restored." One more print. "Look at the hand-plastered walls in the dining room. See those bumpy things? They're friezes. Workmanship like that is rare. So are the Irish-crystal chandeliers and the mahogany woodwork. This house is just begging me to pretty her up."

"Better you than me," Grant said with mixed admiration. "I still can't figure out why you like fixing rotted wrecks."

"I love what I do, and I'm good at it," Clay said simply. "And you know I always give value for my pay."

"That's true. Not like—"

"Hal Hinkley."

"You got it. I guess it's a good thing you were hired and not Hinkley."

Clay sighed. "I praise God for that. The Ashworth had a narrow escape. Hal bid on her too. I had to turn in a low bid to get the job, but I couldn't let that scum ruin another old home."

"Can you bring it in under budget?"

Clay ran a hand down the back of his neck. "I won't make it under on this one. As it is, I'll have to work hard to stay within budget. Pray a lot too. But you know I have the experience to pull it off."

Grant assented, and his prematurely gray hair caught the light from the turn-of-the-century art lamp by his side. "I have the last eight years' worth of contracts, and you've showed me satisfied-customer letters to prove it. But why did you put yourself in this tough of a work situation? You've been turning down jobs left and right for years now. Why'd you take on this particular one?"

"The Ashworth's a gorgeous house," Clay said, grinning sheepishly. "I couldn't resist. Besides, like I said, I don't want to see another century home trashed. Remember the scandal over the Bigsby restoration?"

Grant winced. "Who in this area doesn't? It's too bad the owners couldn't get the charges against Hinkley to stick."

"You can't get a thing to stick to slime. And that's what someone who does shoddy work and uses poor-quality materials is. Pure slime. Last I heard the house is falling down around the Bigsbys."

"And the warranty's run out."

"Of course. The day after it did, the plaster began chunking off the ceilings."

"The guy's still out there scamming customers. I'll bet he wasn't happy to learn you were bidding against him."

"You got that right. And even less happy when he learned I got the job. He called this morning. I guess the banker, Magnolia Bellamy—can you believe that Southern name?—phoned the others before me."

"Any pithy comments from Hinkley?"

"Oh, yeah. The man has a gift for true eloquence. He said—and I quote—that he was going to show those dumb hillbillies they'd made a mistake by not hiring him."

"He would have gone over swell in small-town Virginia."

With a wave, Clay dismissed his rival. "I'm just glad for the challenge. I love a tough one, you know."

Grant rolled his eyes. "What about this Magnolia Blossom you'll be working with? What's she like?"

"Bellamy, Magnolia Bellamy. She sounded coolly efficient on the phone—as least as much as a pure, melted-honey, Southern accent can sound. But I've never had a problem with a banker. I'm sure we'll work well together."

Grant lifted an eyebrow. "You versus a Southern belle. Mmm . . . might be interesting."

Clay rose, energized by his desire to start the new project. "Who cares about the banker? I'm just glad I can spare Miss

Louella Ashworth the trouble Hal's last employers had. I can guarantee her satisfaction. Nothing's going to happen to her house while I'm there."

❧

Today Maggie would meet the carpetbagger, a short seven days after she'd hired him. She hated even the thought of it. For goodness' sake, her job could very well depend on the outcome of his efforts.

Despite the eight years she'd worked at the Bellamy Fiduciary Trust, Maggie knew that Mitchell Hollings, the bank's president, took her at face value—*her* fragile-featured face. Why, she suspected he even thought that her pale blonde hair's lack of vivid color demonstrated a similar lack of gray matter in her brain cells.

She was tired of Mr. Hollings's inane assignments. He routinely assigned her the most ridiculous accounts—those he believed wouldn't amount to much and wouldn't cost the bank much should she fail. Like the Bellamy Community Church's loan for a new steeple. How many upright congregations had interesting, challenging business dealings? The BCC had borrowed the money, had the steeple built, and paid the loan. Ahead of schedule.

"I'm going to make sure this Marlowe fellow brings in this project under budget," she promised herself. It was the least she could do. After all, Miss Louella had not another penny squirreled away in her egg-poor nest. She couldn't afford to make some hotshot Yankee any richer than he already was.

Maggie had the sneaky suspicion that now that Clay Marlowe had the job, he'd start nickel-and-diming the minute he stepped foot in the mansion. Demanding an enlarged budget to line his pockets, of course.

But he'd have her—Magnolia Bellamy—to deal with first.

The intercom crackled to life. "He's here," Ruby hissed. So much for Maggie's warning to act normal.

Pressing the Talk button, she stood. "Show him in." She then rounded her desk, straightened her pale green linen skirt, and tugged down the peplum of the matching jacket.

The door opened. One look at the Yankee and Maggie had to fight to keep the dismay from groaning out of her.

The man towered over her, filling the doorway. From his wavy brown hair to the tips of daunting black boat shoes, he probably measured seven feet, if not more—NBA material for sure, she thought. His unusual gold-colored eyes opened wide, and his mouth gaped to match. He hadn't been expecting someone like her—*that* was clear.

How on earth was she going to keep that giant's toes from creeping over the line when even his little one could squash her flat?

Well, she'd just have to take control of the situation. "Come in, Mr. Marlowe," she said, pretending not to notice his unflattering reaction to her and ignoring her unnerving response to him.

The large man let his mouth creep up on one side. "Thank you. It's a pleasure to meet you, Ms. Bellamy." He extended a hand toward her.

"*Miss* Bellamy, if you please." She took the paw with a certain qualm, which proved all too valid when he wrapped her fingers in his warm, work-roughened clasp.

Ooo-eee! This man was trouble. All of him—cat gold eyes, brawn, and gentle, manly grasp. Her hands were certainly going to be full with this fine kettle of Northern fish.

Discreetly she reclaimed her hand. "Please take a seat. We have much to talk about before you start the job."

His powerful, athletic stride brought him to the antique leather wing chair Miss Louella had occupied only a week earlier when Maggie had broken the distasteful news to her. Would the chair support that much man?

When it didn't collapse under him, Maggie stepped back behind her desk. Taking her seat, she met his gaze. "I hope you understand this is a significant project."

"Oh?"

"Why, yes. The Ashworth Mansion is a treasure of the Confederacy."

His mouth quirked up a hair more. "How's that?"

"Well, Mr. Marlowe—"

"Clay."

Maggie arched an eyebrow. "Not very formal, are you?"

"Formal went out with the last century, *Miss* Bellamy. Call me Clay."

Something about the way he said her name made Maggie feel he was making fun of her, yet no smirk marred his handsome face, no chuckle rumbled out with his words. She decided that paranoia might be flying over this cuckoo's nest.

"Very well, then. Clay it is. Where were we? Oh, yes. We were discussing the importance of this historical treasure. Why, the Ashworths entertained Stonewall Jackson overnight, right within those very walls. It's a testament to the Confederacy, I'll have you know."

His eyes twinkled, and this time she saw him fight to keep his lips from curving further.

She fixed a reproving glare on him. "I see you hold our past's treasures in contempt, Mr. Marlowe."

"Clay. And I do no such thing. It's just . . . a friend warned me that many Southerners think they're still fighting the Civil War."

Maggie again rose. "You *do* mean the Great War of Northern Aggression, don't you?"

When he bit down on his lip, Maggie *knew* he was laughing at *her*.

Paranoia was not her problem. The carpetbagger was. For someone who always functioned at a disadvantage on account of her height, blonde hair, and blue eyes, laughter at her expense didn't sit any better with her than a lead balloon did. "Perhaps we hired the wrong man. It's not too late to call another candidate. We haven't signed any contracts yet."

That sobered the yucking Yankee. He straightened in the chair. "You don't want to do that, Miss Bellamy. I am the right man for the job."

"Not without a flyspeck of respect for what you're about to partake in."

He blinked at her words. "I have a lot of admiration and consideration for the homes I work on. I take my work seriously. I just don't take *myself* too seriously."

"And you're saying I do?" she said defensively.

"Maybe a bit."

She gave him another once-over. "I can see working with you is going to present quite a challenge."

Clay smiled mischievously. "Funny. I was thinking the same about you."

Irked by his attitude, Maggie forced herself back into her chair. "I believe we need to discuss how we will handle matters."

"Fair enough."

Maggie picked up the contract the bank's attorney had drawn up. "You report to me, Mr. Marlowe—"

"Clay."

"Of course. Nothing happens at the mansion without my approval. Do you understand?"

He stared at her, then nodded curtly.

Maggie saw that he hadn't liked her condition, but it couldn't be helped. She had too much riding on this account. Maggie continued. "I'll disburse funds as the restoration goes forward. And I must warn you ahead of time: there is absolutely no budge-room in this budget. Miss Louella cannot squeeze another penny out of her turnip. Do you understand?"

A disgusted look drew a furrow between his dark brows. "What? Budge-rooms or turnips? Or that you're going to hold the purse strings tightly?"

"I believe we understand each other," she answered, wondering if the understanding would extend to the next item on her agenda. If he was anything like most other contractors she'd come across, he was going to squawk louder'n a peacock on the prowl.

"The final condition I must impose," she said firmly, "is about the key. I'll be keeping it at all times."

"Impossible!" he erupted. "I can't work that way."

"Then you're not the right man for the job."

"Of course I am, but what you're suggesting is ridiculous."

"I'm not suggesting. I'm telling you how it's going to be. And it's not ridiculous. I'll meet you at the site every morning at seven o'clock, and I'll inspect the day's work before you finish for the night. There'll be no problem with doing things my way."

As she spoke, Clay Marlowe had begun to pace her office, his size and energy filling the room to capacity. Leashed power fueled his every move, his slightest gesture. Maggie found herself admiring the man.

"Oh, flapjacks!" she murmured. She couldn't afford to admire him. She had to maintain control of the situation. She had to ensure the success of the account. She had to make sure the Ashworth Mansion was returned to its former glory. It was the least a daughter of the South could do for its posterity.

Finally Clay drew to a stop before her desk. He leaned over and planted ham-sized fists on the gleaming, hundred-year-old walnut top. "Fine. I'll play it your way. But if you cause us a problem, a delay, or a cost overrun, it'll be up to you to fix it. I won't be charged with whatever your whims cost the job."

When he'd first leaned over her, Maggie's breath had caught in her throat. His eyes had burned with passion, determination. His indignation had rushed from him in waves. His strength had radiated from the knotted muscles in his forearms.

Clay Marlowe was a force to be reckoned with.

So was Magnolia Bellamy.

It was just as well each recognized it from the start. She stood and stared him square in his golden eyes. "I'm so pleased you defer to reason, Mr. Marlowe—Clay. Now, I would think you'd like to see the mansion, wouldn't you? This is an excellent time for me to give you a tour. Will you follow me?"

As they left her office, she could have sworn the giant behind her was gnashing his teeth to a pulp. But since she wasn't his dentist, she paid his irritation no mind. She had a job to do, and she was going to do it.

Minutes later, Clay hung on to the door handle of the cobalt Miata as if his life depended on it. Which it probably did.

Not only had he had to fold himself into a small package to fit into the tiny vehicle, but now the Magnolia blossom next to him was driving like a raving maniac.

"Gorgeous day, isn't it?" she asked in that thick, leisurely accent of hers as she screeched to a stop in front of the mansion.

After a few seconds and a couple of deep breaths, Clay's heart slowed from its recent hummingbird beat to something resembling human. He popped open the Miata's door, desperate to stretch his abused joints. "If you say so."

"Why, of course it is!" she exclaimed. At least that's what Clay assumed she said. "Just look at all that yummy sunshine and the bulbs beginning to show," she expounded. Only to Clay, her words sounded more like, "Jes look a'tall th'yummy sunshahn, an' th' bulbs beginnin' ta show."

He made a noncommittal sound, just to let her know he'd heard her enthusiasm, then focused on working the Miata-induced kinks from his body.

Miss Bellamy continued, clearly oblivious to his condition. "There it is, Mr. Marlowe. The Ashworth Mansion."

Clay craned his neck to see . . . and froze. The reality of the house was worse than even the most graphic photograph had portrayed. He inventoried missing shingles and broken windows, a sagging porch with flaking paint, and a shutter on an upstairs window that creaked as it flapped listlessly in the breeze.

Even in its state of disrepair, however, Clay couldn't help but admire the home. The Victorian flourishes that embellished the structure might have struck some as excessive, but not him. He'd always enjoyed the whimsy of turned wood and turrets, of decorative trim that wasn't necessary but beautiful.

He considered those touches representative of life. One always had to deal with the necessities, but it was a pleasure and a blessing to acquire the extra bits that made life more enjoyable. Not lavish extravagances, of course—those simply wasted God's provision. But the details that brought enrichment into people's daily existence, in Clay's mind, were part of the joy God meant for his children to experience.

The Ashworth Mansion had the requisite turret—added years after the original construction—its top covered in fish-scale shingles. Gracefully turned spindles edged the verandah, and where its supports met the roof, gingerbread curlicues—also a later addition—further softened the appearance of the structure.

He noticed the teak double doors with leaded glass. Then he saw it. *The* window. In the middle of the second story a circular stained-glass piece of art had retained its original magnificence and now captured his imagination. Against a sky blue backdrop a dove soared above a cloud, with the sun its triumphant background.

Freedom, Clay thought. That bird made him think of the freedom God gave Christians through his Holy Spirit. And for Clay, that kind of freedom and peace had been hard won. The fabulous window indeed looked out of place in its paint-bare frame.

Clay knew that, were his lawyer with him, Grant would urge him to flee from the site. But Clay had committed to restoring the wreck, and now, after finding the window, he knew he would see the project through. Besides, he'd given his word, and he always kept it.

"What do you think?" Miss Bellamy asked.

Clay gave her a wry grin. "A lesser man would be discouraged, so you're lucky you hired me."

"If you insist on demeanin' our treasure, then I'll have to consider our contract null—"

To Clay's relief, a shout cut her off. "Hey, Mag!" called the redheaded woman zipping by.

Miss Bellamy spun around, stiffened, then waved with half-hearted intent. "Hi, Lark."

Intrigued by her response to the greeting, Clay asked, "Who's that?"

"Curious, aren't we?" Maggie shot back.

When he shrugged, she said, "My older sister, if you must know."

"Hmm . . . you don't look at all alike."

Her taut stance grew a coat of ice. "So I've heard, Mr. Marlowe. Shall we?" She gestured toward the mansion, having effectively put him back in his place.

Or so she probably figured. Her reply only served to pique Clay's curiosity further. He just didn't know why.

In silence he followed Maggie up the steps to the verandah, his weight wresting creaks from the old planks. The risers would need replacing. He hoped the interior floors were in better condition, especially since he'd noticed the intricate parquetry in some of the photos Maggie had sent him and he'd rather preserve than replace.

"Do be careful comin' inside, Mr. Marlowe—"

"Please. I prefer to be called Clay. And you . . . ?"

He knew she wanted him to call her Miss Bellamy. Various expressions crossed her face as she struggled with his question. Finally she said, "Call me Maggie. If you must."

He bit back a laugh. That had cost her, more than he thought it should. Why? "Thank you. As you were saying?"

She grew flustered. "Oh! Yes. I suggest you watch your head as you come inside. The doorway's not built for men your height."

"Hmm . . . made 'em short, didn't they?"

Her eyes spit blue flames. "No shorter'n in the Union."

Grant *hadn't* been kidding. "Easy, there. I wasn't casting aspersions on your Confederacy. I only meant that men were shorter last century—as a general rule."

She gave him a top-to-toe look. "In this century they don't make them as tall as you. How tall *are* you?"

"Not that tall. I'm six-foot-four."

She studied his frame again. "Are you sure?"

He laughed.

She didn't.

"Of course I'm sure. Want my driver's license?"

She looked tempted but then waved dismissively. "Your height's not important—so long as you don't crash into the chandeliers and chip the crystal."

Clay chuckled again, amazed by what a Southern accent

did to a simple word like *chandelier.* Coming from Maggie
Bellamy's lips, it evoked lush images of elegant, sumptuous
evenings with music and romance. "I'll be extra careful
around your chandeliers, Maggie."

She whirled. "They're not mine—oh!"

With an ominous *crack,* the board beneath her feet sagged,
and she lost her balance. Time seemed to slow as Clay reached
out to catch her.

But petite, blonde, and blue-eyed Maggie Bellamy was
made of sterner stuff than that. She fought gravity with the
same dignity she wore like a mantle, and her sheer grit kept
her from crashing to the dirty floor. She pulled herself upright
and straightened her jacket.

"I'm quite all right—"

"Yoo-hoo! Maggie, dear. Ruby said you'd be here."

The woman's voice seemed to bolster Maggie, who met
Clay's gaze and smiled—for the first time since they'd met.

Clay felt as though someone had launched a missile attack
on his gut. What a punch the dainty lady carried! What a
transformation that smile performed on her beautiful features.
The lines of her face softened, sweetened, as if glowing from
inside. He wondered what it would be like to be the reason
for that smile.

He shook his head. He had to be nuts to think like that
about a woman as prickly as Maggie Bellamy.

"Come on in, Miss Louella," she called. "But be careful. I
nearly fell on a loose board."

"Oh, I know, honey," answered the newcomer as she closed
the front door. "This old house is showin' her age."

"Unlike some other ladies," Clay said, stepping forward to
offer his hand to the elegant woman. "Miss Ashworth, I
presume?"

Shrewd gray eyes evaluated him. "Aren't you a charmer?"

"Only honest."

"Let's hope you're as good at what you do as you are with that glib tongue, son."

Clay did something he hadn't done in years—he flushed.

Maggie laughed.

He coughed. "Miss Ashworth, you're a beautiful woman, just as your home is a beautiful house. I'm sure you're aware of both truths. It's a pleasure to meet you, and a welcome challenge to restore the Ashworth Mansion."

"Maggie, dear," Miss Louella said, turning to face her, "are you sure you didn't hire one of the Southern boys after all? One cursed with a Northern accent?"

Maggie-dear answered, irony in her voice. "Maybe the *boy's* full of Irish blarney."

"We're Scots, ma'am," Clay countered. "From the borderlands."

"And can a Scotsman bring life back to this gem of southern American gentility?" Miss Ashworth asked.

"It's what I do best," he answered.

"Not hardly," murmured Maggie.

"I hope so, son," said Miss Ashworth, ignoring Maggie, to Clay's relief. "Because I don't intend to lose the last of my inheritance on shoddy work."

"Trust me, Miss Ashworth. I know what I'm doing. I put my reputation on the line with every job."

"It's not your reputation you should worry about, Mr. Marlowe," said Maggie. "It's your vanished freedom that'll give you problems if you so much as think of pullin' a fast trick around here. I'll call the law down on you faster'n fleas can flick from dog to dog."

Maggie's words raised for Clay the only specter that could perturb his peace.

The threat of jail.

TWO

Did she know?

How could she?

Clay examined Maggie's face but found no indication of advance knowledge. She merely wore an expression of warning, of future trouble if she didn't get what she wanted. In this case, what any employer—or banker, he should say—wanted from an architectural restorer.

He cleared his throat. "You have my references, Miss Bellamy. You're welcome to phone my previous clients. They'll tell you I usually come in under budget and ahead of time. My work speaks for itself."

Clay determined to stand on God's promises of protection. Even if he still didn't understand why God had failed him that other time.

"Just a friendly warnin', Mr. Marlowe."

He raised an eyebrow. "If this is what Southern friends are like, Maggie—"

"For heaven's sake," said Miss Louella, "I want my family home rebuilt, not fought over like a bone between dogs.

Maggie, honey, you should have listened to me about Buford. He's not the one for you. You've taken to behavin' like him."

"Why, Miss Louella, Buford's perfect. Every time I look at his wrinkly face, I melt right into a puddle."

So the pretty banker liked older men. Much older men.

"Into a puddle of piddle, perhaps," retorted Miss Louella.

Good grief, and incontinent, too! Clay looked at Maggie with distaste. Was she so money oriented that she'd latched onto some kind of senile sugar daddy?

Maggie shook her head. "Let's leave Buford out of this, shall we? What matters is the Ashworth Mansion. And Mr. Marlowe's—"

"Look," Clay said, cutting her off, "I much prefer to be called Clay, and I hope you begin to do so." He turned to Miss Ashworth. "I'd be honored if you'd call me by my first name, too."

With a gracious nod, the older woman said, "And I'm Miss Louella to friends."

Southern through and through, he thought, *and hardly offering true friendship.* Clay was sure he was being tested. "Of course, Miss Louella. I value your trust, and I give you my word to do my best on your house. My boss expects no less of me."

"Your boss?" Maggie queried sharply. "I thought you worked independently."

He smiled. "My boss is a Jewish carpenter, and I do everything to honor him. A Christian can do no less."

"Or more," said Miss Louella, smiling. "Well, I'm mighty comforted to know that, despite your unfortunate birth north of the Mason-Dixon, you know what's really what. I feel much better knowin' a son of the Father will be fixin' my home."

He'd passed a test, if not yet graduated. "I'd appreciate your keeping me and my work in your prayers, ma'am."

"Of course."

With an impatient flick of her graceful hand, Maggie said, "On Sundays I'm sure *Clay* will want to join you for services at the BCC, Miss Louella. But here at the construction site what's goin' to count is what I can touch and see."

"Still a follower of Thomas, I see," Miss Louella added.

Tipping up her chin, Maggie answered, "I have my doubts." She then shot Clay a hostile look. "About *everythin'.*"

"It'll be my pleasure to dispel them," Clay countered. "All of them." *Is this woman's doubt why you brought me to Bellamy, Lord? Show me what I can do.*

A skeptical expression hardened Maggie's pretty face. "We shall see."

With perfunctory statements, she proceeded to guide him through the house. During the tour, Clay wondered why she'd bothered to hire him if she didn't want a Northerner here. He wasn't the only restorer around.

Then he remembered: Hal Hinkley.

At least she'd had the sense to hire him instead of Hal, Clay thought later, after refusing Maggie's offer of a ride. He preferred walking to his boardinghouse to endangering his life in her Miata again.

He hadn't driven to the bank earlier that day since he'd wanted to get acquainted with the town. Bellamy seemed a nice place, with its vintage business section and gracious brick and frame homes, many sporting porches shaded by tall, aged trees. The residents waved and smiled, although he couldn't help but wonder how long that friendliness would last after they heard his admittedly Northern accent.

Clay grinned. That Maggie Bellamy was something else. She really took her Southern roots—not to mention herself—seriously. He wondered what lay behind that controlled facade, that unexpected formality, that intense seriousness.

And her doubts about God.

Even during the time when he felt God had let him down, Clay still hadn't doubted God's majesty, his power. He had only wanted to know why. Why it had happened. Why to him. Even though he feared he'd never know . . . in this lifetime.

So why did Maggie doubt God?

Clay felt a surge of the curiosity that often challenged him as much as did the most fabulous historical wreck. It urged him to dig deeper, to get to know the pretty banker, to learn what made her tick.

And especially what might attract a beauty like Maggie Bellamy to a wrinkly, incontinent old man named Buford.

At 6 P.M. the tinkling of the widow Sprague's bell called Clay out of the nap he'd decided he needed after his initial encounter with Maggie Bellamy. By the time he'd returned to his boardinghouse, his head had been spinning.

So he'd spent some moments with God, mulling his experience over, then he'd given his body the rest for which it clamored. Now the bell and accompanying savory scents wafting into his room awoke a bodily clamor. Due to his eagerness to see the mansion, he'd missed lunch. His stomach was reminding him of that, with a vengeance.

He clattered down the stairs of the large home, pleased to note how well it had been maintained. Not quite as old as the Ashworth Mansion, Mrs. Sprague's house had been built around the turn of the century. While it was no mansion, it boasted of generous rooms, solid oak trim and banisters, and excellent, hand-plastered walls. This house was proof that top-quality original workmanship lasted through time.

In the dining room, he joined the other boarders at the oval table. Mrs. Sprague had said she had only him and two others at the moment.

"Hi," Clay said, holding out his hand to a teenage girl. "I'm Clay Marlowe."

The young woman blinked behind her large glasses. "I'm Suze McEntire. Pleased to meet you."

He shook her hand. "Pleasure's mine."

Turning, he pulled out the chair at the unclaimed place setting and acknowledged the older gentleman across the table. "Clay Marlowe," he repeated.

"How'd'ye do, son?" the slender man boomed in a surprisingly robust, non-Southern voice. "Willard Johnson— Willie—at your service."

Clay placed his napkin on his lap. "Dinner smells great."

Willie Johnson's blue eyes twinkled. "Don't let our landlady hear you call it dinner, son. It's supper in these parts."

Clay rolled his eyes. "Another of those unwritten Southern rules, then."

Willie nodded. "Meant to trip up a man."

"Seems local ladies like to do that."

"Ah, but they're the loveliest of women, and don't you forget it."

Suze bounced her gaze from man to man.

A swinging door opened and Mrs. Sprague appeared, bearing a large steaming platter. Thick slabs of pot roast bathed in dark, rich gravy covered its surface. Clay's stomach cheered the food's arrival—loudly.

Mrs. Sprague arched a delicate brown eyebrow. "Somethin' tells me you're hungry, Mr. Marlowe."

The gesture struck Clay as familiar, even though he knew he'd never met the woman until that morning when he'd checked in. "No need for the tact. I'm starved, and I'll admit my stomach has no manners."

"Then let me serve you first," Mrs. Sprague offered.

"No, please. Beauty and age before uncouth." He gestured toward Suze and Willie in turn.

A smile tipped his landlady's lips. "Oh, mercy, we have a Northern charmer here."

"No, ma'am. Just a man whose mother made sure he learned some manners—unlike his stomach."

Willie chuckled. "I'll bet that learning was done by means of a wooden spoon across the bottom and soap across the tongue."

"Something like that."

After Mrs. Sprague had served the others, she hurried back to the kitchen and reappeared bearing heaping bowls of mashed potatoes and fresh, steamed asparagus.

"You've prepared a feast," Clay said. "I didn't expect this when you suggested I take meals with you and your boarders, but I'm glad I took your advice."

"I like to cook," Mrs. Sprague said graciously.

"Unusual these days in a woman so young," commented Willie, eyeing his plate with obvious anticipation. "You're a treasure, my dearest Cammie. Some smart young buck'll realize this soon."

Clay studied his blushing hostess. The name suited her. Simple, sweet. She'd seemed too young to call her *Mrs. Sprague,* but since she had introduced herself that way, he hadn't had any other way to address her.

And she *was* young, clearly in her twenties, her wholesome face pretty and unlined. Light brown hair framed her features in a smooth fall that curved in at her jaw, and her figure under the voluminous apron struck him as strong, healthy, and well exercised.

"Now, Willie, you know I'm still in mournin'," she said in her gentle voice. "And I'm much too busy runnin' my business to worry about men." She glanced at Suze, who'd been following the conversation in silence but with avid attention, then at him. "Mr. Marlowe—"

"Clay, please."

"Thank you. Clay, I've always said grace since my mamma taught me as a little girl. I hope you'll join us."

He smiled. "I consider it a privilege to thank God for his provision."

As heads bowed in reverence, Clay felt, for the first time since arriving that morning, a measure of peace about his new job. If nothing else, his living situation had the earmarks of becoming a true pleasure.

Unlike wrangling with Miss Magnolia-Blossom Bellamy was likely to be.

At seven o'clock sharp the next morning, Maggie pulled her Miata to a stop in front of the Ashworth Mansion. As she'd expected, the Yankee was waiting for her. It wasn't that she was late or anything, she'd just figured he'd want to make a point about the key.

As did she. So with a simple nod of greeting, she went up to the front door and opened the house. Without a word, Clay sauntered past her, tipped a finger to his forehead, and proceeded into the bowels of the place.

Maggie turned on her heel, irked that he'd bested her, even if only by such a minimal thing as a cocky gesture.

She tore away in her car, pressing the gas pedal harder than she should have. Not unpredictably but still distressingly, a starchy-uniformed Cecil Wiggon caught up with her.

It figured! A lousy start to this day was now bringing another ticket to her name. It was just her luck. "Don't say a word, Wiggon. I know the drill." She pulled out her driver's license and handed it over to her erstwhile kindergarten class-mate. "How're Jill and the boys?"

"Fine, Mag. How's Buford?"

"A treasure, Wiggon. I can't imagine what I did before I got him."

Wiggon hunched bony shoulders. "Beats me. But maybe you'll be countin' on him for transportation if you make me give you one more ticket. You got more points on this thing than a compass."

Maggie groaned. "You're not just going to give me another warning?"

"No way. I clocked you doin' sixty-five in a thirty-five zone. Maybe the best thing for you *would* be to lose your license."

Maggie couldn't believe her ears. "How can you say that? I don't have time to waste walking anywhere. I'm too busy."

Wiggon stuck his pen back in his pocket, then tore the ticket off his pad. "Maybe that's your problem. You're too busy. An' I ain't sure what with."

She sighed. "Oh, work. You know."

"Dunno, Mag. Seems you weren't always like this."

"I grew up, Wiggon. I have business to take care of." Like the insolent Yankee she'd left at the Ashworth Mansion.

"I just want to make sure you keep on livin' long enough to take care of all that there business. Indy-style drivin' down Main Street ain't gonna do it."

"Come on, Wiggon, give a girl a break. Just tear up that ticket. For a kindergarten blood sister united with you against Mrs. Odenkrantz's rule of terror."

"Not even. Slow down, or the next one's the last one." He stood firm, holding out the ruinous piece of paper.

Maggie grumbled some more but took it anyway. It was all Clay Marlowe's fault. What right did he have to be so self-assured, so smug, so . . . big!

And well-referenced. Strong. And good-looking. Experienced. And sweet-talking.

Oh, no! What was she doing letting the creature get to her like that? She had more important things to worry about—

like her job, and whatever piddly busywork Mr. Hollings had for her to do next.

She'd bet her next year's salary that no one had ever dug up busywork for Mr. Capable Cocky Yankee himself. That irked her even more.

After pulling into her parking spot without her usual screech of tires, Maggie closed the car door with utmost control. She entered the building and didn't slam that door either. She didn't even bang her office door against the rubber doughnut Ruby had installed in the spot where the knob had dented the wallboard in previous bangings.

See? She could handle anything—even Mr. Marlowe. It had nothing to do with her height, her blonde curls, her fluffy name. She was a capable businesswoman. She just had to prove it to Mr. Hollings, her sisters, and to everyone else in town.

※

At six o'clock that night, Maggie drove to the mansion, ready to inspect the premises and lock up. She'd expected to find Clay on the verandah but was surprised when he was nowhere in sight. He'd better not have gone AWOL without *her* leave, especially not with the door wide open. Why, teenagers could have a field day scoring goals through the windows, shooting baskets in the chandeliers.

"Well, hello there," said the cause of her wild speculations. "I hadn't realized it was time to close up."

Maggie reached into her suit pocket and jangled the keys. "It's that time," she said, clipping her words. She hated being caught at a disadvantage. And for some obscure reason, she especially hated it when it was the carpetbagger doing the catching.

Get ahold of yourself, girl. "How did your day go?"

Although he gave her a look that said he was fighting a laugh, she gave him credit for not even cracking a smile. "I enjoyed my first day on the job. I spent my time inspecting everything. Got some measuring done, checked for termite damage—"

"Oh, dear! I had no idea."

"Don't worry. I'm pleased by how structurally sound the house is. I found no evidence of termites."

"Thank goodness."

"On the other hand, I found more dry-rotted wood than I expected."

Maggie's eyes became slits. "I sincerely hope you remember my warning."

"In vivid detail."

The momentary silence grew awkward until Maggie said, "I must be going. Buford's probably dying to see me."

To her surprise, Clay clenched his jaw. If he hadn't been so polite, she suspected he might have sneered. Well, some people! "Good evening, Mr. Marlowe—er, Clay."

Without waiting for his response and without inspecting the house, she locked up and hurried to her car. She hated to think about seeing him again tomorrow morning. Tomorrow evening. Every day without a precise end in sight, until this project was over.

But on Friday, four days later, she realized she'd managed to see him day after day, until the first week was practically over. And to her utter amazement, neither had killed the other—yet.

Still, Maggie suspected they'd have plenty of excellent opportunities before the job was done. At least by now she'd reached the point of wry humor when she thought of him, as she did on her way to lock up the mansion this clear, honey-suckle-scented evening.

As usual, she was forced to call for him when she arrived. "Clay! It's closing time."

"All right, all right," he yelled from somewhere in the back of the house. "Be right there."

True to his word, his heavy tread ran up some stairs. From the sounds of it, he was taking more than a few steps at a time. Minutes later he popped into the foyer, a cobweb drooping over his right eye.

She smiled. "Looks like you got down and dirty."

He returned her smile—with alarming results.

Watch yourself, Magnolia Bellamy.

Wiping his hands on the rear of his dirt-streaked jeans, he approached. "You could say that. I spent some time in the attic, then went down to the cellar about an hour ago. Which reminds me . . ." He turned and headed for the kitchen. "I found something Miss Louella might think interesting."

"Really? What is it?"

He reappeared, a small black book in his hand. "It looks like a diary or journal. Asa Ashworth's the name inside the cover."

Excitement bubbled up in Maggie, and she held out her hand. "A diary! Captain Asa's diary! I can't believe our luck. Oh, Clay, Miss Louella's going to be tickled. Asa Ashworth was her great-granddaddy. She'll think this was worth paying you to come here."

Clay relinquished the book, and Maggie respectfully took it. "Oh, look! The first entry's in 1865; it starts near the end of the war. This is an absolute *treasure* for our town. You have no idea what it means to me."

"Enough to see me as something other than an invading enemy army?"

Maggie stiffened. She'd forgotten. "That remains to be

seen, doesn't it? I'll let you know once your job is complete. I operate on what I can touch and see."

He spun on his heel and left the house, muttering. Maggie thought she heard "Oh, ye of little faith."

THREE

WHEN CLAY ARRIVED AT THE ASHWORTH MANSION EARLY Saturday morning—after being forced to ask Maggie to come with him and open the house on a day that wasn't a regular workday—he found the place surrounded by women of a *certain* age. "What—?" he managed to begin.

"Oh, you must be that darlin' Yankee who found dear Asa's journal," gushed a slight, white-haired lady with a twinkle in her faded blue eyes as she trotted up to him. "We're beholden to you. Why, it's a monumental find, a veritable treasure, and you so sharp as to spot it in the—where did Maggie say you found the journal?"

First the mansion was considered a treasure, thought Clay, and now the dusty old diary has become one, too. The Bellamy residents definitely had treasure too much on their minds. The house might become a treasure *after* he was done with it, but the journal looked like every other Civil War diary he'd seen.

"Mr. Marlowe?" the lady asked. "Are you feelin' poorly?"

"Oh. No, not at all. I was in the attic—"

"That's right," cut in another lady with tight rolls of lavender hair marching down her head and turquoise eyeshadow blazing from her eyelids. "She said you were snoopin'—"

"Now, Myrna, how can you say such a thing?" asked the first one, outraged. "The boy was hired to fix the place, and surely he must get acquainted with the house in order to do so. Why, I wouldn't call that snoopin', would you?"

The colorful one sniffed. "Florinda, *sugar*, the man's a Yankee. Remember . . . ?"

Florinda took Clay's arm in both her frail hands. "Don't you pay no never-mind to her. She's just an old lady, lost in the past."

Clay fought the urge to chuckle. An aged pot was calling an equally ancient kettle black.

Florinda went on. "Come right along with me, son. Some of us in Bellamy are far more progressive. We keep up with the times."

"Yes, ma'am" was all he could muster and retain a modicum of politeness.

"Florinda Sumner, you can't go monopolizin' the only gentleman here this mornin'." The speaker, the embodiment of Clay's notion of the grandmotherly breed, held out a napkin-covered plate in soft-looking, plump hands. "Here, Mr. Marlowe. I baked you some biscuits and filled them with our finest Virginia ham."

Myrna shook her lavender head. "You'd a'taken the first Yankee to your mama's silver long's he'd had his teeth an' hair, Sophie Hardesty. Honestly, a body wonders where your patriotism lies."

Sophie didn't even flinch or glance at Myrna. Instead she smiled at Clay. "Go on. Everyone says I make the best biscuits in town. Try our good Southern cookin' here, Mr. Marlowe. It'll do you a world of good."

All the while he was being wooed by geriatric flirts and

plied with cholesterol-boosting goodies, other senior citizens milled around the front porch. Clay hoped none would put her foot through an unsound board. He feared the redoubtable Miss Magnolia-Blossom Bellamy would find some way to blame him for that—on the basis that it might inflate the cost of the restoration, of course.

He knew this situation called for the utmost tact and caution. "Miss Sophie," he said, hoping he'd used the properly Southern form of address, "I just finished breakfast at Mrs. Sprague's, and she's been doing her best to bring me up to snuff on Southern cooking. I'm a convert by now, but I'd be honored to try one of your ham biscuits."

He munched quickly, nodded his pleasure, and allowed himself to be led by Florinda up the mansion's front steps.

Myrna gave another sniff. "Bribery will get you only so far, Sophie. An' flattery does no better, Florinda. The man's a Yankee an' a carpetbagger an' he can't be trusted. If you all have lost your senses, I surely haven't. *I* will keep an eye on his every move."

Groan.

"What was that?" asked Sophie. "Oh, dear. I surely hope the biscuits didn't give you dyspepsia, honey." Sophie thrust the platter into the hands of a newcomer, who wore a pair of sweatpants, a turtleneck, a cardigan, and a raincoat despite the bright morning sun overhead. "Be a dear, Philadelphia, and hold these a moment."

Sophie rummaged in the massive handbag dangling from the crook of her elbow. "They're in here. I know they are. Why, I put them in a couple of minutes ago. Now where did my digestive powders get to?"

Digestive powders? This had gone on too long. "Miss Sophie, please don't go to any trouble," Clay urged. "I'm fine. What you heard was just . . . a . . . murmur. Yes, yes, a murmur of satisfaction. Your biscuit was delectable, and I thoroughly savored it. It hit the spot, and now I'm ready to tackle my work. But I must ask all of you to stay away from the house. The floors aren't sound, and I would hate for anyone to be hurt."

Florinda turned to Philadelphia. "Isn't he a marvel? So mindful of his elders. Why, where on the dear Lord's green earth did Magnolia find him? He's a treasure."

There they went with the treasure business again.

"A gem," Miss Sophie concurred. "A true gem!"

"We can only hope not a counterfeit one," Magnolia Blossom stated in her least-complimentary tone as she strode up the walk. "Ladies, I agree with Mr. Marlowe. He's here to work, and you must let him get to it. Miss Louella can't afford this project to run overtime—or budget."

"Contrary to popular Confederate belief, Maggie," Clay said, struggling to hold on to his temper, "Yankees have been known to hear well enough the first time. I heard your budgetary concerns that morning in your office. Since I haven't even asked for the first disbursement, I see no reason for you to suggest I intend to swindle anyone out of anything."

A series of wheezy, elderly gasps burst forth.

Maggie had the grace to blush. "I never said you meant to swindle—" she said in a suddenly molasses-thick accent.

"Pretty close, Maggie," Clay said, forced to cut off her defense. "You've come a hair shy of calling me a thief, and I don't appreciate it. Especially since I've done nothing to merit your suspicion, much less the accusation."

To his satisfaction, she tightened her lips to a white line, then nodded. "Point taken, Mr. Marlowe—"

"I *still* prefer Clay. I mean no disrespect when I call you Maggie, and I never lose sight of who has the power to call the shots here."

At that, she averted her brilliant blue gaze, the red in her cheeks deepening. "Ladies," she said again, "it's time to leave *Clay* to his work."

With a minimum of grumbling, the seniors flocked off the mansion's porch and onto the tree-shaded sidewalk.

After a hard look at Clay, Maggie climbed into her Miata and tore away, dust and bits of road debris spitting out from under her tires.

The woman was a menace on the road, Clay thought. If not generally speaking.

And *speaking* might be the operative word; latter-day Confederate warrior Maggie Bellamy possessed a bayonet-sharp tongue.

"The meetin' will come to order," announced Savannah Hollings from the podium in the basement of the Bellamy Public Library later that evening.

Maggie dashed into the room and slipped onto the first available chair. It wasn't that the Bellamy Garden Club had *that* many members; it was simply a matter of her tardiness rendering the choice seats unavailable. She much preferred to sit close to the door; other attendees must have had the same thought since they'd already occupied those convenient chairs. Because the door was located closer to the front of the room than the rear, Maggie was forced to sit smack in the middle of the first row.

Roll was called. By the time the last meeting's minutes were read, Maggie had looked at her watch a dozen times and had tired of fighting the yawns that beset her.

". . . Myrna Stafford's new business."

Maggie bolted upright. Finally. The reason for her invitation to tonight's meeting of the inoffensive, innocuous, and uninspiring Garden Club.

Savannah went on. "As we know, dear Magnolia was forced to hire a Yankee to handle the restoration of our town's greatest treasure."

Regretful sighs stirred the stale air.

"A mighty fine Yankee, if you ask me," inserted Sophie Hardesty.

A titter rippled across the room.

"Nobody did, *sugar,*" retorted Myrna, exhibiting her mastery of the ladylike Southern put-down. "Especially since Maggie an' I have our doubts about his motives."

"Motives, my foot," scoffed Florinda. "Just by lookin' into his eyes you can see he's as right as rain. That boy is no more a swindler than I am."

The room erupted into verbal mayhem. Half the gardeners sided with Florinda and Sophie, while the other half shared Maggie's and Myrna's doubts.

"He's a carpetbagger—"

"Get on now! Carpetbaggers went out with the last century—"

"He's not one of us—"

"But he has marvelous references—"

"Which he might have forged—"

"Ladies, *ladies!*" Maggie had had enough, now that her diligence in checking out the foreigner had come into question. She sprang to the podium and edged Mrs. Hollings to one side. "I thoroughly checked those references. I spoke with every one of them *after* cross-referencing them with local phone directories. Mr. Marlowe's reputation in the restoration business is as he portrays it. My questions arise from my own patriotic historical perspective.

"You know I want that precious home restored—but not merely because I love everything flavored with the past. Consider this: What could be better for Bellamy than to present it with a genuine tourist attraction? A *Confederate* tourist attraction."

Myrna stood. "Precisely. But you all know Yankees haven't stopped invadin' in the century an' some since they crushed our noble Confederacy. Look at what they've done to Atlanta, with all the traffic on those highways an' those unmannerly sports teams."

A few gray heads nodded. Others cocked as Myrna's contention was considered. Still others shook mild denials, while a few bobbed up in indignant objection.

Maggie glared at Myrna. "I don't think incendiary comments will help our cause. What I care about is protecting Miss Louella's interests."

"And our Southern heritage," offered Miss Louella, the woman who stood to lose the most, as she marched down the center aisle to the lectern. "As an Ashworth, I made sure the man was qualified to do the work. Just one look at the fat file Maggie put together reassured me of her choice. But seein' as he's not one of us, I don't believe he *could* hold our history in the regard it deserves."

Maggie smiled. "Precisely my concern, Miss Louella. As a loyal daughter of the Confederacy—"

"Nobody questioned your motives, Magnolia," said Miss Louella in a tart tone, "so you don't have to put up such a strong defense. My concern is what he's doin' at the house. Even though he doesn't have a key, I'd like to hire a guard— especially at night, when who knows what he might do."

A chorus of *oohs* and *aahs* chimed in.

"Miss Louella," Maggie responded, as if she were reasoning with a child, "I surely wish we had the funds to hire a guard, but you more than anyone know how tightly I must hold the strings on this project's purse. I can't authorize a penny more'n I already have."

Miss Louella frowned. "Then how do you propose we keep your Yankee honest?"

"He's not *my* Yankee!" Maggie protested. "And I'm open to suggestions. Ladies?"

Murmurs again swept the room, but no one volunteered any ideas. Maggie agreed with Miss Louella's valid concern. A guard would be ideal, but their budget being what it was, ideal and real were far from one and the same.

"Myrna?" she asked, growing desperate.

The head adorned with lavender sausages shook from side to side. "No idea."

Maggie spied a lace hanky waving to her left. "Magnolia! Magnolia, dear," called Philadelphia Philpott in a whispery voice.

"Hush, now, ladies," Maggie urged the group. "Philadelphia has something to say."

The gathering grew silent. "Thank you," susurrated Philadelphia, tucking the cotton shirt around her turtlenecked chin, then wrapping a cardigan across her narrow chest. "I may have an idea."

Maggie waited, knowing the meek and timid woman had struggled to put herself as far forward as that. When nothing more was forthcoming, she figured a word of encouragement was needed. "And that is . . . ?"

Philadelphia gulped, then paled. She twisted her slender fingers and stared at her clunky orthopedic shoes. "If I recollect rightly, you recently acquired a rather imposin' companion, did you not?"

Maggie's eyes widened. "Why, Philadelphia Philpott! What a splendid idea. Since my darling Buford has cozied up to living with me, he's made me feel as safe and snug as a bug in its rug."

Miss Louella nodded. "You may have somethin' there, Philadelphia."

"You don't think the Yankee is more than a match for your Buford?" asked Myrna, skepticism on her hard, thin face.

Her loose, Gibson-girl do quivering, Sophie Hardesty bounced up. "We ought to give the boy the benefit of the doubt, ladies. Our country still runs on the 'innocent until proven guilty' standard."

"I know, Miss Sophie," Maggie inserted. "We're not accusing Clay of anything—yet. And the guard will ensure we don't ever have to. You all know that prevention is the weightier part of any cure. Just in case we've taken a viper of a Yankee into the bosom of our town, I think supping with him should be done with a mighty long spoon."

Miss Louella waved the discussion aside. "A guard's the best way to go. Barrin' some other burst of brilliance, Buford's our best bet. But how should we do it? Lock the poor fellow in the mansion every night?"

Maggie frowned. "I'm not sure that would work. He'd miss me. He gets lonely during the day as it is. That wouldn't be fair to the poor dear."

"Then that's the answer," stated Myrna.

"What's the answer?" asked Maggie.

"Why, you."

"Me?"

"*You'll* be our guard," Myrna elaborated, as though Maggie lacked a lightbulb's worth of intelligence. "With Buford at your side, of course. No one else knows Louella's situation quite as well as you do, an' we all agree you're determined to see the mansion brought back to its original grandeur."

Agreement was unanimous. Even Sophie and Florinda, Clay's ardent cheerleaders, approved of the idea.

Maggie looked around the room. "I must admit I can't find any reason to object. Except for my need to sleep."

"My Mitch does need you wide-awake days," warned Savannah Hollings, who'd remained silent until then.

"I never forget my responsibility to the bank, Mrs. Hollings," Maggie said. "And that's why, as the officer in charge of Miss Louella's loan, I feel duty-bound to guard the bank's interests. I'll do it."

Applause followed her declaration. Although she thought the idea full of merit, it didn't halt the flock of butterflies in her middle. Something about Clay Marlowe unnerved her, yet she'd just agreed to protect Miss Louella and her mansion from any effort on his part to swindle her.

Remembering how the man had bested her, if only by his self-assured attitude, Maggie hoped bringing Buford, her peerless protector, along on her nightly rounds would put her in the catbird seat. In dealing with Clay, she feared she was going to need every advantage she could scrounge up to keep from having her goose toasted by a Yankee of William Tecumseh Sherman's ilk.

🌿

As the door closed behind Maggie, Miss Louella Ashworth released a breath of relief. "Well, now, fellow members of the Garden Club," she said, "as your duly elected and newly installed president, it's my honor and privilege to bring up our next matter of business."

Bending down, she retrieved the canvas tote bag she'd hidden behind the podium. With dramatic flair, she withdrew a handful of paperbacks, then another, followed by a final fistful of well-worn tomes.

"What do you think you're up to, Louella Ashworth?" demanded Myrna.

Louella, knowing well the theatrical value of a long silence, smiled and waited. When every eye in the room was riveted on her stash of reading material, she went on. "These, dear friends, are my prized collection of Marvin Pinkney novels."

"What do they have to do with this year's public beautification project?" asked Florinda.

"Absolutely nothin'," said Louella.

"Then why are we wastin' our time watchin' you play with a pile of dusty old detective books?" challenged Sophie, evidently still irked by what she'd called the group's uncalled-for suspicion of a fine specimen of young manhood.

"Patience, my dear, patience. I'll tell you . . . ," Miss Louella said with such a conspiratorial smile that all the women of the Garden Club scooted expectantly to the edge of their seats.

FOUR

IT WASN'T GOING TO BE EASY, HE KNEW, THE FOLLOWING Monday.

In fact, it was going to be tougher than breaking into the Bellamy Fiduciary Trust. Not that Clay had any intention of breaking into anything, but he viewed asking Maggie Bellamy for the first disbursement of funds in the same vein as bank-vault busting.

It would take care, caution, and more guts than he feared he had. The delicate lady was a tiger when it came to her business dealings. Or maybe she only turned feral when it came to her much loved Confederacy.

Clay shook his head. Who cared? He had to ask Maggie for money, and he looked forward to it about as much as he would root-canal work—without the benefit of anes-thetic.

He stared at his hand, hovering mere millimeters from her office door. If she had learned anything about his past, that knowledge would make things worse between them than they already were.

Marshaling his determination, he bypassed the doorknob and knocked.

"Come in," said the woman uppermost in his mind, her Southern-scented words honeyed and appealing.

He knew better than to be fooled. "Hello, Maggie. May I have a minute of your time?"

She dropped the sheet of paper she'd been reading into a file and gestured him to the wing chair at his right. "Have a seat."

Clay sought the right words. He had to; the lady was formidable. He wondered why. What made Maggie Bellamy such a tough cookie beneath the luxurious, feminine, ladylike, magnolia-blossom exterior?

She seemed to have an inordinate need for respect; her actions and attitude demanded it. Like when she'd asked him to call her Miss Bellamy instead of Maggie.

Being a man used to getting what he went after, Clay knew he'd find out—one way or another—but not today. He had business to conduct. "I'm sure you've been expecting this visit."

At her nod, he continued, "As you know, I've spent the past week inspecting the Ashworth property. I've made a detailed list of the work that needs doing and projected a work schedule for the entire restoration. I'm ready to hire subcontractors and order supplies."

Maggie's rose-glossed lips pressed together. "You're right," she said. Clay noticed that her words showed nervousness and stress by the way they mushed together; he'd come to know his nemesis that well already. "I've been expectin' this visit. And, to be honest, I was wonderin' why it hadn't happened earlier."

At least she hadn't argued. "Fair enough. You see, I'm cautious in my work. I don't jump in blindly. Before I spend the first penny, I like to know everything about the project.

Since I was in San Francisco when we first discussed the Ashworth Mansion, I didn't get to see the premises until last week. I wasn't going to add up interest on Miss Louella's account until I was ready to spend her money—wisely, at that."

Maggie must have liked what she heard, since her lips loosened into their normal, attractive curve. "I must commend you, Mr.—Clay. That's a most fiscally prudent way to proceed."

He grinned. "Relax, Maggie. I'm not out to hurt you or Miss Louella. Not even your beloved Confederacy. It's in my best interest to succeed in this job. Sooner or later you're going to believe me. Even if it kills you to admit it."

She flushed. Clay admired what the rosiness did to her porcelain skin. It reminded him of . . . well, a flower petal. Velvety, exquisitely tinted. And feminine—very, very feminine.

If Magnolia Bellamy wasn't so confrontational, Clay suspected he'd be in danger of falling for her. As it was, her thorny nature made it impossible for him to even think of her in those terms. He didn't much care for armed combat during dates.

So why was he thinking along those lines anyway?

He leaned forward and propped an arm across her desk. "You'll cut me a check then?"

She opened a drawer and withdrew a blank form. "Mm-hmm. I don't suppose you can hire plumbers and electricians or buy wood-strippin' products without money, can you?"

He chuckled. "I'd love to do business that way, but the barter system doesn't work in restorations. Most subs don't need their homes restored, and lumberyards aren't particularly interested in my services, either."

She smiled and slipped the cashier's check into the printer to the left of her computer. She tapped out a handful of characters, glancing at the folder she'd opened at her right.

As Clay followed her gaze, he caught sight of the open file and the letter she'd dropped when he'd walked into the office. Seeing the name there made him feel as if a pine flooring plank had smacked him on the head: Hinkley Home Renovations. Dated as of last Wednesday.

What was Hal up to now—with Maggie?

Worry churned Clay's clenched middle. He studied the woman at the computer, noting the fragility of her neck, bared by her upswept hairstyle. Her downy cheek glowed with health; her delicate hands evoked the movements of a dancer.

Maggie, despite her efforts at toughness, was no match for Hal Hinkley. That crook would leave figurative heel marks all over her—not to mention, more than likely, costing her her job and trashing Miss Louella's house in the bargain.

Oh, yeah. True to his slimy form, Hinkley would then lie and grease every palm in town to avoid prosecution.

Thank you, Father, Clay prayed, *for keeping Hal from winning this particular account. Help me prove myself worthy of the trust Maggie's so grudgingly placing in me. Help me prove myself to her.*

Without a word, he took the check she extended a moment later and stepped toward the door.

"See that you spend it wisely, Clay," Maggie warned as he grasped the doorknob.

His clasp tightened. "I always do, Magnolia Blossom . . . er . . . Bellamy. I always do."

⚘

The Union was at it again.

They'd resumed the Great War of Northern Aggression. Maggie didn't appreciate being its first casualty.

"Magnolia Blossom," she fumed, pacing the width of her office. "How dare that Yankee call me that? He complains about my business savvy, then stirs up a hornet's nest of trouble by calling me *that*. It just shows what a monumental lack of brain cells these Northern carpetbaggers have."

Her intercom crackled to life. "Maggie?" asked Ruby.

Maggie pressed the proper button. "Yes?"

"Is he gone?"

Oh, yeah. And lucky to be gone, too. "Just left."

"Then you'd better skeddadle to Mr. H's office. He wants to see you."

Oh, dear. What now?

This was turning out to be the most hackle-raising day. After the routine opening of the mansion this morning, she'd come to work to a waiting stack of petty correspondence. Then the scalawag had showed up. Now her boss wanted something with her.

It couldn't be anything good. Good news came to you; bad news called you in. Or so it was in Maggie's experience.

Had Clay cashed the check already? Before the printer ink had even dried?

Had the teller alerted Mr. H that fast?

Why couldn't anyone trust her to be capable? Why couldn't they understand she had the situation under control? Why couldn't they accept her for the serious businesswoman she had become?

It couldn't all be because of her name, her ringlets, her blue eyes, her height. Was there something about her that told people she was somehow lacking?

What was it that betrayed her greatest fear?

※

If Clay didn't know any better, he'd swear gremlins had invaded the Ashworth Mansion. Two weeks after Maggie had released the first construction-loan disbursement, Clay stood staring at the stripped, sanded, and prepped mahogany-paneled and bookshelved walls of the library. He'd planned on applying fresh stain today, but now he couldn't.

His outrage at the destruction before him was so great that he didn't know how to contain so much anger.

A neat row of even, circular holes lined the bottom of the wood panels, hideous in their symmetry. No insect or animal had accomplished this. The holes had been bored with a drill bit; he'd worked with wood long enough to recognize the results.

But who?

"Hey, Hobey!" he called, hoping his masonry subcontractor hadn't yet left to pick up the special mixed-to-match mortar he needed to refurbish the chimneys.

From the other side of the open window he heard a loud, "Yeah, Boss?"

"Come in here a minute, willya?"

"Comin'."

Moments later, the floor sang an alarming soprano as the three-hundred-pound hulk of Horace Hobey entered the library. Clay pointed to the damage. "What do you make of that?"

Hobey scratched the thick ruff of grizzled hair growing below the shiny crown of his head. "Sure do look like you did a great job, only . . . I cain't figger what you're aimin' to do with 'em holes."

Clay shot him a glare. "That's the point. *I* didn't do it. I found them a minute ago when I walked in here. Do you know who might have ruined the wood like that?"

The mason frowned. "Don't know nobody so dumb as to wreck stuff that expensive. It's some of that mahogany from near the *ee*-quater, ain't it?"

Clay nodded, his frustration at the senseless destructiveness seething inside him. "I'd go further than calling this dumb. In my book it's criminal. Vandalism is against the law. Whoever trashed these walls had better find himself a top-notch lawyer. I'm going to press every charge I can come up with as soon as I know who's to blame."

∦

A week later, Hobey stormed into the parlor where Clay was scraping the last bit of century-old finish off the fireplace mantel.

"You better come take a gander at this, Boss," the large man said, his stolid features burning an intense puce.

"What happened?" Clay asked, unease wriggling in his gut. After the hole-boring incident, more strange things had happened. Nothing quite as dramatic as the defacement of magnificent pieces of vintage wood, but each morning he had found tools in different places from where he was sure he'd left them the night before. Other tools he hadn't found at all, and he'd needed to purchase new ones.

"I cain't talk 'bout it, I'm so steamed. You best just come see."

Feeling the slap of Hobey's ire, Clay followed him out of the mansion to the last chimney Hobey and his crew had worked on. Clay's unease crystallized into rancid certainty. "Who?" he roared.

"Don't look at me, Boss," responded Hobey, his jaw protruding pugnaciously, his beefy hands fisting.

Clay laughed at the thought. "Never. You're too picky *and* too professional to come up with something like that."

"Garbage," Hobey spit out.

Garbage it was. The precise chimney work of the previous day had been torn apart and then rebricked. Not a single brick of the freshly constructed chimney lined up with another. And the mortar . . . well, it had been *liberally* applied, with the resulting globs and plops adding to the impression of deformity.

Clay ran a hand through his hair, then rubbed the base of his skull, where a thunderous pain had instantly lodged. It didn't forecast a good day ahead. "There's nothing to do but tear it out and do it over again."

Hobey snorted. "You didn't hafta tell me. I ain't gonna leave it like that. Horace Hobey don't do junk work."

"That's why I hired you."

Somewhat mollified by Clay's words, Hobey clumped off, barking orders to his men. Clay, however, stood before the defaced masonry, no longer doubting his suspicions. Someone *was* sabotaging him. What he didn't know was who—even though he had his suspicions.

Or why.

But he'd find out—soon.

🌿

"You know, sugar," Maggie said to Buford one evening a couple of weeks after they'd begun their patrols at the mansion, "I'm not getting any sleep."

Over the counter separating the kitchen from the living room, Buford's soulful eyes followed her as she lifted the lid to check on his favorite liver dinner.

"These sleepless nights can't be doing you any good, either. Why, you need your rest. And I haven't seen hide nor hair of any Yankee high jinks. If he'd come asking for another chunk of change, it'd be a horsehide of another color, but I'm of a mind to go ask the Garden Club to either take turns with us, or let us quit."

Buford cocked his head but remained silent, his gaze riveted on Maggie. "D'you think, honey," she asked as she flipped her chicken breast on the broiler pan, "that I might have misjudged Clay?"

Buford blinked, then settled himself more comfortably on the living-room couch in Maggie's small apartment.

"Okay, okay, I can't put the burden of this on you. I have to decide what I think of the man myself." Maggie thought back on all their encounters to date. "You know, he's never done or said anything even a teensy tad off. Maybe that's something to worry over. Do you find the way he please-and-thank-yous the elderly ladies suspicious?"

Buford shook his head, his pendulous cheeks quaking.

"Oh, all right. Maybe it *is* a matter of his mama's good training. He doesn't go *too* far with what he says, you know. No lies or anything like that. It's just . . . he's just . . . too perfect to be real. Then there's the Yankee business, to be sure."

Buford sneezed.

"Bless you," Maggie said automatically, mounding fresh greens in a bowl for her salad. Buford, poor dear, was getting over a case of the sniffles—which reminded her to add some brewer's yeast for B vitamins and orange rind for bio-flavonoids to the pan with the liver. "Clay Marlowe scares me, if you really want to know. I'm afraid if I don't watch myself, I could fall hard for him. Where would that leave me, Buford? I'll tell you where. Right here in Bellamy, nursing a heart broken and discarded by a smooth-talking, good-looking Yankee."

Buford clambered off the couch, padded through the living room to the kitchen, and damply nuzzled Maggie. His response to her fears was a heartfelt, and to her way of thinking, concurring *"AWWWROOOOOF!"*

F I V E

CLAY HAD THOUGHT THE FIRST TIME WAS HARD.

Hah!

Compared to what he knew he'd face today, that had been a cinch. He stared at Maggie's office door with trepidation as he tried to orchestrate the words with which to ask for a second disbursement of funds ahead of schedule.

He could too easily envision the tough lady-banker's reaction. His request would draw a single crevice between her brows; her lips would purse; her blue eyes would narrow; her cheeks would flare with color. What would proceed from her sharp tongue was anybody's guess.

Lord, he prayed, *I need a way to prove to this woman that I've done no wrong. Words would be good, but a change in her heart would be even better. What I need most is your protection. I couldn't stand to have happen again what happened all those years ago, when I was nineteen.*

Feeling better after asking for God's help, Clay knocked, then opened the door without waiting for a response. "Maggie, we have to talk."

She jerked away from her computer and blanched. Her fingers betrayed a tremor. "Wha . . . ?"

Great. He'd handled this one well. Barging into her office barking like a rabid rottweiler was not the way to win her over. "Let's start again," he said, "with my apology first of all. I'm sorry for the way I walked in here. I startled you, and that was never my intention. Please forgive me."

By now, matching red circles had popped out on her otherwise-white cheeks. Then her eyes hardened.

Oh-oh. Maggie wasn't going to make this easy.

"Apology . . . accepted," she said, giving him a regal nod. What she didn't say, but he could swear he heard anyway, was *"But it better not happen again."*

She waved him over to the wing chair and, with icicles embellishing her words, asked, "To what do I owe this . . . *peculiar* honor?"

"Ah, Maggie," Clay said, frustrated, "I'd rather be scorching my brains in the Sahara right about now than saying what I have to say. But there's no avoiding reality. There have been some episodes of—" he inhaled deeply—"vandalism at the mansion."

Alarm widened her blue eyes, and her fair skin turned ashen. "Vandalism?" she whispered.

His rage at the injustice of the senseless acts pushed him to want to pound something, to vent his helplessness in a howl, to . . . to . . . but instead he said quietly, "Yeah. Damage. To the Ashworth Mansion."

"How bad?"

Thinking of what he had to do next, he said, "Bad enough."

"What kind of damage?"

He surged to his feet. "You want to know?"

As she nodded, he began pacing. "I'll tell you. Then maybe you can help me figure out who did it—and why."

He dropped back into the now-familiar-in-its-discomfort wing chair and rubbed his tight and sore neck. "First there were the holes someone bored into the mahogany paneling in the library."

"Oh no," she said with a moan.

"Oh, yeah. It took time and money to match the filler, patch in the holes, sand the panels again, and finally stain and finish those walls."

Maggie closed her gaping mouth. "You said that was first. What else has happened?"

Ticking off two fingers, he said, "The chimney came next. I have to tell you, it was enough to make this grown man want to cry."

"Will you *please* tell me what happened?"

To Clay's Northern ear, Maggie's words, "Willupleeeeese tell me whahappen?" sounded like something reminiscent of that morning's grits.

He almost smiled, but the situation was too grim. "The chimney bricks Hobey's men had just replaced were knocked out, then stuck back together like a bunch of pick-up sticks. And what they did with the mortar was criminal. Lumps. Clumps. Drips." He shook his head. "The mess had to be redone. Don't forget, we use a special-order mortar so that it matches the existing stuff."

"More time wasted," she murmured.

"More money spent," he bit off.

That jolted her from her distress. She rose to her full petite height, crossed her arms across her chest, and tossed back her mane of shimmering blonde curls. "Ah s'pose y'wan' mohr."

Clay's newly bilingual brain translated automatically.

"No, I don't *want* more. If someone hadn't messed with work that had already been done, I'd have had the right amount for this stage of the restoration. But since someone showed no respect for another's property, irreplaceable property as a house this old and beautiful is, I've been forced into the lousy position of *needing* more."

"I assume these things have been fixed by now."

"Of course. What do you think ate up the money?"

Her eyes slitted into cobalt blue lasers that beamed right into his soul. "I don't know. You tell me. So far you've said an invisible someone sneaked in right under your nose, drilled holes in wooden walls, and trashed a chimney. Didn't it occur to you to tell me about this right after it happened? When I could see the evidence?"

Clay's cheeks burned. He'd known he should have called her, but with her uncalled-for suspicions fresh in his mind, he'd hoped to squeak by without alerting her to the trouble. He'd been wrong, and he knew it. "I have no defense other than I hoped to fix everything without running up the cost," he said.

She waved her slender arms. "How could you have thought that? Especially since you just said you had to order more of that custom mortar."

He couldn't tell her without catapulting her suspicion. "Wishful thinking that led to poor judgment."

Her honey-brown brow curved as she tipped up her chin. "I do believe we finally agree on *somethin'*. Now, what do you propose to do about this situation? One where I can't corroborate your story, and I have to take you at your word."

Groan. "What do I have to gain by running short of money, Maggie?"

Blue eyes accused him of unmentioned—as yet—atrocities. "You could be lookin' to persuade me to increase Miss Louella's loan."

Clay snorted. "You've made it absolutely clear you won't do that."

"Maybe you figure this is the best way to make me do it. All the while your pockets are bulgin' with the fleece you're shearin' from us."

"I don't appreciate your questioning my integrity."

"I don't appreciate havin' to worry over your motives."

"My only motive is to restore the Ashworth."

"How am I to know, since your original bid is now wingin' away from the nest?"

"Because I've given you my word."

"Which is worth . . . ?"

"Everything to me. Or nearly everything."

"Aha!" A slender finger stabbed in his direction. "There's a little waffle there."

His anger rising, he counted to ten before replying. "I only meant that my relationship with God means everything to me. After that, my word, my integrity, who I am, are top priority. It's that way because, as a Christian, I'm responsible to represent God's Son, Jesus."

Her spine straightened to an icy rigidity as she bit off her next words. "I only see a Yankee—like so many who came to feather their carpetbags after the war. And all I know is that I gave you a sum for the first phase of the work. Now, ages shy of the next disbursement, you're in my office askin' for more, and I can't even verify what you've said. I know Louella calls this my 'doubting Thomas side,' but I believe a good banker has to doubt and question everyone's motives."

"A drop of faith would do you a world of good," he said sadly, considering the bleakness of a faithless existence. *Just maybe,* he thought, *God's purpose for my presence in Bellamy isn't only the restoration of the Ashworth Mansion. It's possible I've been sent to restore Maggie's faith.*

He paused, aware of the enormity of that task, then said plainly, "I'll need that second disbursement."

"I suppose it can't be helped now. The work will stop if I don't do as you want."

"Pretty much. I need to pay for the re-enameled bathroom pieces so the plumbers can finish that job, and the kitchen pipes haven't been ordered yet—I need a deposit. Then I have to pay for the wallpaper that recently arrived, and the outside wiring has to be finished."

Maggie tensed her lips and turned her back on him. "Very well," she said, her words clipped. "I'll write the check ahead of time. But I will *not* do it again. I expect no further need for funds until our next pre-agreed disbursement date. Do you understand me, Mr. Clay Marlowe?"

He clenched his fists at his sides in controlled, righteous rage. "I've always understood every word you said. What I have trouble understanding is why you choose to use them in such antagonistic ways. I haven't questioned you, your honesty, or your competence. *Yet.*"

She gasped and spun around, hurt in her blue eyes.

What had he said to cause such an extreme reaction in Maggie Bellamy? Clay wondered. Without meaning to, he'd daubed salt on some raw inner wound. What was it? And who or what had caused it?

As he strode out of her office, he promised himself he'd find out, before he left town.

🌿

Maggie had known Clay would be trouble from the moment she was forced to hire him. Once she'd clapped eyes on him, she'd had nothing but trouble. Now he'd thrown her greatest fear in her face.

The louse.

Well, he hadn't done it intentionally. He couldn't have known how badly Maggie needed to prove her competence. Still, he'd done it; he'd given voice to her deepest fear.

How was she going to get beyond that fear? Especially now that the words he'd said were figuratively smacking her with a two-by-four.

Maggie had always seen herself as the filling in the Bellamy three-sibling sandwich cookie, with driven, exceptional, and successful Larkspur two years before her, and cozy, warm, earth-mother Camellia two years behind her. Maggie was considered the light and fluffy stuffing between those two.

No wonder she had her share of uncertainties, insecurities, and doubts after playing that role since childhood. For years, she'd suspected that most people had to hold back the urge to pat her on the head. She figured the minute anyone looked at her, they discounted her as a decorative, empty-headed blonde. Man, did she hate that abominable stereotype! It certainly wasn't the best position from which to face down a delinquent borrower or potential swindler.

And her height? Just because she was about as tall as an average twelve-year-old didn't mean she had the maturity and competence of one. Or did it?

Just because her hair was pale gold didn't mean she hid a vacuum of air under it. Or did it?

The contrast among the sisters the townspeople had nick-named "the three Bellamy Blossoms" because each was named after a flower had always made Maggie overly aware of her fragile appearance. Lark's dramatic-redhead vibrancy left Maggie looking washed out and wimpy. Cammie's all-American, girl-next-door good looks and maternal ways left her feeling inadequate and weak.

Her sisters' personal successes hadn't helped matters, either. The beautiful, striking Lark had taken off right after high school graduation, put herself through college, lost her South-ern accent, and then landed a fabulous job with the *Baltimore Sun*. Now she was twenty-eight, and the whole country knew her byline. Recently the energetic, *tall* redhead had come home to concentrate on her latest project: her own, recently launched literary magazine.

And baby Cammie had always known what she wanted

from the moment she could voice those desires. "I wanna be a mommy," she'd stated every time she was asked.

When she'd married her high school sweetheart, David Sprague, at nineteen, Cammie got her hearth and home. The mommy part was currently in the works. True, the marriage part had ended in tragedy four months ago, when David's car had crashed on his way home from work one snowy night. But Cammie had used her lifelong craving for a family to see her through the difficult transition. Over the past couple months she'd turned her house into a boardinghouse—in essence, a home for the lonely—and she seemed to thrive in her new capacity as mother to those in need.

Of all the sisters, only Maggie seemed to flounder—when she shouldn't. She had her job, which she'd worked hard to land, starting as a typist at the bank the summer she finished high school, then working her way up to teller, and finally snagging the promotion to loan officer nine months ago.

Then why did everyone seem to cast a jaundiced eye her way? Why couldn't they believe she could do the job?

She did—didn't she?

"Oh, flapjacks!" she muttered, frustrated that she was once again wasting time mucking around in her doubts. And she didn't have the necessary intestinal fortitude right then to put her lousy relationship with her sisters under a self-help microscope. Not when she had to thwart a too-handsome-for-her-own-good Yankee primed to leave her holding the empty bank bag.

🌿

She wasn't going to get away with it. No way was Clay going to let that snippy Magnolia Blossom cast a shadow on his business or personal reputation. He'd prayed too much and worked too hard salvaging his future to let a woman with a century-plus-old chip on her shoulder thwart him.

Someone was setting him up, and Clay wasn't going to take the fall for anyone else this time. He was older and much smarter. He was *not* going to let anyone charge him with bilking an old lady out of her money. He would catch the worm red-handed first.

Kneeling by the overstuffed armchair in his room at Cammie Sprague's home, Clay closed his eyes and Bible and prayed aloud. "Father, I'm in another situation I don't know how to handle. The restoration isn't going well."

Hah! When had he become a master of understatement?

"I have no idea who's behind the vandalism—well, maybe an idea, but nothing sure. I doubt it's anyone on the crews I hired." He thought about his subcontractors as he had many times before, only to come up with the same unhelpful conclusion.

"Then there's Maggie." Just the thought of her made him want to smile . . . and growl.

"She's the most intriguing, infuriating female I've ever met. And she's out to get me, just because I was born in Gettysburg! How can I work around that?"

Clay had no idea, but he figured God did.

"I need your strength and courage. I can't afford to be accused of wrongdoing again. The last time nearly tore me apart. You know I always honor your commands. I don't have malicious intent, much less criminal. Maggie baffles me with her bristly nature, her hard-nosed suspicion. And even though I'd like to know more about her, maybe help her find her way to you, I'm afraid to get closer to her."

He sighed, knowing he'd hit the crux of the matter. "Oh, God, I know. I need to lose my fear and do your will, not mine. Will you please take over this mess?"

When he received no heavenly response, he argued further. "I feel such a pull toward that contentious Southern belle, but I also need to protect my career—and my carcass. I don't know what I should do. So give me the right words to say to her, show me what I've missed seeing, and guide me through this mess so that, in the end, my work will bring glory to you."

🌿

"The meetin' of the Bellamy Garden Club will now come to order," Louella Ashworth announced, smacking her gavel against the wooden lectern with relish.

The chatter dwindled to a dull roar. "Goodness gracious, ladies. It's not as if you all haven't seen each other for months. We have important matters to discuss tonight, and I for one want to get home at a decent time."

"Marvin Pinkney's latest is good, then?" asked silver-haired Sarah Langhorn, owner of The Blissful Bookworm, with a sly grin.

"*All* of Marvin's books are good," Louella pronounced.

Sarah nodded. "With a title like *Slaughtered Secrets of Castle Stembley,* you know you have a Marvin classic." Sarah was another Marvin fan, but she couldn't hold a candle to Louella's loyalty—in Louella's opinion, of course.

"I suppose that's goin' to give you more ideas for some club activities," Sophie Hardesty said.

"Of course," Louella said with a sassy wink. She continued, "Ladies! Ladies! We must get to the business at hand. Sandra, did you decide which nursery you'll buy the petunias from?" Turning to the other side of the room, she scanned the group. "Darla, is the planter schedule done?"

Seeing the women's affirmative responses, Louella drew a satisfied breath. "Wonderful, just wonderful. Now we can get on with our new business with the latest Pinkney novel," she said as excitement shimmied up her spine. "And I've found just what we need to accomplish it."

With a great flourish, Louella pulled a scarlet shopping bag out from under the podium. "Greasepaint, ladies. Black greasepaint."

Some jaws dropped. Others' eyes sparkled with anticipation.

Florinda leaned toward Sophie. "We're sure enough in trouble with her as president."

"And they're worried about Yankees?" Sophie queried.

Louella chose to ignore the gapers and dissenters. "And we need a uniform, too," she said, drawing out the words for emphasis.

"What kind of uniform would that be, Louella?" asked Sophie, suspicion in her voice.

"Why, sisters in sleuthery, we're goin' to wear leotards."

SIX

"Mornin', Maggie."

Maggie heard the familiar greeting as she stood at the corner of Main and Fourth, waiting for the light to change. Turning, she saw her younger sister, Cammie, leave the Bellamy Professional Building. The glow on Cammie's face suggested she'd just had her monthly prenatal visit.

Maggie faked a smile. "Everything's well, I hope."

Cammie's radiance upped its wattage. "I can't describe the feelin' I get when I hear my baby's heartbeat. God's miracles are so awesome that they leave me breathless, humbled, and full of joy."

Maggie wrinkled her nose. There it was again—one of the biggest bones of contention between her and the youngest Bellamy Blossom. That matter of God and all his goodness. Maggie hadn't felt his goodness in a long, long time. Not since their parents' deaths, when Maggie was eight. She had taken the loss hard; she'd had an especially close bond with her mother. To counter her sisters' increased hovering, she'd worked to toughen up. And she'd stopped buying anything she heard in Sunday school, even though Granny Iris had made sure she attended every week.

To change the subject, she asked, "And you're due . . . ?"

"Around October. I can't wait to hold my little one in my arms."

The satisfaction on Cammie's wholesome features made Maggie's middle lurch. Why couldn't *she* achieve the same measure of joy in her life that Cammie had? Maggie would even settle for contentment. Because everyone seemed to discount her most basic capacity to survive—as if she couldn't even cross a street without getting splattered by an oncoming speedster—she always felt the need to go the extra mile, to give every situation absolutely all she had, to prove herself more than an accident of favorable genetics.

This urge intensified in the presence of her so-capable sisters.

"Hey, Mag!" Lark called out as she idled her cherry red Ford Escort at the curbside, waiting for Cammie to get in.

Maggie's stomach sank.

"Fancy seeing you outside the halls of finance during work hours," said Lark, her attempt at humor falling flatter than a flopped soufflé on Maggie's ears.

"Oh, you know," Maggie said noncommittally, swallowing her frustration, "we slaves to our jobs must crack our whip at those we command. I'm on my way back to the office from the Ashworth site."

As soon as she mentioned her largest assignment to date, her sisters looked at each other, startled. "Can you handle something that complicated?" asked Lark in her usual blunt way.

"I heard the project will involve a lot of responsibility," added Cammie, concern in her voice.

Maggie forced herself to huff out the painful breath stuck in her chest. "Camellia," she said, keeping her voice cool, reasonable, and mature sounding, "I've managed to work with lots of money for years. Of course the restoration involves complicated transactions and a great deal of money. That's what loan officers do. They handle loans. Of large amounts of money. For big jobs."

"Yes," countered Lark, "but you've never had to do it by yourself. You've always worked with someone else. When a bank puts out so much money, a great deal of liability falls on the person in charge."

"So what you're saying," Maggie said fiercely, "is that I'm incompetent."

Lark hesitated. "No, of course not." Then she hurried to say, "It's just . . . the magnitude of the project that concerns us. What if something goes wrong?"

Maggie gulped, remembering all that had already gone wrong, and forced her features to conceal her anxiety. "So? Problems always arise in business. I'll handle them with the expertise my years in banking have given me."

Cammie's expression grew more troubled. "Yes, but Maggie, it's the pressure, honey. Can you handle it?"

"Camellia," she said through gritted teeth, holding back the urge to scream . . . to cry. "I wish you'd remember I'm two years older than you. Just because I'm six inches shorter doesn't mean I'm not as fully adult as you are."

Cammie flushed. "I never said that."

Noting the evidence of guilt, Maggie stared her down, waiting until Cammie averted her gaze before saying, "You implied it. You imply it every time you talk with me."

"Not at all, Mag," argued Lark, backing up Cammie. "We're just concerned for you. After all, you're our sister—"

Maggie gathered up the last shred of her courage and pride. "But if you can't dredge up a smidgen of respect for me, then what kind of sisterhood can we have? Think about it, *sisters.*

When you come up with the right answer, you know where to find me."

"But, Maggie—"

"Come on, Mag—"

The light finally changed again, offering her escape. Crossing the street, Maggie made certain to look both ways, in case the two in the red subcompact were watching.

"Hand me that sheet of 220, willya, Hobey?" Clay asked, pointing in the direction of the sandpaper with his chin.

"You know I know nuthin' 'bout wood, Boss. I'm a mason, 'member? Bricks an' rocks. So what's 220?"

Clay chuckled as he rubbed his fingers over the wood paneling he was working on. "We use 220-grit sandpaper to prep the wood for the stain. That's it over there by the cans from the paint company."

"Gotcha, Boss. Here you go."

"Thanks." Clay began sanding, relishing the feel of the wood under his hands.

"Shame, ain't it?"

"If you mean the vandalism, it's worse than that. It's criminal. I can't believe someone would do something like that."

Hobey shook his massive head. "Me neither. Y'ain't got no idea who coulda done it?"

"No. If I did, they'd be behind bars already."

"Sure 'nuff, an' I'd a'helped you put them there."

"I know, Hobey." Clay cast a questioning glance at his sub. "What are you doing here today? I thought you guys had finished the masonry."

Hobey's ruddy cheeks darkened. "Well, I just got to likin' workin' with you, an' I got to feelin' rotten 'bout all this—" he waved toward the library and the chimney—"so . . . I wanted you to know that if there's anythin' I could help you with, I reckon I'd be happy to. Long's I ain't got 'nother job goin'. Which I don't. Not until next week."

The large man's generosity deeply affected Clay. "Your offer means a lot."

Now even the mason's earlobes blazed scarlet. "Ain't nuthin', Boss. Just what's right."

"What's right?"

"Yeah. I'm a Christian, see, an' I'm called to do unto others as—"

"You'd have them do unto you."

"You . . . ?"

Clay nodded. "Brothers in Christ."

Hobey grinned. "Amen."

Growing serious, Clay sent a question heavenward. God's answer resounded in his heart. "I have to tell you something about me before you commit to helping me. It could affect you, your business, your reputation."

Hobey's shiny forehead grew furrows. "Ain't nuthin' wrong with you, Boss."

"In a way, you're right," Clay admitted, "and I appreciate your support. But there's a black mark against me."

Clay didn't go out of his way to make a secret of his past, but neither did he go around broadcasting it or volunteering the information in his résumé. Although he knew he had to tell the older man so that Hobey could decide how closely to associate with him—and for that Hobey needed full knowledge of the pertinent details—Clay still struggled to tell the tale that could kill this burgeoning friendship.

"I'm waitin'," the bricklayer said, his voice starched with stone.

Clay glanced down at the stripped but unsanded floor. "I've . . . a record."

"Well, the wife has boxes and boxes of 45s and LPs, too. Ain't nuthin' wrong with that," Hobey responded.

If he hadn't been feeling so tense, Clay would have laughed. "Not *that* kind of record. I mean a criminal record."

Hobey's mud-colored eyes widened. "Get outta here. Ain't no way you done nuthin' wrong. I seen you workin'. I know what kinda man you are."

Emotion prickled the back of Clay's throat. "Thanks, Hobey. Your reaction is incredible. But it's true. When I was nineteen, I did eighteen months in prison for embezzling."

"Well, then, them courts went stupid the day they sent you up." Hobey crossed his arms over his massive chest, the expression on his broad face mulish. "Ain't no way you stole money from no one."

Clay exhaled in relief. "You're right, Hobey. I didn't take a penny. The History Club at Yorkville University required all its members to volunteer at the local Historical Society. When a huge sum disappeared from its account, we came under scrutiny. I was singled out as the likely culprit. I didn't do it. However, since I was a flat-broke, scholarship sophomore and the recently elected treasurer of the club, the university authorities and the cops looked no further. Opportunity, need, and accessibility convinced all concerned of my guilt. Plus the public defender's office assigned me a kid fresh out of law school who didn't care if I rotted in jail. So by the end of that surreal year, I was in prison—and my scholarships were given to other students deemed more worthy than a con. Although I could have earned an undergraduate degree in jail, I knew my dream of becoming an architect died the day the jury foreman read the verdict. If it hadn't been for Jesus . . ."

"Amen, brother. I reckon that's the only way a man comes out of that without turnin' into a rattlesnake kinda guy."

"You have no idea." Clay shuddered, remembering the fights he'd witnessed, the immorality he'd rejected, the two murders that had happened while he was there. Although Clay's future had seemed bleak through human eyes, his spiritual eyes had learned to focus on his newfound Savior during that time in prison. With the Lord's help, he had envisioned the end of his jail term and a fresh start. And, although he hadn't known how he would make his way through his new life as a Christian and an ex-con, he had known with every fiber of his being that he wouldn't do it alone. Jesus would always walk at his side.

His talent at carpentry, inherited from his father, who'd died when Clay was fourteen, had offered him hope. His love of history, absorbed from his mother, who'd died when Clay was eighteen, had given him the idea that eventually enabled him to support himself. He'd learned everything he could about restoring homes. And through hard work and word-of-mouth recommendations from client to client, he'd built a good, solid business over the years—with scrupulous honesty as his trademark.

"So what makes you think that's gonna affect what I do?" Hobey asked, his stare challenging.

"Associating with an ex-con—even one who's now been cleared of all charges—isn't healthy for a businessman. Especially a con who, because he was born north of the Mason-Dixon, is being judged a criminal by someone who doesn't even know his past."

Clay knew human nature well enough to know that, if Maggie knew about his prison time, she would see his prior conviction as proof of a lack of integrity and would likely condemn him without considering his side—just as the justice system had done. They'd found it impossible to believe that an orphaned scholarship student might be innocent of embezzling.

"Who's the fool?" Hobey's bottom lip pushed out.

"I'd rather not mention her name."

"The littlest Bellamy Blossom, ain't it?"

Clay's eyes widened. "How'd you guess? At least, you guessed if you meant Maggie."

Massive shoulders rose, then fell. "Sure I mean Maggie. She's the puniest of the Blossoms."

"Blossoms?"

"Yeah," Hobey said, laughing. "Ever since their granny Iris's and mom Iris's time, all the Bellamy women have been called flower names. Town calls 'em 'Bellamy's Blossoms.'"

Clay's lips quirked into a grin. So he'd not been too far off thinking of the tart-tongued banker as Magnolia Blossom. "So how'd you know she was the one?"

Hobey met his gaze head-on. "She stands to lose the most if the man she hired turns out rotten."

"Doesn't look that way to me. Miss Louella's the owner."

"Miss Louella might lose money, but she'd still keep the house. Maggie . . . she could lose her job."

"Why?"

Hobey's *tsk-tsk* ricocheted through the empty house. "Son, you seen the way she looks."

Visions of gold curls, blue eyes, and diminutive delicacy danced in Clay's head. "Yeah, but what does her beauty have to do with it?"

"Well, it's like this. She ain't got a whole lot o' sense. Or at least that's what folks what knows her better'n I do say."

"She doesn't strike me that way," Clay said, returning to his sanding so Hobey wouldn't catch his burning interest in this latest turn of the conversation.

"She ain't no taller'n a mite, is as hardy as dandelion fluff, and none too old. If I recollect rightly, she's just turnin' twenty-six. Them's three strikes against the lady."

The memory of their encounters had Clay shaking his head. "I don't think I can agree with you, Hobey. She's been tough as polyurethane every time we've faced off."

The mason scratched his ruff of hair. "Ain't that the stuff you put over finished wood to protect it?"

Clay nodded.

"I hear it's pretty brittle, too. Kinda like Maggie. I figger she's gonna crack into a jillion pieces if she cain't get this job done."

Clay thought over his friend's assessment. "I do know she's determined to see it through. And she's not about to give me a penny more than we agreed on."

"That's no surprise. What d'you need me to do?" Hobey queried.

"Grab a rag from the bag in that corner, and wipe down the panels I finished sanding. Then I'll run the shop-vac so I can start staining first thing tomorrow morning."

As Hobey did what he was told, Clay thought about Maggie. Could her brambly behavior be due to her vulnerability? Could fear of losing her job be making her impossible to work with?

Was everyone in town so blind they couldn't see she was tougher than her Southern belle exterior suggested?

Maybe. If nothing else, he grew more determined than ever to find out what made the beautiful Miss Magnolia Bellamy tick.

🌿

The next day, Clay's most recent suspicions about Maggie were proven true. At 11 A.M., who should *tap-tap* her high heels across the room but the Steel Magnolia herself!

She was checking up on him—not once, but twice a day.

He felt hunted, and a twinge of fear tightened his stomach muscles. He'd been in this position before.

"How can I help you?" he asked, forcing his painful thoughts aside.

She came closer. "Ah'm jus' doin' mah job, Clay."

Hmm . . . his quick-to-translate brain told him the mush she'd voiced meant she was as nervous as he. If so, then why had she bothered to come during the middle of the day when it struck him as easier to snoop after she'd chased him out in the evening?

"Be my guest," he said with a wave, hoping she didn't catch the tenseness in his voice.

As he returned his attention to the panel he'd started staining, Maggie's small cream pumps entered his line of vision. He refused to think of the way she affected him just by her presence—of the way her eyes made him want to come closer while her tongue made sure he stayed away. He especially refused to think of what might happen if she ever dropped the porcupine act.

He was still attracted to her—even though he knew she wasn't a Christian. It was the most disastrous attraction he'd ever experienced.

"Oooh," she murmured, distaste in the sound. "What's that stink?"

Clay glanced at her, noting the crinkling of her nose. Across the rippled skin lay a dusting of the faintest freckles, a detail he hadn't noticed before. Something about those tiny dots of color struck him as . . . endearing.

Uh-oh. I'm falling deeper into trouble here. Remembering her question, he said quickly, "I don't notice anything unusual."

"Well, I do."

He turned to see if he could identify the source of the smell and noticed she stood right over the open can of stain. "Bet you this is what you smell," he said, tapping the open can. "It's the stain for the wood panels."

She leaned closer and sniffed. "Ew! That's it all right."

As he sniffed in turn, he caught the sweet hint of flowers,

a soft, warm fragrance that was all woman. It tugged at him, entreating him to come closer to its source.

Whoa, boy. "Seen enough?" he asked roughly, returning to his panel.

"For the moment," she answered, her voice betraying her surprise at his sudden change of tone.

"Then since you've assured yourself I'm not conniving to steal Miss Louella blind, I suggest you get back to work and let me do the same. I'll see you at six."

From the rapid tattoo of those heels, it seemed Maggie couldn't get away from Clay fast enough to suit her.

Fine. Things were back as they should be.

Clay continued smoothing color onto the rich wood, but his thoughts refused to move away from Maggie. Her unfounded suspicion always brought to life the misery of his past ordeal. And the remembered pain gave birth to fear—fear that it could happen again.

Clay wasn't sure he'd survive another prison term.

Why couldn't everyone be like Hobey? Yesterday's conversation with him had brought Clay a satisfaction he couldn't ever remember experiencing before. He'd bared his soul to a virtual stranger, and that stranger had treated him with compassion and respect.

That stranger had taken him at his word.

In Clay's estimation, Hobey was the best example of a Christian saint around—as flawed as any other human, yet filled with the Savior's love, looking at another with Christlike eyes.

"Oh, Father," he murmured out loud, his heart so full he didn't know what to do with the emotions swelling in it, "thanks for Hobey's friendship. His faith in me is so encouraging, especially when I have to deal with Maggie's contempt."

Bowing his head, Clay couldn't stop a tear from dampening

his lashes. "It still hurts, Father. The memories burn in my gut—the fear that those who learn about my past will think less of me." The ache roiled in him, bringing bile to his throat. "Why can't there be more Hobeys? The world would be a much better place. And why does Maggie feel the need to be so suspicious? Why must she doubt me based on my place of birth?"

As if God had spoken out loud, Clay knew the answer. *Because she doubts God.*

That's when Clay realized just how dangerous the pretty banker was. Her lack of faith in God left her with nothing to claim, nothing to hang on to in times of trouble. All she knew, as she'd said, was what her senses showed her.

If the evidence against him looked bad—which it already did, from Maggie's point of view—her faithless nature would lead her to the same conclusion at which others had arrived a lifetime ago.

❧

At 11:45 that night, Clay slipped out of his bedroom without making a sound. The rooming house was silent, too—the peace of night a pleasure. Too bad *he'd* found no similar peace since Maggie's visit to the job site earlier that day.

As he'd silently consumed Cammie's delicious supper—he assumed it had been delicious, as everything she prepared always was, but he'd tasted none of what he'd chewed—he'd come to a conclusion: Since the strange occurrences at the Ashworth Mansion continued unabated and since he was the one whose future was in jeopardy, then he would take the only possible precaution left to him.

He would guard the mansion through the night.

When he'd sleep, he didn't know. Maybe he didn't need to worry about sleep, though. If Maggie Bellamy pointed her graceful finger at him and named him a swindler, he could be looking at years of prison time to do nothing but sleep. He'd never forgive himself if he failed to keep that from happening to him. Again.

He tugged the hood of his black sweatshirt further over his face, glad he'd decided on the black running shoes last fall. It wouldn't help his cause if a local cop caught him skulking around the mansion.

Descending the stairs, he held his breath. Only a few more steps to go, and he'd be on his way, undetected.

"What's wrong, Clay?" Cammie asked from behind him, her soft voice robbing him of thirty years of life. "Can't you sleep either?"

Ordering his heart to quit thumping, he forced out a smile for his landlady. "Nope. I thought a run might tire me out."

She cocked her head and gave him a doubtful look. "I don't know. I've read that exercise before bedtime makes it harder to fall asleep."

"Hey, I'm not sleeping as it is, so I may as well give my heart a good workout." As if her sudden appearance hadn't already done that.

"I guess." She followed him down the remaining steps, then went to the kitchen door. "I'll stick with my chamomile tea. It seems to help, and it even tastes good."

"Well, if I have no success with the run," he said, gently teasing his hostess, "I'll try your tea when I get back."

She smiled. "I'll leave the box on the table for you. I hope you find your rest."

"You too, Cammie. You and your baby need it."

As he left the house, his mouth turned grim, and his resolve strengthened. No one was going to put him behind bars again. Especially not for vandalism he didn't do.

Clay would stand guard at the Ashworth Mansion every night until the restoration was completed—even if it was the last thing he ever did.

SEVEN

CLAY APPROACHED THE ASHWORTH MANSION IN THE clear moonlight, his admiration for the venerable home greater than ever.

With the moonlight softening the harshness of neglect, the mansion showed the promise of what it might be once Clay restored it. He couldn't help but stop and stare. Then he realized he wasn't doing himself any good standing on the sidewalk. Who knew what was happening out back? Who knew if Maggie really locked up the place as she insisted she did every night?

That was his greatest fear. What if she had something to do with the vandalism?

The possibility horrified him.

But what could she possibly gain from it? Was she capable of such destructiveness? such treachery?

He didn't know, but he meant to find out—just as he meant to learn everything about Maggie Bellamy. Not sure how to go about it, however, he'd decided to start at the house, the bone of contention between them, as Miss Louella had said.

Taking care not to make any sound, Clay walked across the far end of the Ashworth property line, making sure not to venture onto Mr. Malloy's manicured lawn. He'd been warned by *Mrs.* Malloy.

As he cut across the yard a moment later, heading for the rear of the mansion, a strange noise came from inside the house.

Aha! His heart kicked up its beat. His blood rushed through his veins. The skin at the back of his neck prickled. Maybe—just maybe—he'd caught the vandals in the act.

He measured his pace, making sure of his step. The last thing he wanted was to stumble and fall over any construction debris that might have been missed by the sub crews at the end of the workday. He didn't want to alert the crooks inside.

Excitement filled him. If he could identify the culprit or culprits, he could finish his job without fear that his past might become his future. He could do what he'd been hired to do, then get on with his life.

His determination redoubled, he carefully approached the back steps. Confident they wouldn't creak since he'd just replaced them, he trod onto the first one.

As if by calculated design, a cloud suddenly obscured the moon, rendering the night pitch-black. At the same time, a bloodcurdling howl erupted inside the house just feet away from Clay.

His heart quit beating.

His breathing failed.

His blood congealed.

Clay stood frozen, horrified to realize he'd heard Cerberus warning him away from that hound's infernal domain. As he stood there waiting for the certain, upcoming attack, irrational laughter bubbled in his throat.

This wasn't the time to remember Greek mythology—never

one of his favorite school subjects. It was merely an inappropriate something his subconscious had dredged up at the worst possible time.

Even if that wasn't the three-headed guardian of the ancient Greeks' netherworld inside the house, the beast posed a danger to him. Where had it come from? Why hadn't he been warned?

Then he knew.

The beauteous and treacherous Maggie Bellamy didn't trust him. She'd probably laid the canine trap in the hope of catching Clay in the act.

Anger surged in him, clearing his throat of the coppery taste of fear. Just wait. Just wait until he saw the suspicious Magnolia Blossom again and confronted *her* with *his* suspicions.

As the cloud continued its path across the stygian sky, the light of the full moon illuminated the mansion's back door. What should he do now? He certainly couldn't try to break in. That would make Maggie's day. But he also couldn't give up. He had to protect his interests; he had to watch out for the vandals.

Eyeing the stoop with a jaundiced eye, he grinned wryly. What he wouldn't do to keep from going back to jail unjustly, he thought. In comparison to a prison cell, the small landing looked welcoming. He'd park himself there, wait for whomever was responsible for the weird stuff going on in the mansion, and in the morning worry about the knots in his spine.

Clay pulled the drawstring around the hood of his sweatshirt more closely against the cool spring breeze. He had no criminal intention. He only wanted to finish his restoration job, then go back home. And if to accomplish his goals he had to sleep outside, well, it couldn't be helped.

His determination stronger than ever, he trod onto the middle step.

"*AWWWROOOOOF!*"

He froze again.

Cerberus didn't.

The scratching on the other side of the door made Clay's hackles rise. He'd just finished painting that door. Since he knew the door was solid, he also knew he wasn't about to become the beast's midnight snack, so he took the final step onto the small porch.

More scraping.

A pitiful whine.

Another deep, bloodcurdling "*AWWWROOOOOF!*"

A complete canine cacophony of yelps and booming barks followed, punctuated by the destructive scratching.

Clay's rage boiled, but he realized there was absolutely nothing he could do but leave. Otherwise, the creature would trash the door, requiring him to replace it rather than just sand and paint it—again—and add to the mounting costs of restoring Louella Ashworth's ancestral home. Clay couldn't afford any more setbacks. No matter that the most overgrown dog—if not a miniature draft horse—had taken up nocturnal residence in the house. At Clay's slightest movement, the beast again howled. Growled. Barked at earsplitting decibels.

Hating this sense of impotence, Clay retreated. What was he going to do? What *could* he do?

As he headed back toward Cammie Sprague's rooming house, his feelings crystallized. Maggie Bellamy stood out as the source of his suspicion, frustration, and fear.

Somehow *she* was behind the debacle with the dog. Clay didn't know how he knew; he just felt it in his gut. She'd better watch out. He wasn't going to let her lock him up again.

At the persistent shrill of her alarm clock the next morning, Maggie was tempted to call in sick and stay in bed. But being too conscientious to do so, she smacked the shut-off button and made her aching body roll out of bed. True, her paid sick days were untouched, but since she wasn't sick, she didn't feel right missing work to catch up on her sleep.

Even if she'd lost that sleep while doing her job.

A puppy yawn from the corner of the room made her smile. "Morning, darlin'," she murmured, then went to rub Buford's sturdy neck, his wrinkly forehead, his solid belly.

The rascal wriggled with joy at her attention, and Maggie basked in the pleasure of dog ownership. "And there are those who say you're the wrong one for me!"

Buford rolled over, sat, and cocked his head, his expression comically quizzical.

"Precisely!" she exclaimed. "The moment I saw you, I fell in love. Now that I've had you five months, I know you were the best decision I ever made."

The puppy nuzzled her hand. Maggie grinned. "Not enough for you, sugar?" She rubbed the wrinkles between his eyes, then up higher on his skull, finishing with a pat to each of his folded-down black ears.

Although at nine months Buford was technically still a pup, he stood twenty-seven inches at the withers and weighed in at one hundred pounds. Solid and muscular, he was a perfect specimen of the bullmastiff. When full grown, her baby would probably weigh what his sire did, a massive one hundred and thirty pounds, and be a powerful force.

His bark already sounded full grown, as it had last night at the mansion. Maggie's heart had nearly stopped when he'd let out that first howl. It *had* been a good idea for her to guard the mansion with Buford. Her baby barked at even the drop of a needle into a haystack, so he was the cheapest and most effective guard around.

Last night she'd thought for sure they were about to catch the vandal, but Buford's guard-dog efforts had driven away whoever had been outside.

She was glad. She'd gotten her baby for that most salient talent of his: Bullmastiffs were known as fearless protectors, had in fact been bred through the years to protect what and whom they perceived as theirs. Maggie had wanted a companion she could depend on when she felt her weakest, her least able. Nighttime was the worst; she was all alone—until Buford entered and brought the pleasure of his presence into her life.

"Enough now, darlin'," she said, then hurried to shower. A rushed half hour later, Maggie had dressed in a blue linen suit and off-white moderate heels and pulled her hair into a sleek French twist. After crating her rascal to prevent puppy mischief, she dashed out to the car. She was running late, and Clay was sure to be waiting at the mansion.

When she pulled up to the curb, she found him sitting on the verandah. "What took you so long?" he asked.

"Overslept," she answered truthfully, then ran up and opened the mansion.

Turning to head back to her car, she found her gaze snagged by his. A foreign shimmer ran through her, disconcerting her. How could he do that—look into her soul like that? What did it mean?

"Oh, flapjacks," she said crossly, looking away.

"Flapjacks?" he asked, humor in his voice.

"Do you have a problem with that, Mr. Marlowe?"

He chuckled, shaking his head. "No, Miss Bellamy, none whatsoever."

Holding herself erect, she descended the steps and started back down the brick walk.

"Mornin', Maggie!"

Startled, she looked toward the sidewalk. "Oh! Mrs. Langhorn, how are you?"

"Fine, honey, and you?"

At that moment, the most uncouth yawn hit her, making it impossible to respond.

"My, my," said the bookstore owner, shaking her trademark silver pageboy as she came down the sidewalk. "It looks to me like you need to catch some rest. Your granny Iris always said you tried too hard. She was right, you know."

Her cheeks blazing, Maggie said a bit defensively, "The work's got to get done. But you know that. You're a successful businesswoman, too."

The trim, navy-suited lady smiled. "I think I've finally arrived to where I can acknowledge my success."

"I should hope so," Maggie said. "I know I spend plenty at The Blissful Bookworm."

The woman's shrewd, sideways scrutiny had Maggie regretting her words. "Haven't seen you there in a while," her late grandmother's friend said.

Maggie waved vaguely. "Too busy, Mrs. Langhorn."

"Nonsense! A good read will do you wonders. Why, look at the Garden Club. Everyone has finally come to understand what Louella and I have been saying for years. The latest Marvin Pinkney novel will cure what-all ails you. At least, for a couple of exciting hours."

Maggie wrinkled her nose. "He's not my type."

Penciled-in pewter brows rose. "You just haven't given him a chance."

"One book was enough."

"But there's so much to be learned from his tactics," Mrs. Langhorn insisted.

"I'm afraid that as a loan officer I don't need to know much about international intrigue, murder, or mayhem."

"You'd be surprised how much of his knowledge can come in handy—even in little old Bellamy," Mrs. Langhorn countered cryptically.

"Oh?" Maggie queried.

The glint of a true Pickney fan brightened Mrs. Langhorn's small dark eyes. "Why, sugar, Louella has assigned our members a chapter of Marvin a night. As homework, you see."

This supercilious secret agent was a role model for the biggest busybodies in Virginia? "Huh?"

With a pat to her sleek bob, Mrs. Langhorn answered, "Indeed. We're benefitin' from it enormously."

"The bookstore, maybe."

"That, too. But it's the Garden Club I mean. We've learned so much, and are puttin' it to *excellent* use."

Stumped about what Mrs. Langhorn meant, Maggie remained skeptical. "If you say so."

More sage nods. "I do, honey, I indeedy do." Mrs. Langhorn glanced furtively at the mansion and then smiled. "Now, dear, I must get along. I have the store to open. Have I any hope of persuadin' you to join the club?"

"No, ma'am. I'm too busy at the bank to do much gardening these days. Maybe sometime in the future."

"One can always hope," said the aging purveyor of quirky secret-agent books as she hurried on her way.

Maggie stared after her.

"What do gardeners want with a two-bit 007 clone?" Clay asked.

Maggie turned, realizing she'd somehow managed to forget his presence. "I have no idea. But then we're talking about the Garden Club."

Again that puzzled expression caused Clay's smooth brow to crease. "That says it all?"

"To those from Bellamy," she responded.

"And to those from elsewhere?"

She shrugged and started toward her car.

"Care to explain?" he asked, following her, his voice louder, intractable.

She gave a vague wave. "Too long an explanation. Too little time."

"Some other time, then."

She looked at him then and recognized his steely determination; it matched her own. "Maybe. If I have the time. It doesn't have a thing to do with you."

"Maybe not. But I'm curious."

Maggie slipped behind the wheel. "Funny, you don't look like the cat curiosity did in."

She turned the key, and the Miata's engine purred to life. As she burned rubber pulling away, she could have sworn she heard him growl. He sounded nothing like the feline she'd compared him to but remarkably like Buford had last night.

When Maggie was leaving the office for her midday check on the mansion, Ruby's voice came over the intercom. "Maggie, Mr. Hollings wants to see you in his office."

"Now?"

"What do you think?"

"But it's my lunch break."

"Not today it isn't."

Tamping down her irritation, she capitulated. "I'll be right there."

As she strode down the carpeted and wood-paneled hall toward her boss's office, Maggie mentally flipped through all her current projects. None came to mind as potential cause for the summons.

Except the Ashworth Mansion.

As she knocked on Mitch Hollings's door, she prepared herself mentally for the battle ahead. Too bad each time she faced Mr. H it felt like going to war for her career, her reputation, her self-worth.

"Come in, Magnolia."

Donning a smile, she closed the door behind her. "How may I help you, Mr. Hollings?"

"Dunno that you can, missy." He waved an unlit cigar in the direction of the leather settee in front of his vast desk. "It's more of me wantin' to help you."

"I'm afraid I don't follow you, sir."

"You will. Just sit." For all his gruffness, Maggie knew Mitch Hollings was a good, honest man. If he had too wide a skunk's streak of good-ol'-boy running down his back, well, that was just the fly in his ointment.

He flicked his Bic. "You mind?"

She did, but didn't think it would do to object at the moment. She checked the window and rejoiced in its open position. "Go right ahead, sir."

When the noxious fumes filled the air around his head and wafted in her direction, he leaned back in his leather chair. "It's like this, Magnolia. The restoration of the Ashworth ain't going too well, it seems like to me."

"Oh, no, sir. Everything looks lovely. The paneling in the library is magnificent, and the chimneys are solid once again."

"Nah," he said into an exhaled puff of smoke. "I'm not meanin' the house itself, and you know it. I mean the money—our business here at the bank."

"Oh."

"Yes, Magnolia, oh. Where's the money goin' so jackrabbit fast?"

"Well, sir," she said, searching her suddenly blank mind for a workable explanation, "Mr. Marlowe found that more flooring was unsound than he'd initially expected, so that accelerated the need for the second installment of the construction loan."

The bank president's tufty black eyebrows scooted together. "Floorboards? Don't b'lieve it, Magnolia. Must be more to it than that."

"We're also in need of authentic nineteenth-century doors, doorknobs, and bathroom fixtures. I imagine they're quite expensive."

Mr. Hollings's dark head shook from side to side. "Not enough there, girl. You need to keep a closer eye on this guy Marlowe. Whaddaya know about him, anyway?"

Maggie's cheeks warmed. "His reputation's the best, sir. I'd never have hired him otherwise."

"But is he honest?"

"From all accounts. I checked every reference."

"Did you run a check on priors?"

"Prior whats?"

"Convictions. For all you know, the guy's a con."

Maggie dismissed the suggestion. "I doubt it. His references went back to his early twenties. They all sparkled. Besides, he doesn't strike me as a jailbird."

Mitch Hollings rose. "What would it take for a man to strike you as a jailbird?"

"Oh, I don't know. Maybe a rough manner, a tattoo or two, beady eyes. You know. A shiftiness in his behavior."

"Ever hear of white-collar crime, Magnolia?"

"Sure, but Clay Marlowe's a carpenter by trade. He's not an office worker."

"Still, I'd be settin' more comfy here if you'd have him checked out."

Something about the prospect felt wrong to Maggie. But she couldn't decide quite what—or why. "Of course, Mr. Hollings. I'll do it as soon as I have a moment."

"See that you do, Magnolia. I've a bad feelin' on this one.

I'd hate this account to go sour on you. You know how important it is."

Maggie's middle clenched. "Of course, it's important. All my accounts are."

"Then count yourself warned. I don't want Louella hurt. Or you."

"Thank you, sir, but I'm on top of the situation."

His black eyes grew shrewd behind the cloud of putrid smoke. "I wonder, girl. I really have to wonder."

Maggie rose, anger and fear impelling her. "No need for that, Mr. Hollings. I know what I'm doing. If you'll excuse me, I'll go right back to it."

With a nod, her boss dismissed her. Maggie forced herself to open the door gently, although her instincts were to yank it. *Hard.* But she closed it—gently, too—and marched down the hall and out the parking-lot door.

Clay Marlowe had better be prepared to answer some questions, she thought furiously. Her competence had again been questioned—and all because of him, that Yankee scalawag.

E I G H T

As Maggie ran up the front steps of the Ashworth Mansion—fuming—she heard a guttural roar inside the house.

"What's going on here?" she asked, rushing in the direction of the dining room, from where the sound had come.

She skidded to a standstill when she reached the open double doors. The sight before her was enough to bring a grown woman to tears. As it nearly did.

The gorgeous fireplace, which had been faced with exquisite delft tiles, stood denuded of its decoration, the ceramic squares neatly stacked to one side. As if that weren't bad enough, the intricate parquet floor had . . . well, lost its intricacy. The lighter rectangles that brightened the geometric pattern were scattered here and there, as if a careless domino player had tired of his game.

But this was no game. The holes left in the pieces of wood were painful to view—as were the rage and anguish on Clay Marlowe's handsome face.

To Maggie's surprise, not a curse spewed from his lips.

Rather, he formed another wordless sound of rage, frustration, and helplessness.

"Why?" he asked a moment later.

"You tell me," she answered, in complete accord with the sentiments on his features. "I can't conceive of anyone doing such a thing."

His eyes narrowed. "Can't you now?"

His steely stare sliced at Maggie. The implicit accusation stung her. "What on earth do you mean?"

"Never mind," he replied, turning away. "What did you want?"

An unexpected pang of sympathy struck Maggie at the sight of his sagging shoulders, his lowered head. "I just came on my regular visit to see how things were going. But I never imagined I'd find things so . . . catawampous."

He looked at her over his shoulder, and she caught the upward tilt of his lips. "If that 'cat' word you used is a Southernism that means something like being caught between the devil and the deep blue sea, then, yeah, that's exactly how things are."

"Well, they've certainly gone from bad to worse."

"I'm back to square one."

"You may even have your back against the wall after this."

He scoffed. "I'm not licked yet."

Maggie cocked her head. "Do you mean that if this is the whole ball of wax in their bag of tricks, they're barking up the wrong tree?"

"What do you think? If *they* think they're going to make me beat a hasty retreat this way, then they've got bats in their belfry. I'm more determined than ever to batten down the hatches and bear the burden and the heat of the day. They'll have a battle royal on their hands, and I promise you, I'll beat their band all hollow."

Admiration surged in Maggie. "My goodness, Clay Marlowe, you sure do have a way with words. For a Yankee."

To her amazement, the man burst into deep, rich laughter. In fact, he roared with it. Robust peals rang through the room and out into the rest of the vacant house.

Maggie felt torn. Half of her quivered with indignation. After all, she knew instinctively that he was laughing at her compliment, hard to believe as that might be. The other half of her wanted to acknowledge the appeal of Clay's laughter. The masculine sound tripped up and down her spine, sending shivers through her.

She'd never felt this way before, so attracted to someone so wrong for her. Especially since he was, in essence, laughing at her. "What's so funny, if I might ask?"

Clay notched his laughter down to a rumble. "You."

"How dare you!" Maggie exploded, her pride nicked.

"Now don't go puffing up like a cat . . . or should I say a catawampous?"

"I'll have you know, that's a perfectly good word. And it has nothing to do with cats."

"I figured that much out, Maggie," he said, a twinkle in his feline eyes. "I'm not stupid, and I didn't park my smarts on the other side of the Mason-Dixon line."

"If that's the case, then what *were* you laughing at?"

"You." At her renewed sputter of objection, he held his hand out. "Wait. I mean that what you said was hilarious."

"Oh?" she queried, her skepticism running rampant.

"Yeah. You just told me I have a way with words, and all I did was counter your clichés with more of the same."

She scoffed. "I'll have you know, I do not use clichés in my conversation."

"Wanna make a bet?"

"Of course not. I'm a banker, not a profligate with my money."

"I don't wager either, but you're a fount of clichés, idioms, and maybe a proverb or three. Mangled, too."

Why did everyone accuse her of that? "Not at all. I use the English language in inventive ways. I enjoy putting a different twist to the familiar. That way, I can't be called boring."

Again, Clay Marlowe indulged in that unbridled display of hilarity that challenged Maggie's temper. This time, though, she'd had it. "What now?"

"You. Again."

"How so?"

"You're all sorts of things, Magnolia Blossom—like laced up tighter than a Victorian lady's corset, a workaholic of the first degree, a Confederate jingoist, and stubborn to the point of intransigence. But I can promise you this: you are *not* in any way, shape, or form, boring."

Maggie frowned. Had he insulted her or complimented her? Or both?

She studied Clay, waiting for her answer. "Oh, flapjacks," she said without thinking, then glared at him. "And don't you dare laugh at that, too."

A patently false expression of innocence brightened his face. "Wouldn't dream of it."

"Hah!"

"No, really."

Maggie flung her arms heavenward in surrender. The man was impossible. With everything he did—every word he uttered—he drove her nuts, confused her, and unfortunately, fascinated her, too.

Despite the evidence against him, some bizarre, unreasonable quirk inside her had kept her from launching an in-depth investigation of Clay's past as Mr. Hollings had suggested. She hated Clay for it—or at least she tried to tell herself she did. She didn't trust him, but she grudgingly admitted that she might, under different circumstances, come to like him.

All of this was utterly insane, of course, since Maggie was certain Clay was behind the monkey business at the mansion. Granny Iris had always warned her three granddaughters to beware of Yankees with hungry pockets, and Clay had all the earmarks of one.

She was insane to even think of liking the man—especially since circumstances were no different than they had been fifteen minutes ago.

She surveyed the latest mutilation. When she glanced back at Clay, the humor had vanished from his face. "What are you going to do?" she asked, sobered.

"Only thing I can do. Fix it again."

"You mean, you'd finished with all this?"

"Pretty much. I was waiting to do the windows before applying the topcoat to the floor."

"No wonder you were so upset."

"Still am. But it won't do the house or me any good to feed my anger."

She shook her head. "That's not natural, you know."

"What isn't?"

"To deny you're angry at what happened."

"I'm not denying it. I'm just choosing not to act on it." He gave her a long, and in her mind, measuring look.

"But if you didn't do it—"

"I didn't," he cut in, his words precisely chiseled.

"Then you have every right to be angry and to look for the one who did it. Justice, you know."

"Oh, I am angry. I want the culprit brought to justice. But I'll leave that to the chief justice," he said, jerking his chin skyward.

"Oh," she said flatly. "You mean God."

"I mean the one and only God, Maggie. My long-term goal is to honor him with my life. My short-term goal is to restore this house to the best of my ability. And if by doing that I can help apprehend the guilty party, then God, who loves truth, will be honored."

"Whatever you say," she said, not buying his logic—not after her experience with God. "If you're not guilty, don't you want to prove it to everyone?"

Clay sighed. "I did to begin with. I even tried to catch the criminal at his game. But when my efforts failed, I realized I just needed to turn the mess over to God and get back to my business of fixing the house."

"Doesn't your reputation count?"

"More than you'll ever know."

"Then why don't you do something?"

"I have. I've taken myself out of God's way because he can handle the situation better than I can. And I don't have to prove anything to him."

"I don't know," Maggie said slowly. "I just don't buy it. It's not *natural.*"

To her surprise, he nodded. "You're right. It's *super*natural. It's God's way, not man's."

"I . . . guess. If it works for you, then fine. But I have to see—"

"And smell and touch and hear and taste. I remember what you said. That's too bad. You're missing the very best there is. God's infinite love."

"That's my choice, Clay." Uncomfortable with the latest turn of the conversation, Maggie walked over to the fireplace. She ran a hand over the mortar with its ghostly squares marking where the tiles had been. "Yours is to go on with the restoration. What will you do first?"

"I'll sort and replace the parquet as best I can."

"Then?"

"Tomorrow I have an appointment to meet the manager of an architectural salvage firm in Baltimore. I need to pick out doorknobs, bathroom fixtures, maybe a door or two, and some lamps. I refuse to put that off and let my schedule fall so far behind. Not for some sick thug who gets his kicks from watching me run circles around his tricks."

Maggie barely heard his tirade; a phrase had caught her attention when he'd begun. "Hmm . . . an architectural salvage firm," she said, turning the concept over in her mind. "If it's what I think it is, that trip sounds fascinating."

"Only if you like old homes."

"Why do you think I'm in charge of this particular account?"

"None of the other bankers had time to handle it?" he asked with a mischievous grin.

"Nope. None of the other bankers could stand the smell of old wood, the creak of old floorboards, the guttering of old lights. Since Miss Louella and the ladies of the Garden Club knew I share Granny Iris's passion for history and antiques, they wanted my knowledge on the mansion's side. I love it all."

He gasped and clutched his chest theatrically. "You mean we have a shared interest?"

She nearly giggled. "Truth is sometimes stranger than fiction."

"I'll say."

"So what does an architectural salvage company have in its . . . warehouse? store?"

"Warehouse. They have lots of neat old stuff. You name it. They have floorboards, windows, mantels, lamps, bathtubs, sinks, whole barns, even. Anything old that came from a building, basically."

"That does sound neat," she said, deciding then to take a trip into Baltimore one of these weekends and snoop out the place. "Where is it?"

Instead of answering, Clay grew quiet. As if pondering the

secrets of the universe, he rubbed his fingers over his chin. Abruptly he said, "Wanna come?"

"You mean . . . with you?"

"Well, I didn't exactly have a trip with a terrorist in mind for you."

She'd better not look at his gift horse's teeth too long or too carefully. "Sure! I'd love to. What time?"

"I figured on leaving at eight tomorrow morning. We'll be there all day—maybe even eat supper in town. Can you take the time away from work?"

Maggie knew everyone at the bank would be stunned when she announced she was taking a day off, but she couldn't make herself turn down Clay's invitation. She didn't dare examine why any too carefully. "I have plenty of vacation time coming to me."

"Well, then, I guess we're set."

"For tomorrow at eight o'clock sharp."

Neither Maggie nor Clay could come up with a thing to say after that exchange. Finally, desperate to end the silence, Maggie leaped for the first conversational gambit she could think of. "How will you fix the floor?"

"Here, let me show you," he answered, his relief evident. "Grab a bunch of the wood pieces and join me in this corner."

As he moved toward the far end of the dining room, Maggie bent to scoop up a handful of rectangles, suddenly determined to learn how to repair parquetry. Not that she had any immediate use for the talent, since she lived in Bellamy's only apartment complex, but her dreams were grand. Almost as grand as the Ashworth.

Clay's generosity in sharing his knowledge wouldn't go to waste. Not as his hard work had done at the hands of a vandal.

If a real vandal had indeed been at work.

For the first time it occurred to Maggie to wonder why she hadn't shared with her boss her own suspicions about the Yankee she'd hired—and suspected from day one.

The two-hour drive to Baltimore was . . . interesting. Or so Maggie thought as Clay parked his maroon pickup truck behind a massive building. He'd suggested she choose some music, but after inspecting a selection of classical stuff she didn't recognize, she opted to turn on the radio.

That hadn't worked either. He'd objected to her country western station on the basis that life had enough true hard-luck stories to be forced to listen to more while he drove.

She'd countered that she didn't have that high a brow and that classical music consisted of nap-inducing sounds that should have been retired at about the same time the composers did.

They'd then driven in charged, irritated silence.

To Maggie, it had seemed as though they'd never reach their destination, but ultimately the country roads decked in blossoms gave way to bumper-to-bumper traffic and exhaust fumes. When Clay pulled up behind the brick behemoth, she figured they'd arrived.

Thank goodness! Now she could lose the taciturn man at her side and explore the treasures in the cavernous warehouse by herself.

"Maggie? You have to be careful in there. The stuff's dirty, rough, and although these guys try to watch for nails and other dangerous things, it's not a museum."

"Give me some credit, please. I did dress for the occasion."

Clay smiled—for the first time that day. "I'd love to see what you think is appropriate for roughing it."

Maggie glanced down. "What's wrong with what I'm wearing?"

"Oh, nothing—for an afternoon's shopping at the nearest mall or dinner at a friend's house. But linen pants and a silk blouse are more fragile than this place has ever seen."

It was Maggie's turn to glance askance at her companion. "Knowledgeable about women's clothes, are we?"

"No. Just experienced in architectural restorations. I often work with the decorators and am familiar with linens and silks."

Maybe. Then again, maybe not. Clay *was* extremely attractive. Maggie didn't imagine his social calendar stayed empty long.

"I'll worry about my outfit. I want to see what's inside."

"Then let's get going." He held the gray-painted steel door open and followed her inside.

In the dark, mawlike entrance, Maggie felt tinier than ever. Above her, ceilings rose thirty feet in the air, and the space before her was lined with racks of items and stacks of wood. As her vision adjusted to the dimmer lighting indoors, she found no rhyme or reason to the arrangement of things in the gargantuan storage bin she'd entered.

Then the gleam of brass caught her eye. Following its call, she found herself staring at a jumble of old, frayed, cloth-covered electrical wires and even older lamps. Among the certifiable fire hazards, she found a lovely milk-glass-and-brass shade topping a tarnished green base. The piece was perfect for the mansion's parlor—once restored, of course.

"Clay! Look what I found."

As she wrestled with the wicked cord attached to her find, she waited for Clay to acknowledge her words. When no response came, she turned and saw him scaling a skyscraper of boards. When the slab of wood on which he stood wobbled, she caught her breath.

"Clay . . . ," she called in warning.

Evidently he didn't need her caution or her concern, for he balanced on the loose plank, then dropped down to a less precarious perch. His attention never wavered from the materials he'd gone to inspect.

Again Maggie felt unwanted admiration creep up on her, and not just for his undeniable good looks. It seemed as though Clay's strength went through to his character. In spite of her disinterest in his faith, she was attracted to him because he stood firmly on his convictions, voicing them without apology. She appreciated a man who could speak his mind and heart so openly.

Then there was his obvious talent. She'd inspected at least a dozen sets of photographs depicting his earlier projects. The before-and-afters were impressive.

Even his work ethic matched hers. He was always at the mansion waiting for her, and in the evenings, she practically had to drag him away to close down for the night. The men he worked with seemed comfortable in his presence, and she'd never heard him raise his voice to any of them during the many visits she'd paid to the site.

From all she'd seen and experienced of Clay Marlowe, he appeared a paragon of virtue. Still, because her job was riding on the line, she felt she had to exercise caution around him. She couldn't afford to be taken in by his handsome face. She had to forget the stray thought that had crossed her mind in the ravaged dining room yesterday.

Teetering on a mountain of fine old floorboards, Clay caught Maggie watching him. He'd felt her attention, if not her gaze, during the drive into town. She'd unnerved him.

Especially after they'd debated the merits of country

music—none, in his unbiased opinion—and classical pieces—priceless and infinitely enriching to the human intellect, again in his unprejudiced opinion.

Not that Maggie had agreed. She'd gone as far as to suggest a similarity between the string section of one world-famous European symphony orchestra and the caterwauling of a pair of hungry tomcats fighting for a single fish.

But she'd known her love-'em-and-leave-'em-crying-buckets tunes and stars. And she'd sung along with the single song he'd tolerated in a clear, sweet soprano, her features alive with enjoyment.

She'd had no qualms about telling him what was wrong with his choice of music. Nothing much seemed to intimidate the woman.

So why had Hobey hinted about her low self-esteem? Was her antagonistic approach to life a cover for self-doubts? If so, he knew one way to heal her. The best way. Maggie Bellamy had to meet her Maker. She needed to come to Christ.

NINE

AFTER LOADING A MINIWAREHOUSE'S WORTH OF MERCHANDISE into Clay's truck and arranging to have the rest of their purchases delivered to the site the next day, Clay and Maggie climbed into the cab, wincing at the humid heat that had built up as the day had progressed.

Clay glanced at Maggie. "Air?"

"Please!"

In her Southern vernacular, the word possessed at least six syllables and flowed from her lips with the sweetness of honey.

Clay grinned. Maggie Bellamy could be a pleasure—when she dropped her contentious attitude. Right now it looked as though the hope of relief from physical discomfort would go a long way toward improving her disposition.

Nothing, however, seemed to disrupt the appeal of her beauty. She'd pulled her blonde waves away from her face with plain silver clasps that stood out among the gold of her hair. The green of her clothes reflected in her expressive blue eyes, turning them aquamarine. Her obvious enjoyment of their outing lent a rosy glow to her fair skin.

Yes, Magnolia Blossom was well named. Elegant, feminine, delicate, lovely.

Dangerous.

To him.

She'd stated her position from the start. She had not one iota of trust in him, and she'd have no problem turning him in to the authorities—on just the merest suspicion. Telling her about his past was something Clay couldn't risk, no matter how much she intrigued him or attracted him. No matter how much he recognized her need for God.

He had no intention of backing away from what he suspected God was counting on him to do; he *would* share his faith with Maggie at the right time. But he also had to watch himself. Because she wasn't a Christian, he couldn't get involved with her, regardless of how easy and appealing it would be.

Then it hit him. *What if . . . ?*

"No!"

"Come again?" Maggie asked.

Good grief! He'd objected to the ludicrous thought out loud. He couldn't very well tell her that for the shortest spit of a second he'd wondered if God hadn't brought them together, inciting the interest Clay felt for her as part of his eternal plan. For Clay. And Maggie.

No way!

She'd probably see his interest in her as some nefarious scheme to bamboozle money out of her. Which was the furthest thing from Clay's mind.

The only thing on his mind was a normal, healthy relationship with a woman who appealed to him in so many ways. No red-blooded male could fail to notice how gorgeous Maggie was—or to appreciate her determined nature, her work ethic, her persistence. She loved history as much as Clay did—even if she had it skewed toward the Confederacy—and the respect she showed Louella and the rest of her cronies was admirable.

Too bad Maggie was the wrong woman for him to like. He'd be nuts to think of her as a part of God's plan for him.

"Nothing," he mumbled, noting she still stared at him as if he'd grown another nose.

"You often talk to yourself like that?"

Only when you make me crazy. "Never."

"Mmm . . ."

He squirmed under her scrutiny. "What does that mean?"

"One would assume *never* means just that—never. And here you just did. Talk to yourself, that is. It would seem you don't notice when you do it."

You're doing it again, Maggie. Making me stark raving bonkers. "Must be something in the air."

She laughed. "All I can smell in the air is the bay. We're almost at the waterfront, aren't we?"

Phew! New subject. He grinned. "I've been heading that way. I figured we'd catch an early dinner—*supper* at the Inner Harbor."

She gave him a suspicious look. "So long as you don't expect me to eat scaly or slimy sea critters."

Clay's jaw gaped. "You mean . . . you don't eat seafood?"

She gave him a what-are-you-stupid? kind of look. "Is it scaly? Is it slimy? Then of course I don't eat it."

"You don't know what you're missing."

"Oh, but I do. Scales and slime."

"Come on, Maggie. Fish only have scales while they're in the water."

"Um-hmm."

He sighed in exasperation. "The scales are gone by the time your meal's served."

The stubborn set of her jaw became more pronounced. "I still know they were there when the critter started out."

He tried another tack. "I've never had any seafood that was slimy."

She fired a determined look at him. "Shrimp shells are slimy, octopi are slimy—don't even mention squid to me—clams and oysters and scallops are slimy."

A grin escaped his control. "Okay. How about lobsters? There are no scales or slime on them."

Maggie shuddered delicately. "It's those beady eyes . . . and those claws . . ."

He laughed. What else could he do? "Okay, you win. I'll take us where I can have my weekly dose of scales and slime, and you can have your feathers or fur."

"Oh, dear," she cried. "If you put it that way, I guess I'll only be havin' my roll and iced tea."

"Cheap date, are you?"

Her eyes widened. "Of course not! This isn't a date. Why on earth would you say that? It's business. *Business,* you understand?"

Hmm . . . the lady seemed to protest more than he thought the comment merited. Could she be fighting the same attraction he was?

At the red light, Clay peeked at Maggie, seeing the flush on her cheeks, her averted gaze. When she looked directly at him, what he saw in those beautiful eyes got him. Questions. All sorts of questions—the dangerous kind he'd been asking himself ever since they'd met.

There was no doubt about it. Maggie wasn't immune to him.

Although he should have been alarmed by his discovery, the male in him set up a victory cheer. It felt great to know he wasn't alone in this insanity.

"What was that you said?" he asked, knowing perfectly well.

As he turned into the parking lot he always used when

visiting Baltimore's Inner Harbor, Clay got another clear view of Maggie, who was now intertwining her fingers in her lap.

"Business," she said in a tight voice.

But as he took the parking ticket from the ticket-dispensing machine, he caught her looking at him again. The confusion in her eyes gave her away.

"We're here," he announced. The meal would become impossible to eat if he didn't rebuild a rapport between them. Among all the things he already associated with Magnolia Blossom, he didn't want to add indigestion to them.

"Ever been here before?" he asked as he took her elbow and led her into the Rusty Scupper.

She shook her head, but to his surprise didn't pull free from his grasp.

He persisted—if only for the sake of his stomach. "I think you'll like it. They serve fur and feathers. Oh, and rolls, too."

She glared at him—thank goodness. That he could deal with.

"I'll have you know," she said in a familiar, uppity tone, "a lot of people don't enjoy seafood."

"Yeah, but I'm not eating with them. I'm eating with you."

A hostess bearing menus approached. "Two?"

"Yes," he answered, releasing Maggie's elbow so they could follow the woman between the tables.

He missed holding her, even though it had only been for a few minutes and in an impersonal way. Through the silk of her sleeve, Clay had felt the movement of her slender arm, the warmth of her skin. He'd liked it—too much.

Business, she'd said. He should remember that's all it should be. *Could* be. Reconstruction business.

The Lord's business, too.

"So," he said, once they sat facing each other, "are you hungry?"

"Mmm . . ." she answered, pulling the menu up higher.

He grinned. Oh, yes. Maggie Bellamy was fighting the same crazy feelings he was. They were both playing with fire. Its warmth felt delicious.

"Rats!" he said quietly when he realized where his thoughts had strayed.

"I don't believe you," she stated, the menu dipping.

"Huh?"

Blue eyes met his. "You said there were rats. I *know* nobody serves rats, even though they're covered in fur. And there aren't any runnin' around the floor. So stop teasin' and choose your scaly, slimy meal."

Uh-oh. She had good hearing. "I didn't say that . . . I mean, there are no rats here. It's just an expression . . . oh, never mind." She really was making him nuts. "Go ahead and choose your feathers and fur."

When the waitress took their orders and retrieved the menus, Maggie asked for chicken. Clay ordered shrimp.

Through the window by their table they watched the powerboats on the harbor zip by. Farther out, majestic sailboats glided over the calm water. Across the way, the geometric lines of the Baltimore Aquarium caught the early evening sunlight, reflecting the glow off its many panes of glass. Behind the aquarium, an erstwhile warehouse boasted the familiar logo of the Hard Rock Café, and midway between that and the Scupper, a mall filled with specialty shops and a Planet Hollywood attracted hordes of customers.

"Lively place, isn't it?" Clay said to break the silence.

"Amazing how much it's changed in the last ten years."

"I love it down here. There's so much to do, to see."

She gave him a knowing look. "I suppose you come for the symphony."

"Guilty as charged," he answered, remembering the last concert he'd attended. The orchestra had performed Aaron

Copland's *Appalachian Spring*—one of his favorites. "Do you ever come down this way?"

"Of course. The Orioles are here."

"Ah. Baseball."

"What else is there?"

He chuckled. "I never would have thought—"

"What?" she asked, sparks flashing in her blue eyes. "That a woman might enjoy sports? Why, that's the most chauvinistic, idiotically backward notion—"

"Hold it, Maggie," he said, cutting off her diatribe. "I was going to say that I wouldn't think you take much time off for entertainment. You strike me as very focused on your work."

She reminded him of a balloon that had just met its first—and last—pin. "Oh. Well, yes, I am dedicated, but I love the Orioles. My daddy used to bring us down when we were little, and I went whole hog for the whole shootin' match and whooped it up good."

With awe-inspiring control, Clay kept a straight face at her latest turn of phrase. "So you root for Maryland's team even though you're a Virginian?"

"Virginia doesn't have a team."

"So you adopted Maryland."

"Maryland *sports.*"

"Not the state?"

"Not at all."

"Why not? What's wrong with Maryland?"

"Nothin' . . ." she said as the waitress placed full plates of food in front of them. "If your preference runs to wishy-washy, teeter-tottering states."

"What does that mean?" he asked after bowing his head for a brief, silent prayer.

Her chicken-laden fork paused an inch away from her lips. "Don't they teach history up North?"

Clay groaned, suspecting what lay ahead. "Again?"

"Always."

He swallowed his shrimp, fearing a date with Pepcid tablets lurked in his immediate future. "Something to do with the war, right?"

"Of course," she said, waving her now-empty fork. "Marylanders' sympathies lay with the Confederacy, as well they should have. But the state stood to lose too much money if they seceded, so they hemmed and hawed fit to beat around the bush, wafflin' long enough to feed the whole Confederacy breakfast."

Clay fought another grin. He wondered just how well she knew her history. "If I were you, I'd watch what I say about Maryland."

"What do you mean?"

"Virginia did its share of wavering."

Blue eyes blazed again. "But the minute Lincoln called up those seventy-some thousand troops, we made our decision and seceded. Maryland didn't pay a whit of attention to his blatant display of intended aggression against sovereign states."

He grinned again—with mischief. "Ah, but not *all* of Virginia seceded."

Indignation made Maggie sit up tall. "Why, of course we did. Richmond even became the capital of the Confederacy."

"What about *West* Virginia?"

She stuck the last baby carrot in her mouth, chewed, swallowed, then said, "West Virginia's an apple of discord in the Confederacy's eye. They did a Benedict Arnold to their sister Southern states by glommin' on to the Union like that."

"Not quite." At her quizzical look, Clay went on. "Yes, the western counties of Virginia decided they wanted nothing of the Confederacy, formed a new state, and seceded . . . but from *Virginia."* At Maggie's look of outrage, he quickly stated,

"But you should know that. After all, your neck of the woods had to have considered that possibility."

"Why, I never . . . !"

"Well, you'd better, because it's in the history books."

The waitress removed their plates, replacing them with a brownie à la mode for Clay and a kiwi sorbet for Maggie.

Dessert did nothing to sweeten the combative look on her face. "But—"

"Face it, Maggie. The Civil War became a nightmare. Too many lives were lost. It was a tragedy for the entire nation. The only good that came out of it was abolition and the reunification of the country. It's now been over for more than a hundred and thirty years. Let it go."

She didn't come back with a retort. Instead, she stared out the window, spooning frozen kiwi pulp into her mouth. Then in a soft voice she said, "I can't. It's who I am."

What a weird thing to say, he thought. "No, it's not. You're Maggie Bellamy, loan officer at the Bellamy Fiduciary Trust, history buff, country-music fan, antique lover, friend of elderly ladies, and sister to a bike-riding redhead. You're not a relic from the past."

"You don't understand, do you?" she asked, her eyes growing sad at the mention of her sister. He wondered why, but not for long, since she said, "My roots are in the South. My ancestors fought for what they believed in. I belong to that honorable tradition, and I'm proud of it."

Certain he knew how she would answer, he still couldn't help asking, "You honor the tradition that gave us the horrors of slavery?"

Maggie shook her head. "Never. Slavery was wrong. But so was the North's decision to force their will upon sovereign states. That's why the South attacked Fort Sumter—the Union refused to withdraw their troops from the new nation's territory. Slavery was just the excuse the North used to destroy a form of democracy different from theirs. *That's* in the history books, too."

He sighed. "We're not going to resolve a matter so many gave their lives for years ago, so how about if we head on home? I see you're done with dessert."

Maggie nodded and pushed away from the table. "I need to use the ladies' room. I'll be right back."

As Clay watched her graceful walk, he couldn't help but admire her again. Not because she moved so well, but because she stood up for what she believed. Even when she was wrong—in his not-so-humble opinion.

What troubled him, though, was the way she'd said the Confederacy was who she was. Maggie was a lot more than a descendant of Civil War soldiers. She was a smart, competent, articulate woman. He again remembered his conversation with Hobey.

Maggie seemed to have no idea how special she was, but Clay knew just who could teach her. "Lord," he uttered quietly, "give me the right moment to tell her about you, to show her how much you love her, how precious she is in your sight."

"I'm back," said the object of his prayer.

Clay stood, wondering if she'd overheard him talking to God. From the bland expression on Maggie's face, he figured she hadn't. If she had, given her agnostic bent, she would likely be tearing into him right now. "Then we're off," he said, clasping her elbow again and noting, to his dismay, how much pleasure the contact gave him.

The ride home was pensive rather than strained. Surprisingly, it wasn't their political-historical debate Clay remembered. It was the fire in her eyes when she argued a point.

There was no doubt about it: Maggie Bellamy was a passionate woman. The more he came to know her, the more that passion fascinated him. What would it be like to be loved by Maggie?

Then he remembered something distasteful—Maggie and her geriatric lover. What was his name? Beauregard? Buford? Some such Southern name. And the guy was incontinent, to top it off.

Maggie wasn't immune to Clay. Last time he checked, she wasn't married, either. Could that other relationship have ended without his learning about it? She had no reason to tell him such personal things, after all.

"How's Buford?" he asked, curiosity getting the best of his manners.

"Wonderful! The darlin's the joy of my days. I don't even like to remember what life was like before him."

Great. He'd asked. Now he knew more than he'd wanted to know. Still, something egged him on. "How long have you two been together?"

"Nearly six terrific months now."

Swell. "I see."

Gritting his jaw, he forced his gaze forward. But when she slipped a golden wave that had escaped its clasp behind her ear, the lovely motion of her hand caught his attention again. He remembered how she used those feminine, expressive hands to emphasize a point.

As he completed the drive to Bellamy, he thought about the straight line of her nose, the curl of her eyelashes, the curve of her cheek in the rosy light of the setting sun. The flattering glow of dusk made her skin look even smoother than usual. Could that cheek be as velvety as it seemed?

Would her hand feel as soft in his as it looked relaxing in her lap? Would the skin of her palm feel as warm as her elbow had, or would nerves make it cool to his touch? Would she let him hold her hand to find out?

In spite of himself, Clay wanted those answers. He wanted

to know Maggie better, as the lovely, complex woman she was—even if she did provide a threat to his career, his future.

Once in front of Maggie's apartment building, Clay ran around the car to open her door. But she beat him to it. Since the sun had set miles before they'd reached town, he insisted on walking her to her door.

As she fumbled in her purse for her key, he said, "I had a great time."

She shot him a mischievous grin. "In the presence of a Rebel, no less."

"You're more than that, Maggie, much more. And you should know it."

Before he voiced his last word, he knew he'd made a mistake. Maggie's eyes opened wide. The air between them grew charged, dense with the pull that had existed from the moment they'd met.

Clay found himself drowning in a sea of blue, the vulnerability in her beautiful eyes drawing him deeper into the heart of them. Closer to her.

Crazy. This was totally, incredibly, stupidly crazy. But he could no more move away than he could make his heart stop beating. He let his arms encircle Maggie's slim form, lowered his head, and felt her warmth. The intoxicating scent of flowers and woman sent his senses reeling. As he covered Maggie's lips with his, the sweet heat of the caress burned all common sense right out of his head.

TEN

CLAY WISHED SOMEONE WOULD SHOW HIM THE BEST WAY for a man to kick himself after doing something mega-stupid—like losing his mind over a woman.

He'd never let anything like this happen to him before. Because of his past, he'd had few romantic relationships. He'd date a special lady a few times; then when he felt something deeper than friendship might grow, he'd either tell her his story or back off in fear of her potential reaction to it. He'd learned through bitter experience that soon after those painful conversations, broken dates and excuses would begin. Before long, a "Dear Clay" letter followed. So he'd taken to keeping his distance from women, certain none could ever love a con.

An innocent con, but a con nonetheless.

Yet here he'd gone and kissed the one woman who, without any prior knowledge of his past, was ready to throw the book at him.

Why had he found so much to like about Maggie? Especially when there was so much *not* to like about her. Like her misguided defense of the Confederacy, her sharp tongue, her readiness to argue any point, her suspicious nature, and most important, her rejection of Christ.

That last one felt like a boulder crushing Clay's heart. How could he be so attracted to a woman who'd turned her back on God? It didn't make sense. They had *nothing* in common.

They didn't like the same music.

They didn't eat the same food.

They didn't even enjoy the same sports. She liked baseball, the slowest game invented, while he liked soccer—fast, brainy, *and* physical.

They had absolutely nothing in common.

Well . . . they both liked history, even if they did view it from different perspectives.

They both loved antiques and century homes.

They both took their careers seriously and worked hard.

They both were outspoken about their convictions, even in the face of opposition.

But that wasn't enough to warrant the powerful pull she had on him, was it?

They argued every time they came in contact. Clay doubted they could spend much time in each other's presence without at least one verbal battle. And their disagreements always swung around to the matter of his character sooner or later. Maggie thought him capable of swindling Louella Ashworth out of her money.

He could have accepted her initial suspicions since they'd never met before they'd signed the contract. But after she'd had time to watch him work, to see him for the man he was, Maggie had seemingly chosen to remain blind, expressing her lack of trust every chance she got.

She might as well have hired Hinkley. Then she could have put her distrusting nature to excellent use. Then she'd have had good reason to think her restorer was out to gouge Miss Louella.

As he turned onto Main Street after bidding Maggie good night, Clay's thoughts remained turbulent despite the peace of the small-town night.

Maybe Maggie deserved to wind up with a guy like Hal as a restorer. After all, she'd been in contact with the guy even after Clay started work on the mansion. He remembered that day when he'd walked into her office and seen the letter from the louse sitting smack on her desk.

Why had it been there? Had she been lining up a replacement for him as far back as that? If so, then it meant that she'd been sure Clay wouldn't finish the job.

Why?

How?

Did she have inside information?

Inside what?! he thought with a start.

The more he thought about it, the tighter his stomach knotted. A sour tang bit into his chest. He wished he had his trusty pack of Pepcid tablets with him, but he'd left it on the dresser in his room at Cammie Sprague's house.

As he rolled down the quiet, moonlit streets of Bellamy, Clay again admired the attractive houses, the clean streets. It was a good place, a pleasant town. He wished it didn't harbor so much danger for him—especially from a woman out to get him.

Minutes later, he pulled into the alley behind the Sprague home, parked the car, got out, and leaned against the wooden fence of the neighboring house. With every passing minute, his questions jelled more and more.

Hal had bombarded Clay with rage and offensive words as soon as he'd learned Clay had won the bid to restore the Ashworth Mansion. The slap of Maggie's knee-jerk suspicion had followed that initial salvo. Then Hal's letter on her desk had scored a slug in Clay's gut. Suddenly Clay realized he needed to view these past facts in the light of the ongoing vandalism.

It all added up. Maggie was in cahoots with his most bitter rival, and Clay had been dumb enough to kiss her. A kiss that still thrummed on his lips. A kiss he wanted to repeat, but couldn't.

She'd made a fool out of him, but that didn't mean he'd let her send him back to jail.

⚘

At noon on Monday, Maggie left her office, as had become her habit, and headed for the Ashworth Mansion, dread now tensing her shoulders, nerves chilling her hands. She'd somehow managed to unlock the place that morning without having to meet Clay's gaze. Not that she hadn't felt it focused on her every second she stayed in his presence. Now, in order to do her duty, she'd have to see him, speak with him again.

She wouldn't be able to avoid those all-too-seeing cat gold eyes. Saturday evening's kiss hung between them like a block of moth repellent at the door of a woolens warehouse.

Both of them shared the same apparent goal—restoring the mansion—but something kept them from reaching it. To Maggie, the vandalism made it clear that her suspicions about the handsome, fascinating, infuriating, devastating kisser were anything but unfounded.

Why had he done it? Was he trying to smooch her past her wariness?

If so, then he'd missed the boat when he'd booked romance on the *SS Maggie.* She was not the kind of woman to be swayed by a trip to a fabulous antique-treasure trove, a meal at the classy Inner Harbor, or a knee-melting kiss at her front door.

She wondered if she'd ever again manage to talk to Clay

without staring at his lips, especially since she could swear she still felt their pressure against hers. The heat of his mouth against hers had stunned her; the support of his tender caress around her had thrilled her. She'd realized in those few delicious moments how lonely she was.

That had terrified her, and it still did.

She had nobody in her life but a dog. Her sisters . . . they were siblings only in a biological sense. She had Miss Louella's friendship. Well, they were more like close acquaintances brought together by a shared interest. While Buford was a love, he would always be what he was: a dog. He'd never be the one to hold her through the lonesome night, to bind up her hurts, to cheer her successes, to dry her tears when she mourned.

For the first time in her life, Maggie faced the yawning need inside her. To her horror, before her loomed nothing more than that same void.

She cursed Clay for making it all too real to her.

She could no longer deny her inner hunger for . . . more. More love. More passion. Just . . . more. The question was, where could she find that enormous, vague *more?* Who would offer it to her? And at what cost would it come?

As she approached the mansion, Maggie caught sight of the gorgeous stained-glass window in the middle of the second story. She'd always envied that dove soaring across the sky, flying high above the pristine white cloud. She wished she knew that kind of freedom instead of the boggy loneliness she worked to deny day after day.

"Hey, Maggie," Clay called out as she clenched her fists at her side.

That first glance of the man brought the wondrous sensations of his kiss rushing back through her. She cursed him— again—for bringing to raging life the things she was missing.

"Hello, Clay," she said, trying not to give away her inner turbulence. "How's work today?"

In a gesture that had become too familiar in their short acquaintance, he ran a hand through his wavy brown hair and rubbed the back of his neck. "They struck again."

At his words, his gaze seemed to dive inside her, looking for answers she knew she didn't want to give . . . didn't think she could. With difficulty, she turned away from the scrutiny. "What did they do this time?"

He shook his head in disbelief. "They busted out the walls in the bathroom to remove the water pipes. Why? It makes no sense."

"Show me."

Why was he vandalizing his own work? He knew she wasn't going to cave in and give him more money than they'd contracted for. What would he gain from such destruction?

Maggie followed Clay up the stairs, noting the rigidity in his back. He was upset, no question about it. But was it due to her restraint with the money, or did trashing treasures of years ago bother him as much as he said it did?

Then why was he doing it? She came back to that same question time and time again.

At the door to the bathroom he stepped aside to let her look in. The wreckage hit her hard; her stomach churned. Huge, gaping holes showed where pipes had once supplied water to the enameled cast-iron claw-foot tub, the shell-edged pedestal sink, the vintage water closet. The pipes themselves lay in a careful pyramid, like discolored bones awaiting a decent burial.

Tears of frustration stung Maggie's eyes. She blinked hard to keep Clay from seeing how deeply his criminal actions hurt her. When she felt in sufficient control of her chaotic emotions again, she spun around.

"Why? Just tell me why?"

"That's my question for you, Maggie. Why?"

Like a pair of boxers in a ring awaiting the bell, they stared at each other, their eyes full of questions. Maggie felt a powerful urge to shake Clay, to force him to confess, to pry from him an explanation for the unexplainable.

Her icy hands hurt from clenching them. Her neck and shoulders cramped; her head throbbed. How was she going to keep this man from ruining her career? from stealing the last of Miss Louella's money? from destroying the proud, solid, magnificently triumphant structure that had seen so much and survived through so many years?

How was she going to stop this man who had already destroyed her equanimity, stolen her peace of mind, shown her the emptiness of her life? When he'd done it all with one brief, complicated kiss?

Maggie didn't know.

Panic threatened.

🌿

Clay could have cut the tension in the bathroom with a putty knife. He fought his every urge to force a confession from Maggie, knowing she was too strong-willed to cave in that readily. He needed evidence of her criminal actions. Catching her in the act would do the trick. But that dog . . .

Clay stared into blue eyes that made him feel so many things, and his heart cried out. *Why, Lord? Why her? Why do I feel so much around her? Why can't I put her out of my mind, even when we're apart?*

Heaven offered no immediate answer, but Maggie broke the tension by pushing Clay aside and running down the curved stairs. As she threw open the front door, he heard Miss Louella's voice.

"Why, hello, Maggie, dear . . ."

It petered out as Maggie's tapping heels didn't pause.

Clay heard the elderly owner of the mansion say, "I reckon she's runnin' from herself again." Then, louder, she called out. "Clay? Clayton Marlowe, where are you?"

To Clay's surprise, his throat had constricted too much to respond. Yet another sin to lay at Maggie's feet. He coughed the thickness away. "Upstairs, Miss Louella." When he remembered why he was in the bathroom, he hurried to say, "But don't come up. It's not safe here yet, and I'm on my way down anyway."

As he clattered down the stairs, he noticed that the heiress looked impeccable. Her apricot-toned suit brought out the color in her cheeks and enhanced the sorrel and bronze tones of her well-maintained hair. Her eyes remained as alert as ever.

Before he had a chance for a proper greeting, Miss Louella aimed those silver stilettos straight at him. "Did you do somethin' to scare her off?"

"I'd say it's more like the other way around."

A discreetly darkened eyebrow showed interest. "Care to explain?"

"Soon as I have an explanation, I'll pass it on to you, ma'am."

Her gaze focused on Clay until he felt like a five-year-old caught with his hand in the proverbial cookie jar. This woman was nobody's fool. Then again, neither was Maggie.

But he couldn't afford to think about Maggie now. "So, Miss Louella, how can I help you today?"

"I just came by to look around, see how things are goin'. I'm right pleased with what I see, I must say."

It's what you don't see that worries me. "Thank you," he said, fighting back the betraying words.

"And . . ." she added, looking around, "I was wonderin' if

you'd come across any clue as to the whereabouts of my great-granddaddy Asa's treasure durin' your work."

There she went again. "Treasure?"

Miss Louella's eyes widened. "Don't tell me you don't know! How could you not? Remember the diary you found?"

"Oh, yeah. That's right. You and the other ladies called it a treasure."

"Well, yes, it is. But in the diary, Asa says he hid a treasure of the Confederacy in the mansion to preserve it for posterity."

"Really?" he said, surprised. "I haven't seen a thing." *Other than evil at work,* he thought.

"Oh. That's a shame," Miss Louella said, disappointment adding unexpected years to her attractive face. "I guess we must carry on, then. And trust the Lord."

"Always," Clay said, surprising himself with the emotion his voice injected into the single word.

Miss Louella's laser gaze zeroed in on him again. "Do I detect trouble in your response, son?"

"We all have trouble, Miss Louella. You know that."

"Are matters with Magnolia heatin' up?" Miss Louella asked bluntly.

The memory of their stunning kiss flashed through Clay's mind, followed by the more recent charged exchange in the upstairs bath. "You could say that."

As the senior studied him, Clay's discomfort grew.

"Have you ever thought," she finally said, her words measured, "there might be more than triflin' differences makin' you two whomp heads every time you meet? God may have brought you together for his marvelous purpose, and you two may just be fightin' that plan."

Amazed that she could read his thoughts, he blurted out, "That's what I'm afraid of."

She laughed. "You'll do fine, Clayton Marlowe. Just fine,

indeed. No matter how troublesome things appear in the goin'."

He turned to look out the window, wishing for himself a measure of the peace he found in the azalea-rife garden. "That's what I keep telling myself, but things get more and more grim."

"Remember the psalmist's words: 'Weepin' may go on all night, but joy comes with the mornin'.'"

Thinking of his past, his present, his unclear future, Clay faced his employer again. "It's been a very long night already."

"Then the joy will be that much sweeter, if you trust God," Miss Louella said. Again her gaze bored into him, making her words a question.

He sighed. "I do, but I'm growing impatient. It's that old-flesh nature rearing its nasty head, I'm afraid."

"Forgive my presumption," Miss Louella said thoughtfully, "but this seems like a time to consider what Jesus said in Matthew, and pray together: 'For where two or three gather together because they are mine, I am there among them.'" She held out a hand.

Clay felt the need to take it.

As he reached for her hand, a weight fell on his shoulder. "Count me in on this threesome, son," Hobey said, making his presence in the room known for the first time. He met Clay's questioning look straight on. "Came by to see how you were doin'. Seems God knew where I was needed most today, as usual."

That evening as she huddled on her couch, Maggie scrubbed the soft wrinkles on Buford's forehead. Every word uttered, every glare exchanged during that awful bathroom confrontation swirled in her head, over and over, nonstop, making her dizzy with the speed of the gyrations.

She'd cried so much that she felt pretty well dried up, as if the void inside her had swallowed up even her ability to make tears. It seemed to deepen every day, eating up greater chunks of her as time went by.

That was a ridiculous thing to think, wasn't it?

Who wanted to cry anyway? If the void wanted those over-active glands, why, it could surely take them. She was through crying!

Then she heard unwelcome voices out in the hall. Lark and Cammie. The voices were followed by brisk knocking at her door.

"Rats!" she exclaimed softly as she stood, then froze. Clayton Marlowe was a menace. He even had her using his own stupid expression.

Vacillating between the miserable thoughts she'd been wallowing in and the disturbing arrival of her sisters, Maggie wished she could just disappear with Buford. Maybe the two of them could whoosh away to a wonderful paradise where painful memories and people's stereotypes didn't count. She longed for a place where she could come home, feel enfolded in endless love, know what it was like to be accepted for who she was, as she was. And loved anyway.

But that kind of love didn't exist. Paradise didn't exist.

So she sighed and opened the door.

As typical, Lark charged in, every red curl quivering with energy, long limbs eating up the length of Maggie's small living room. Cammie followed, her pace sedate, comfortable, her pregnancy giving her a look of utter contentment despite the frown.

Maggie closed the door behind her sisters, as always wondering at Cammie's unusual, unshakable peace. How did she do it? Where did she find it? Even through an unhappy marriage that had ended in tragedy. And now she was a pregnant widow. She shook her head and focused on the present. "To what do I owe this unexpected pleasure?"

"Cut the garbage, sis," ordered Lark, smacking her fists on her hips. "What's going on at the Ashworth? And what are you doing about it?"

Through sheer will, Maggie forced one breath, then another, into her dead lungs. She felt life return to her numb body, warmth to her cheeks. "What . . . do . . . you . . . mean?"

As if she sensed Maggie's shock, Lark softened her tone slightly. "I heard about the fireplace, the tiles, the floor. What's up?"

How? Where had Lark learned this? Maggie hadn't told a soul. She'd thought Clay wouldn't either. Who had?

Hoping to brazen her way out of this predicament, Maggie got huffy. "Well, if you already know all that, why are you asking me?"

"What are you doing about it?" Lark demanded, not even blinking.

"I'm handling it."

"How?"

"Why do you need to know?"

"Because I'm your sister, and I'm worried you can't—"

"Stop it right there, Larkspur Bellamy," Maggie ordered, steel in her voice. "I'm a grown woman, even if I'm also your younger sister. You don't need to worry about me or my job. I can handle it."

"But, Mag, you've never had to do anything so . . . so . . ."

"So adult? So serious? Needing a modicum of basic intelligence?" Rage boiled in Maggie's veins. "And I couldn't get the dumb chicken across the road he's been crossing for centuries 'cause short, blonde Maggie's even dumber'n the chicken. Right?"

For once, the gutsy Lark had nothing to say. Her jaw gaped too low.

Cammie stepped forward, her hand reaching for Maggie, who pulled away.

The youngest Bellamy Blossom winced. "Maggie," Cammie said gently, "we're worried this is going to hurt you—badly. If what Lark's learned is true, then criminal charges will be pressed somewhere along the line. We don't want you dragged into that mess. We want to help."

Maggie glared at Cammie, who shrank back. "What you mean is that you don't want the Bellamy name muddied, isn't it? You don't want incapable li'l ol' Maggie making both of you successful, happy women look bad."

Maggie was shocked by her own bitter words. Even though her sisters had hurt her more deeply with their words than anyone ever had, she hadn't planned to let her feelings and thoughts out. Certainly not at sweet Cammie, and not even at Lark, who deserved it sometimes.

But maybe at Clay.

"Just go," she said, when she couldn't handle another second of the awful silence. "Please. I'll get through this on my own. I have everything under control."

"I can see this isn't the time to reason with you," Lark said, pain in her green eyes. "Come on, Cammie. She's closed her mind to logic right now."

"No, Lark," Cammie said, heading for the door. "She's closed her mind to love. God's love."

"Don't start in on me just as you're leaving, Cammie," Maggie warned.

"I won't. But you can't keep me from praying for you."

"You're right, I can't. But I can keep you from making me listen to it."

They left. Darkness closed over Maggie, despite her late mother's Tiffany lamp burning brightly on the table.

Renewed sobs ripped through her as fear pelted her like hail in a storm. Maggie sat back down on the couch, and Buford crawled up next to her, trying his best to comfort her.

But nothing worked.

ELEVEN

At 11:15 p.m., with Buford's leash in her grip, Maggie locked the door to her apartment. She was still devastated by what had happened among the three Bellamy Blossoms a few hours earlier.

She hadn't known where all her passion, anger, and rage had been hiding, but it sure wasn't hiding anymore. She'd thought she was in control of her emotions, that she never allowed herself to wallow in the past. But now she realized she'd actually bottled her pain and brewed it up good. With a head rivaling the one on Granny Iris's root beer, it had built up, then burst off its lid and spewed down onto her sisters.

Sure, she resented the way they treated her, and she hated their strained relationship. But none of that was new. They'd always behaved the same way toward each other, and things had gotten worse after their parents had died. Maggie's petite fairness had seemed to draw from them a suffocating sense of responsibility. Unnecessary, of course.

Now things had changed. How much, she didn't know. She didn't even know if she wanted to find out.

Still, she didn't like the way she'd exploded. She'd rather have kept those feelings hidden, where no one else could see the ugliness inside her. If anything, her explosion gave her sisters more reason for their lack of confidence in her.

Buford trotted beside her, his keen nose twitching at interesting scents in the shrubs, his eyes missing nothing in their proximity, his muscular heft comforting in the night. Bullmastiffs had been bred by crossing bulldogs and mastiffs to protect gamekeepers from poachers in old England, and the resulting animals fought to the death to keep their person safe. She was thankful for the sense of security Buford gave her.

And yet, even though she and her canine protector had spent each night at the mansion since the ladies had agreed upon it at the Garden Club meeting, Clay had continued to further devastate Miss Louella's house. How *was* that man getting in? And when?

Maggie arrived every night at 11:30, made sure things were as they'd been during her six o'clock inspection, then stayed until five the next morning—she did need some rest and time to get ready for work. Her schedule didn't give Clay much opportunity to do his dirty deeds.

She doubted he could get in before or after her stints. Before eleven, too many folks took dogs for their evening "constitutional," since this was a residential neighborhood. After five, the occasional early-bird worker or jogger was already out and about.

Nobody had reported any strange occurrences at the house, no odd comings and goings. Nothing weird had happened while Maggie tried to catch some rest in her sleeping bag in the mansion's kitchen.

The only outcome of her vigilance was a bone-deep weariness that increased each day. And night. Maggie's back ached. Her legs had developed an unshakable stiffness. The shadows under her eyes were taking up permanent residence. She looked a fright and felt even worse.

All this led her to believe that Clay had to have had an ulterior motive for kissing her after the day in Baltimore. No man would succumb to the lure of a haggard woman—not unless he had a particular reason to do so.

As she and Buford approached the Ashworth, clouds covered the skinny moon, rendering the night gloomy and redolent with danger. Even though she tried to tell herself her imagination was running wild, she couldn't deny that criminal acts were taking place. Maggie feared that the perpetrator might harm her if he came upon her in her little nest at the rear of the house.

She shot a love-filled glance at Buford. She shuddered at the thought of anyone harming her beautiful dog, and she sickened at the thought of being harmed herself.

Still, duty called her to keep up her watch, and so she let herself in the rear door. Slipping the pack off her back, she spread the sleeping bag in her usual corner, then went to check on the house.

Room after room looked the same as it had when she'd been there at six. Nothing had been disturbed. Since the vandalism had begun, she'd become hawk-eyed. She noted where every hammer lay, where every can of paint sat, where work was only partway done. Nothing was out of place, and she hoped it remained that way.

As she completed her inspection, she thought about tomorrow, when she'd have to check on Clay at lunchtime, when she'd have to meet the man's gaze, glimpse his lips, note the strength in his build and the assurance he wore with such ease.

The kiss still haunted her. It popped into her thoughts when she least expected it. Each time it left her longing for more—more of Clay's warmth, his tenderness, his support.

But that was utterly ridiculous since they were, at best, opponents in the war over the mansion—not allies to encourage each other, hold each other when things went wrong, comfort each other in frustration or rage, cheer each other's successes, help bear each other's failures.

She had to remember that, and she would. Maggie was determined to eradicate visions of Clay's embrace from her nights and memories of his touch from her days.

But hours later, when the night was still dark and thick, Maggie woke up, her heart beating more quickly than normal. She'd dreamed of Clay again, of his kiss. Only in these latest visions it had tangled with the feelings of unworthiness she'd tried to fight since the argument with her sisters.

Instead of the pleasure she remembered feeling in his arms, she felt . . . diminished, discouraged, defeated. She didn't know by what or by whom. Maybe her sisters—and everyone else in town—were right. Maybe she wasn't more than a knickknack to adorn a masterful masculine arm. Maybe her blonde hair did cover a vacant head. Maybe her loneliness revealed a lack of inner . . . richness or value.

A sob broke in Maggie's throat. Buford roused himself from sleep and snuggled his head under her hand. As she rubbed his warm wrinkles, his love made her feel better. Just a tiny bit.

"Get a grip, woman!" she cried out. "Why, you're mucking in misery worse'n a piglet in a wallow of mud. He's just a man. They're just your sisters. Pull yourself together and get back to business. Nothing to it, Magnolia Blo—"

She stopped, horrified. She'd nearly done it—called herself by the hated, wimpy tag people used to refer to her physical delicacy. Called herself by the name Clay had taken to using for the single purpose of driving her crazy, which it now appeared he'd accomplished.

What was she going to do? How was she going to cope? How was she going to keep her job?

She needed that job. It validated her, proved her competence to herself and to those around her. It was proof of her worth as a person, a capable career woman. If she lost it, how would she prove herself worthy of trust? Or prove herself worthy, period.

❧

After her lousy, nearly sleepless night at the mansion, Maggie had trouble staying awake at the office. Despite her exhaustion and her less-than-focused mental state, she couldn't miss Mr. Hollings's pointed stares in her direction.

Each time Mr. H passed her open office door, she cringed, and her breath grew shallow. If big-time reporter Lark had sniffed out the vandalism, had he? If so, why hadn't he said anything about it? Was he just waiting for her to hang herself before firing her?

She didn't want to talk to him.

She wanted to talk to him and get it over with.

She wanted to quit obsessing over the whole mess.

She wanted it to disappear.

She wanted to run away.

But most of all, she wanted the Ashworth Mansion restored to its deserved state. It meant a great deal to her because it represented everything Maggie longed to be: Southern, graceful, mature, beautiful, strong, enduring through time and adversity, firm in its sense of history.

She wished she had a treasure like the Ashworth to give the town, which her ancestors had founded, but she didn't, so she wanted Miss Louella's home restored instead.

Well, she also wanted Clay Marlowe gone from town. Then

she wouldn't feel duty-bound to check up on him every day, as she was about to do.

With a weary sigh, she stood, stretched her stiff spine, and headed for the bank lobby. She yawned as she approached her secretary's desk. "I'm on my way to the mansion."

The heavyset wonderwoman gave Maggie the once-over. "Watch out for the wily Yankee hunk."

Maggie chuckled without humor. She'd thought she had been, but it no longer looked that way. "I surely will, Ruby. Don't you fret."

It was another gorgeous spring day, with the breeze crisp and perfumed with fresh blooms, and the birds singing their joy to all four winds.

Too bad she didn't feel very spring-sprung inside.

As she approached the house, her heartbeat sped, and she felt the odd anticipation that preceded her every encounter with Clay. She could no longer deny her attraction to the man—even when she should be as leery of him as of a snake in the grass.

At the front door she waited until her eyes grew accustomed to the dim indoor light. "Hello!" she called, stepping into the foyer. As always, the beauty of the aged home caught her imagination. The curved mahogany staircase brought to mind balls and parties, ladies in graceful crinolines descending those gleaming steps, gentlemen in black tails waiting to take their hands.

The chandelier, which had been cleaned and rehung, covered a large area of the ceiling, and when lit, rivaled the most spectacular starry sky. The oak parquet floor underfoot glowed with its new coat of finish as she walked farther into the home.

Maggie often wished she'd lived during those historic days. True, they'd been fraught with danger, as the Great War of Northern Aggression proved, but in her opinion, the folks who'd peopled those days had possessed a special dignity. Somehow they seemed to have cared more, to have held deeper convictions, to have considered their values more important than material wealth.

They'd also possessed a measure of faith in mankind or life—she didn't quite know which—but that faith still shone through their writings and the actions they'd taken. She wondered if she'd someday find that kind of faith, a belief to help her through her life.

Although she didn't agree with them since she saw no proof of God, she sometimes envied Cammie and Miss Louella their simple faith. They claimed they'd placed their trust in the "Rock of Salvation," only Maggie had never come close to seeing, feeling, or even stumbling over that Rock. God hadn't been present when she'd needed him most, when her parents had died. So where was he? Was he real?

"Well, hello there, Maggie, dear," a voice said, startling her. "What are you so intent on ponderin' today?"

Maggie jumped and swiveled to see Miss Louella. "Oh, nothing much. The house . . . its history . . . stuff."

"I'm surprised to find you here, honey. You're always up to your eyebrows in work at the bank."

"This is part of my work for the bank."

"Don't you know, Miss Louella?" Clay drawled, appearing in the doorway to the library. "Magnolia Blossom here is everywhere, even when we least expect her."

His suspicious eyes told Maggie his words were nowhere near as innocent as they might sound.

Miss Louella cocked her head. "What *do* you mean by that, son?"

"Yes, *Mr.* Marlowe," Maggie said, her tone a challenge. "Just what *do* you mean by your comment?"

He glanced over his shoulder at the library walls. Maggie remembered the holes bored into the mellow, aged wood.

"She's around here so much," he offered, "you'd think she was part of the . . ."

For a moment Maggie thought he was about to accuse her—*her,* for crying out loud—of the vandalism. Then he finished, "Crew."

Louella nodded and smiled. "Maggie is wondrously dedicated, isn't she? Why, she's as good at her job as Marvin Pinkney is at his."

Maggie grimaced. "What an *interesting* comparison."

Clay snickered. "Gilding the lily, maybe."

"Calling a spade a spade," she shot back, hackles twitching.

"All that glitters isn't necessarily gold," he rebounded.

"Now you listen here, buster," she ordered, fuming. "You're barking up the wrong tree without a paddle! Since actions speak louder than words, you're your own worst enemy. After all, I'm the one who from the start knew we were throwing wide the floodgates with open arms. I knew you were up to no good, and when all the vand—"

"When the vans are emptied, and all the work is done, you'll see how right you were to hire me," he finished, glaring at her. He bobbed his head toward Miss Louella, then shook his head.

Maggie felt her stomach drop to her toes. She glanced at her older friend, and to her dismay, noted how pale she'd grown. "Oh, dear," she murmured, approaching Miss Louella. "Are you all right?"

"I don't know, Magnolia. You tell me. What's goin' on here? Don't say nothin' now, 'cause I'm no one's fool."

It was Maggie's turn to blanch. She shot a pleading look to Clay, whose cheeks had also lost their normal hue.

Then he gave a wry laugh. "Don't you know, Miss Louella? Magnolia Blossom and I aren't the best of friends. I'm a Yankee, and she's a Rebel. Makes for lots of skirmishes in the war."

"War?" asked the owner of the battlefield. "I didn't plan on one when I set to have the house restored. I don't see why you children are blind to what's before your noses. And I can't condone such ungodly attitudes. You should be ashamed of yourselves. Especially *you,* Clayton Marlowe."

To Maggie's amazement, he went from gray to red in seconds. He looked at Maggie, then at Miss Louella. "You're right," he said, his voice low. "I know better, and I shouldn't let my temper run off like that. I have some praying to do." Turning to Maggie, he added, "I owe you an apology, and I ask your forgiveness for my behavior."

Maggie didn't know what to say. She'd never known a man like Clay, who backed down with such sincerity after being called on a transgression. "It's okay," she responded, squirming inwardly. After all, she hadn't behaved like a shining blossom of the South either.

"I don't know what's gotten into you, Magnolia Bellamy. Why, if your Granny Iris were here . . ." Miss Louella headed toward the door, shaking her head. "I declare, it's a sin, is what it is. I reckon I'd best be callin' a meetin' of the Garden Club Prayer Partners to start us off on a real prayin' storm. Maybe then God'll take those scales off your eyes. Mark my words, Magnolia, if you don't open that hard heart of yours to God, you're fixin' to face some hard times ahead."

The slam of the door resonated through the house, just as the indicting words did through Maggie's aching heart.

There was no talking sense to the woman, Clay thought as he walked home at six that evening. No shame in her, either. How dare she stand in that house, argue with him after setting him up, bamboozle Miss Louella, and finally slink out the door like a wounded warrior? Then she had the gall to come back to close up the house, her nose tipped as far up out of joint as any he'd ever seen.

Anyone would think she'd been wrongly, unfairly accused.

Outrageous! That's what she was. *He* was the one *she'd* put on the hot seat. He was ready to get off it.

Then he groaned. She had him thinking in idioms now, too.

The minute he entered Cammie Sprague's welcoming home, Clay breathed the fragrance of roast chicken and a hint of chocolate. His spirits rose, as he anticipated the delicious food his landlady would serve tonight as she did every night.

He ran up the stairs, dumped his folder of drawings and lists on his bed, and went to wash up. When he came back down, he headed straight for the kitchen. "Can I help with anything?"

"Clay!" she exclaimed, her voice warm and cheerful as always. "Everythin's about done, but you can set the table for me, if you'd like."

"For the woman who feeds me better than the average king, anything."

He gathered silverware, sky blue crockery plates, blue-and-white-checked cotton napkins, and tall clear glasses. "How're you feeling?" he asked, noting how her pregnancy had suddenly popped into view.

"Wonderful!" she said, her face glowing with joy. "How about you?"

He winced, then walked through the door into the dining room, unwilling to let the gentle lady in the kitchen witness his inner turmoil. "Frustrated with work, and dying to finish it," he called back to her.

"I've been told I'm a good listener, and I can do that while I clean greens for a salad."

"Thanks, Cammie," he answered, grateful for her generous

offer of friendship. "My work is tough, and while this job's not going as well as others I've done, I have to remember I'm not ultimately in control."

"Mmm . . . isn't that a tough lesson to learn over and over again?" she asked, her voice sympathetic and underscored with apparent experience.

"You struggle with that, too?"

"All the time."

"But you seem so serene, so content . . ."

"Every day I have to turn everythin' over to Christ— deliberately. Otherwise, I find myself worryin' my way to ideas and solutions that lead nowhere but to frustration."

"Sounds familiar."

"I think all believers deal with that. It's in our rebellious, human nature to forge ahead instead of trustin' God."

Clay flinched. "Guilty as charged."

"Would you like to take a moment to pray?"

"Yeah," Clay said enthusiastically.

She gestured toward the clean, scarred kitchen table, turned off the faucet, and wiped her hands on her apron. Clay watched her easy movements, her open expression. He thought of her uncomplicated approach to life, her simple offer of prayer. He remembered her kindness toward her boarders: the elderly Willie said he'd adopted her, and Suze, her resident teen, had found the big sister she'd always wanted in Cammie.

He admired her courage in facing motherhood at the same time as widowhood. And she did it all with unfailing good cheer and genuine faith in God.

Willie was right. Cammie Sprague would make some very lucky man a happy husband. Why couldn't it be him? Why was he so drawn to the beautiful but snippy, highly suspicious Magnolia Bellamy?

"Clay?" Cammie asked, interrupting his reverie. "Do you still want to pray?"

He smiled wryly. Maggie, Maggie, Maggie. She was too much on his mind. "Yes . . ."

❧

Later, as Clay ate, he couldn't escape thoughts of the trouble at the mansion. How were the vandals—by now he knew more than one person had to be responsible for the amount of damage done to the house—getting in?

The dog hadn't sounded like anything he wanted to tackle. That's why he knew Maggie had to be in on the deal. She had the key, and since she was a native of Bellamy, the dog probably knew her. She didn't have to break in, didn't have to battle the canine sentry.

As he did.

The more he thought about the situation, the more he realized he had to get into that house at night. He had to be there to catch the crooks. He had to get past the hound of Hades.

But how?

Staring down at his plate of food, it occurred to Clay that the best way to a dog's heart—better than to a man's, in his expert opinion—was through the critter's stomach. Some tasty treat should at least keep the animal entertained long enough to prevent the dog's tearing a limb off him.

The longer he thought and consumed Cammie's cooking without tasting a bite, the more certain he grew. He had to feed the dog—and not merely food. It had to be something that made dogs go wild.

"Is there a pet shop in town?" he asked.

Voices abruptly broke off to silence. Three pairs of surprised eyes swiveled to look at him.

"Ah . . . yes," Cammie said after a long moment. "There's

the Four Paws on South Main, and The Aerie on Madison and Elm. One sells stuff for furred friends and the other for the feathered ones."

"Thanks, Cammie. That's just what I needed to know. How late are they open?"

Her puzzlement turned to bewilderment, but she was evidently too polite to ask questions. "I believe both stay open til nine."

Clay smiled. "Great."

He felt better already. Inactivity had never sat well with him. He was going to catch the culprit—and maybe as soon as tonight.

An hour after supper Clay made his way down Main Street, impressed by the number of greetings he received as he went. Maybe these Southerners weren't quite as closed as he'd initially been led to believe.

"Good evening, Mrs. Gerhardt," he said, responding to the baker's greeting, and found a bag of cloud-light Viennese pastries pressed into his hand.

As he passed The Blissful Bookworm, Mrs. Langhorn stuck her head out the door. "When will I see you in here, Clay?"

"When I find a minute to read."

"Don't be a stranger now."

"I won't."

As he continued down the sidewalk, the evening breeze fanned the boxes of freshly planted petunias into a purple-pink-white petal dance. Traffic now meandered down the roadway, the hurried bustle of the day no longer in evidence.

On a bench near the corner, a pair of seniors argued over baseball scores. Three boys roller-bladed past him.

Bellamy was a nice town, just as he'd thought upon his

arrival. It appealed to him, drew him, made him long for the community spirit permeating the air. If he didn't already own his dream house in Gettysburg, he'd give serious thought to moving here. After all, he traveled to work; he couldn't very well have the homes he restored shipped to him. To him, home was where he went when his job was done, a beautiful place to relax and prepare for the next project.

He suspected Bellamy would offer that and more. And, even though he was a Northerner, the town's residents had made him feel welcome—for the most part. All but the woman who'd stepped out onto the sidewalk under the carved wooden sign identifying the establishment as The Four Paws Pet Supply.

The woman carried the largest rawhide bone Clay had ever seen tucked under one arm, while in her other arm she nestled an industrial-sized clear plastic sack of crunchy, biscuit-type dog treats. An ear-to-ear smile enlivened her lovely face as she patted the knobby end of the fake femur.

It didn't take a genius to guess for whom the bounty was intended.

T W E L V E

CLAY STARED AT MAGGIE AS SHE STROLLED DOWN MAIN Street. She smiled at passersby, offering friendly comments. Fortunately for her, she was headed toward her apartment, which lay at the opposite end of town from Cammie's home—away from where Clay stood cemented to the sidewalk. He didn't want to speculate what he would have said to her if she'd come close enough to greet him.

It *wouldn't* have been pretty.

The familiar Scripture of Matthew 12:34-35 came to mind, convicting him: *"Whatever is in your heart determines what you say. A good person produces good words from a good heart, and an evil person produces evil words from an evil heart."*

Clay felt the blood drain from his face. A knot formed in his gut. Every confrontation with Maggie came rushing to his memory, each angry, sniping word enlarged, weighted against him. Instead of speaking God's Word to her, he'd challenged, questioned, and alienated her—even though he'd suspected from the start that God had led him to Bellamy for more than the restoration of the Ashworth Mansion. No wonder she bristled every time they met.

He'd spoken what Matthew in his gospel called "evil words," which led Clay to wonder what lay hidden in his heart. The apostle would say he'd acted like an evil man when, as a Christian, he was called to proclaim the truth, the *Good* News.

Clay walked to a bench a few feet away and sat down. *Father, show me what's in my heart—the garbage that makes me act and speak like that. Do surgery if you need to. I want that evil out of me and your peace in its place.*

He figured his prayer would lead to painful self-discovery, just as it had many times before in his Christian walk. But Clay wanted to do God's will more than he wanted to remain in his relative comfort zone. He knew that sin in a believer's heart would never be in God's will.

Since he was meant to speak words of life, of love, of truth, to Maggie, then with God's help, he would.

What about the mansion? his subconscious piped up.

Clay groaned. What about it? He couldn't in good conscience let Maggie continue her ugly game. After what he'd just seen, no doubt remained in his mind. She was guilty—guilty as sin.

He had the duty, as a Christian, to do what was right. So he'd have to collect evidence to bring before the authorities, even if it meant turning in the woman who'd begun to matter to him more than she should have.

He stood, determined to go ahead with tonight's plans. He would befriend the hound, get into the house, and catch Maggie Bellamy in the act. He'd call in the cops, let them take over, and then finish the work on the house and head out of town.

He'd make sure he took with him no regrets.

After all, a Christian shouldn't fall in love with an unrepentant criminal who didn't belong to the family of God.

That kind of romance could never be in God's will.

✿

Armed with an arsenal of freeze-dried liver, chunks of cheddar cheese, and a bag full of desiccated pigs' ears—items he'd been assured were no-lose choices for charming a pooch—Clay set out for the Ashworth Mansion at exactly 12:30 A.M. He was determined to become, if not the hound's best friend, then at least not its bedtime snack.

After disarming the dog, he planned to set up guard in the center hallway of the house. No one would get past him, regardless of where they entered. The kitchen opened to the hall, which emptied into the grand foyer. He would not be budged. He was on a mission.

Since one of the basement windows had a less-than-secure latch and the locksmith hadn't yet installed the new one, Clay was counting on prying it open. True, the beast would probably set up a ruckus fit to wake every soul in Bellamy, but the lock should yield quickly, and he could then make use of the booty he'd bought to keep the dog's mouth busy.

Approaching the house, this time under a full moon, he didn't hear the critter's unforgettable *"AWWWROOOOOF!"* right away. He wondered if Maggie and her cohorts had decided they no longer needed their canine guard. After all, Clay had been scared away on his first attempt.

He headed straight for the defective window. Less than a minute later, it slid up with a squeal.

A growl came from the belly of the house.

Hurrying, Clay slipped inside, pulled the window closed again—this time *sans* squeal—and breathed a sigh of relief. So far, so good. In the dim glow seeping through his unorthodox entryway, he crossed the small room in which he found himself. At the room's door, he paused. Pressing his ear against the solid slab of oak, he held his breath, trying to discern the dog's whereabouts.

Nothing.

Which could be good, if it meant the animal was still haunting the upstairs. It could also be bad, if the monster stood on the other side of the door, holding its breath until Clay made the mistake of leaving his sanctuary.

With a brief prayer for courage and a plea for godly protection, Clay inched open the door. He heaved another sigh of relief when he saw no dark hulk awaiting his exit. Heart pounding and his hands embarrassingly damp, he skirted the piles of junk stored in the basement and reached the bare wooden-plank stairs.

Step by step, he trod the sides of the boards, knowing they offered their greatest support where they joined the walls. The last thing he wanted was to coax a creak from any of them.

At the door to the pantry, he again paused and listened for his nemesis. He heard nothing.

But what if the perpetrators already knew he'd entered the house and were keeping the dog quiet to dupe him?

He swallowed. It was a chance he'd have to take. With another prayer for his safety, he opened the door.

Again, nothing greeted him. Nothing but a darkened, silent house . . . and the thudding of his pounding heart. Still, he'd heard the dog growl. He knew it was somewhere in here with him. He couldn't afford to let down his guard.

Taking cautious steps, he crossed the pantry, a small room lined with glass-fronted, floor-to-ceiling cabinets that had once held all the items needed to feed the home's residents and guests. At present they were laden with decades of dust.

His breath coming in shallow pants, Clay eased open the swinging door between the pantry and the kitchen.

With a single, peace-shattering *"AWWWROOOOOF!"* the beast flattened him. No less than three hundred pounds of wild animal crushed his stomach, his chest. Fangs the size of Swiss Army knives glittered in the moonlight, and the slavering jaws were mere millimeters from his neck. Mad black eyes glared at him. He was about to become toast.

"GRRRRRRR!" the beast offered.

Clay dropped his grip on the bag of pigs' ears and prayed as the hound's head lowered, its next growl thundering against Clay's throat. Sweat poured from his every pore; every bone in his body shook with dread.

The depredation began with a scouring bite of his face. To Clay's shock, it didn't even hurt. It felt as though someone had scraped wet, rough-grade sandpaper over his skin. It amazed him that, in his last hour, he was capable of analyzing how it felt to be eaten by a vicious, probably rabid canine. Dying certainly felt weird.

The beast let out a piercing whine as he went for the other side of Clay's face. Again, he only felt the sandpaper slather. Then the monster began to wriggle. Its whiplike tail beat across Clay's lower body, abusing his thighs. The whine became a . . . *whimper?* No, it couldn't be.

But it was.

The beating on his legs grew merciless.

Another wet-sandpaper strafe attacked his face. The whimpers grew. The wriggling on his torso became brutal. The animal panted, then removed the last bit of facial flesh Clay had left with another rough scrape. Still, Clay felt little, if any, pain. He thanked God for this unexpected mercy as his life was about to end.

Then the animal changed gears. Literally. It suddenly lumbered off Clay and burrowed its nose into the side pocket of his jeans. The whining became excited yelps and yips. The fangs glittered in the light that poured in through the rear window, and Clay braced for the worst.

Riiip! The tear of flesh sounded surprisingly like that of ripping cloth. He grew lightheaded but still felt no pain.

The hound at his side plopped onto the floor and noisily consumed the chunk of thigh it had just torn off. To his right, Clay heard the sound he'd dreaded all along.

"Wh—who's th—the-ere?" Maggie cried, visceral panic audible in her voice despite Clay's half-dead limbo.

"Why?" Clay managed to croak out. "Why'd you do it?"

"C-Cl-Clay?" she stammered.

"Who else, Jezebel?" In the moonlight, he saw her eyes widen, her jaw gape. Before she could offer some stupid excuse for her actions, he said, "You must be happy now. That . . . demon-hound has dispatched me, and I'm off to my eternal reward." The ease with which he could speak surprised him. He was half-dead, after all.

Maggie's jaw snapped up. A questioning look spread across her beautiful features. "What on earth do you mean?"

"What do you mean, what do I mean? Isn't it obvious? The dog has eaten me alive. I have no face left, and my hip is gone. I'm not long for this world."

To Clay's astonishment, Maggie grinned. She glanced at his murderer, then back at him. She began to laugh.

How dare she? He was dying, and she rejoiced. "Jezebel's too good a description for you, you fiend!"

That only made her laugh louder. Tears rolled down her cheeks.

If he weren't so weak from the business of dying, he would have killed her; it would have been justifiable homicide. "How can murder by mauling entertain you?"

She waved helplessly and continued laughing. At his side the canine cannibal sighed his pleasure, then grunted and resumed chomping.

"If you're dyin'," Maggie gasped, "then it's the first death by lickin' on record."

As she resumed her maddening laughter, Clay's temper began to boil. Was that possible? Could a dying man get angry? "What do you mean, death by lickin' . . . er, licking?"

"Only that my darlin' little Buford did no more than lick your face to bits."

His mind seized on a single word. *Buford.* Queasiness stormed his stomach. He shot a glare at the masticating mutt. "You mean . . . *that's* Buford?"

Maggie nodded, her eyes dancing mischievously. "So you see, you're nowhere near dyin'."

"Buford's the Hound of the Baskervilles?"

She laughed again. "He's my darlin'."

"BUFORD IS A DOG?" Clay roared, rearing up from his prone position.

"Why, what else would you have him be?"

Before he could stop himself, he blurted out, "A geriatric sugar daddy with a bladder-control problem."

Her merriment vanished instantly as the familiar light of contention filled her eyes.

Clay's every fiber *uh-ohed* at him. "Ah . . . you mean, he *didn't* eat me?"

"You're a fool an' an idiot an' dumber'n a barnyard chicken, if that's what you think, Clay Marlowe. Not only are you not even nipped bah mah puppy, but you're too fahr from death foh mah comfort."

Maggie's accent had deepened, turning her tirade into tapioca. She propped her fists on her slender hips and glared some more. "How dare you think me capable of such foul behavior? A sugar daddy? You, Clay Marlowe, are plumb ol' disgustin'."

Now her words bore the consistency of yesterday's rice, thick and ripe with the flavor of the South. But after his nearly being killed, her self-righteous indignation struck Clay in the wrong spot.

"What's a man to think when a woman goes around claiming her Buford's a darling and running off her mouth about his attributes?"

"He's supposed to think she has a dog!"

"How?"

"Maybe the ol'-fashioned art of askin' would do the trick."

"Oh, yeah? How's a man to know said woman won't bite his head off just for asking? Especially since she's been known to be snippy at times."

Outrage blared from her face. "Me? Snippy? You're a cannon full of foul words. And you aim 'em all at me, you crazy Yankee."

"I'm not crazy; you're the crook. And I haven't a clue why."

"I'm not a crook, and you're plain stupid for thinkin' that. Why, I'm Miss Louella's friend and staunchest supporter in her efforts to repair her ancestral home. I'd never do a thing to hurt a jewel of the South."

Clay snorted. "Stop the Rebel nonsense, Maggie. Look at the facts, and realize your game is up. You're the one with the key, the dog, and the purse strings. Who else has unimpeded access to this place? Who else is determined to run me off the job? Just so you can find yourself a good ol' Southern-boy restorer you think you can trust more than me. What have I done to earn your mistrust?"

He held his breath, expecting her to bring up his past.

"You stole a kiss," she spit out, then widened her eyes in horror. "Oh, no!" she moaned. "I didn't say that. I mean . . . I didn't *mean* to say that." Her cheeks blazed pink, and her hands fluttered as if to wave her words away. "Just pretend you're a gentleman and forget it, will you?"

Clay grinned. So the kiss *had* left a mark on her, as it had on him. Maybe once she quit her stupid destruction and he finished the job, they could explore the insane attraction between them. By then Maggie would have seen the error of her ways, spent some time in jail, come to understand the importance of God in her life, and ask him to see her through such hardship.

Clay's thoughts came crashing back to the present. "Rats!" he exclaimed. The woman *was* a menace. She had him thinking the most ridiculous thoughts at the most inappropriate times. "I don't have to pretend a thing, and I'll forget what you said as soon as you forget the games you're playing with this house."

Rage wiped embarrassment off her face. "I'm playin' no games with the house. *You're* the one creatin' more work so you can worm more money out of Miss Louella's account."

"I'm doing no such thing. I'm going to lose money on this job at the rate we're going. I haven't asked you for a penny more—even though we need it—so we've limped along for a couple of weeks now."

"You know there's no more money—"

"That's why I haven't asked for more," he said, cutting her off in the hope that a reasonable defense might end her onslaught. "Why you think I'd continue backing myself into an impossible corner is beyond me."

She crossed her arms over her chest and jabbed her chin toward him. "You're the only one who stands to gain from the vandalism."

"No way. You've told me more times than I want to count that you won't give me a penny more than we contracted. What kind of fool do you think I am?"

"A Yankee carpetbaggin' fool," Maggie spit out. "You all came south to make yourselves rich off the Confederacy's misery."

"Stop!" he barked, his frustration raging out of control.

The dog's ears twitched; Buford looked up, then, unimpressed, returned to his goodies.

"Just stop with the Civil War nonsense," Clay continued with more restraint. "We're talking today, tonight. I came to catch you doing your thing. So what have you torn into now?"

"Nothin', you dunce. I've done nothin' but try to steal a nap so I can function in the mornin'. But here you come, pockets full of—that looks like freeze-dried liver! And is that a bag of pigs' ears?"

She laughed again. "Well, no wonder Buford went at you like that! Those are his favorite treats in the whole wide world."

Clay rolled his eyes. "I think we've established that. What we still have to determine is the reason for your presence here in the middle of the night with your wild beast."

"He's not a beast, wild or otherwise. He's a pedigreed bullmastiff, out of champion sire and dam, which I intend to finish as soon as the mansion is restored."

"Finish?" Clay asked, growing queasy again. The mutt had leapt at him, but since he suspected his facial skin was right where it belonged and all Buford had actually ravaged was the fabric of his Levi's and the cache of liver he'd brought along, Clay's feelings toward the animal were not violent. The thought of Maggie killing him made him sick.

"Oh, for cryin' out loud! I'm not goin' to kill my precious puppy. I'm going to finish his championship. In breed. As in the Westminster dog show? You know, blue ribbons, Best of Breed, Champion Whatever of What-Have-You?"

He relaxed. Marginally. "Okay, we've established that you're not a dog killer. But we still can't declare you innocent of vandalism. What were you doing here?"

"Isn't it obvious?"

When Clay shook his head, she continued, "Why, I'm here

to catch you tearin' up the place. I need Buford for protection. I was afraid you'd come armed." Humor danced in her eyes, in the tilt of her grin. "I just didn't count on freeze-dried liver as your weapon of choice."

Buford belched. He stood, then stretched out his front legs, bringing his shoulders and head to the floor while raising his rump ceilingward. He made a contented sound, then padded over to Clay's right side. He nuzzled the torn pocket. When he found it empty, he rubbed his wrinkled forehead against Clay's hand. The pooch then turned adoring eyes to his.

Maggie pointed. "You meant to weasel your way past my guard dog."

"True, but when I went to the pet shop tonight to buy treats, I saw you there, too."

She arched a brow in her patented way. "And buyin' pet supplies is proof of my guilt, I suppose. No matter that I actually *own* a dog."

Clay went on the defensive. "You were here, weren't you? With the only key, right?"

She took a step closer to him. "I'm only goin' to say this once," she stated, her voice flat, measured. "I—did—nothin'—to—hurt—this—house—or—Miss—Louella."

He matched her step for step. "Then listen to me," he responded, his voice low, unequivocating. "I did nothing to harm this magnificent mansion or its owner. I'd *never* do such a thing." His dread of being falsely imprisoned returned full strength. "I'm innocent of all your charges."

Maggie must have heard the sincerity in his voice because she frowned. "Then who did it?"

"Not you?"

"No!"

As they stared at each other, questions whirled through Clay's mind. Only one name came: Hal Hinkley. But if Maggie wasn't helping him, then how was Hal trashing the place? He wasn't in town. Clay would know if his business rival had arrived in the small town of Bellamy.

As he pondered that conundrum, Buford gave a little whine and rose on his hind legs. With stunning strength, he plopped his paws on Clay's shoulders, making him stumble backward, then proceeded to scrub his face with his tongue again.

He grinned. "You're not kidding when you call him a puppy, are you?"

"Of course not. He's only ten months old."

"He's going to be a big one."

"That's one of the reasons I chose a bullmastiff. I wanted protection, security."

"What were your other reasons?"

Maggie's expression softened. "Look at those eyes, that face. Can you walk away from him without them tuggin' your heart?"

Clay did as she asked, and to his surprise, he fell in love with the pup. "You're a friendly boy, aren't you?" he asked, rubbing the wrinkles between Buford's eyes.

The animal responded with another swipe of his blanket-sized tongue and a renewed wriggling of his hind end.

Maggie chuckled. "I think with all that liver he ate you've made a friend for life."

"Could be worse," Clay answered, thinking that perhaps tonight had turned out for the best. Maybe now Maggie would drop her ridiculous suspicions. "So, since we've established that neither one of us came here to do anything illegal, why don't we call it a night? I can use some sleep, and I suspect you can, too."

Maggie glanced at the slim gold watch on her left wrist. "My goodness, it's nearly two-thirty."

Taking Buford's dish-sized paws off his shoulders, Clay eased the animal away. "Time to snooze, by my clock. What do you say?"

She sent him a challenging look. "If you promise you won't come back and damage anythin' else."

"Only if you promise the same."

"You have a deal."

"Shall we shake?"

"Of course."

He clasped her hand in what he'd meant to be a business-like grip, but his fingers disobeyed the minute he touched her. They slipped across her warm palm, over every curve and hollow as his thumb nestled into the notch between her fingers and her thumb. Without any directive from him, his thumb began caressing the back of Maggie's hand.

She gasped.

He met her blue gaze.

The air around them became as electric as it had been the night they'd kissed. Instinctively, he pulled her closer. Her eyelids lowered, then rose again, their movement slow. Her lips parted. She sighed.

He brought his mouth a breath away from hers.

Buford *AWWWROOOOOF*ed the mood to shreds.

They parted, each thinking of what might have been.

THIRTEEN

THE DRIVE TO THE BANK AFTER OPENING THE MANSION FOR
Clay and his crew the next day gave Maggie unwanted practice in the fine art of Dodge 'em Car racing. As she tooled along at her normal speed, all manner of vehicles materialized in her way, forcing her into frequent use of her horn and frantic swerves to avoid collisions. Add to that her latest affliction—unending yawns—and the morning's start was nothing if not harrowing.

She hadn't slept a wink. Even after she and Clay had decided nothing would be gained by their staying at the Ashworth Mansion all night. It was all his fault.

The memory of his big palm sliding across hers, its roughness intimately real, had claimed her thoughts most of the night. His thumb's caress on the back of her hand had soothed her, comforted her, made her long for a similar caress at her back, maybe her cheek. She'd wondered for hours, or so it seemed, how it would feel to be embraced by his arms as her hand had been by his hand.

But it was the almost-kiss that ultimately haunted her.

She'd known he wanted to kiss her. In all honesty, she'd wanted it too. Later, as she'd lain in bed, tossing and turning, Maggie had wondered if she remembered their first kiss correctly. Had it been as warm and moving as she thought? Had his touch been as exciting and welcoming? Had he really wanted to kiss her, or had he done it to woo her into a sense of trust she shouldn't risk?

In the bank's parking lot she slipped into her usual spot and turned off the Miata's engine. She was running late, but she had to pull herself together before facing the work on her desk . . . Mr. H's looks . . . Ruby's questions.

She didn't know the answer to any of those questions, much less her own more immediate ones. Her curiosity had sharpened in the wee hours of the morning. She'd wondered what a *real* date with Clay might be like. How a woman would feel in his company, certain he was with her because of simple attraction. She'd wished she could be that woman. In the final account, Maggie wanted to know what it would be like to be loved by a man like Clay.

That had frightened her.

An attraction to an unsuitable man was one thing, but the *L* word was a horse of another feather, and since Clay was a Yankee and she a Rebel, they couldn't very well flock together.

Every one of her ills that morning had its root in Clay. Last night the man had awakened her from her nap, turned her watchdog into a pussycat by means of a pocket full of liver and a sack of roasted pigs' ears, then kept her from catching any more winks by the mere virtue of his existence. He was a menace. A talented, hardworking, good-looking, frustrating, infuriating, fascinating, Yankee menace.

Maggie couldn't stand to think how attracted she was to him, much less how difficult it would be to say good-bye once his job was done.

That handclasp last night had stolen yet another chunk

of her peace of mind; the near kiss had robbed her of a piece of her heart. No wonder she was a wreck today.

How could she be so drawn to Clay?

Her innate honesty made her consider what she'd refused to believe from the start. What if Clay was innocent, as he insisted? He hadn't behaved like a guilty man last night. His voice had rung with sincerity, his eyes had shone with honesty, his actions hadn't differed much from hers. And she was innocent.

Had she misjudged him?

Then who was ravaging the mansion? Who was going to cost Maggie her job?

Right now *she* was if she continued to sit in her car. With a deep sigh, she opened the door and heaved her exhausted body upright. Every muscle felt as strong as Jell-O, every bone as solid as spaghetti, her head as clear as clam chowder.

The irrational jumble of images running through her mind reminded her she'd missed breakfast. Maybe a biscuit smothered with cream gravy from Ellamae Hobey's Dinner Diner would do the trick. The heavy carbs would give her energy, the fat would quiet her growling stomach, and the protein from the sausage bits . . . ? Well, maybe it would inspire her resolve to stiffen up again.

As she drove to the diner and brought her breakfast back to the bank again, she resolved that she had to avoid Clay Marlowe at all costs—personally, that was. When it came to the mansion, however, she had to stick to the man like dog hair to wool.

She'd be just that welcome, too.

Too bad. Maggie had a job to do—to save. If she lost it, she'd lose her last chance to prove she was more than a useless, pretty face under a dumb blonde's mane.

In her office, no sooner had she thrown away the breakfast debris than a violent pounding assaulted her door. Maggie took the five steps from her garbage can to the endangered slab of wood, her heart in her throat. Had Mr. H learned of the trouble at the mansion?

Turning the doorknob, she took a breath for courage. "Clay!"

He stormed in, forcing Maggie to plaster herself between the wall and the open door to avoid being mowed down. "Who else would you expect?" he roared. "And after you gave your word."

"What are you talking about?" she asked, stunned by his vehemence.

"Don't act so innocent. I don't buy the show anymore. I can't believe I ever did."

"Since I've no idea what you're raving about, I don't need to act any particular way," she said, furious. "I haven't put on a show for anyone, although *you* certainly seem bent on doing that."

Dark brows crashed in a formidable frown. "I have every reason for being steamed," he said, approaching like a dark funnel cloud.

She backed up a step.

"And you know it," he added.

Enough! Stand up to him like the strong businesswoman you are. "You're talking crazy."

"No, I'm not. Think. Maybe a nudge will help. What does the word *toilet* bring to mind?"

She shook her head helplessly. "You know, toilets are . . . toilets."

"C'mon, Maggie." He now tried cajoling. "Just tell me about the toilets."

She raised her arms in defeat. "If you insist. Toilets are utilitarian items that can be found in most structures. They're usually made of porcelain, filled with water, and are where people perform certain necessary bodily functions." Maggie congratulated herself on the serious expression she maintained during her explanation. "They then are flushed so that the refuse is eliminated from the receptacle."

The red in his cheeks darkened. "Stop the nonsense, Magnolia Blossom. Those baby blues and the Shirley Temple curls aren't going to save you this time."

His crack landed a low blow. "They never have, buster, and I don't expect them to." She marched on Clay like Sherman on Atlanta. "They're the bane of my existence, for your information. But since you—" she jabbed his chest—"say toilets tickle your fancy, if you'll speak plain ol' English and ask what you—" another stab at the steely male chest— "*really* want to know, I might be able to tell you. It sure as shootin' isn't about the intricacies of plumbin'.."

He didn't move. "I'll make it as plain as plain can be. Why'd you go back to the mansion and yank out the toilets? Wasn't it enough to disembowel the plumbing from the walls? What's the point? It's going to cost plenty to fix those floors again, and now we have to replace the pipes and joints we replaced the last time. I'm not swallowing these costs."

Maggie's stomach and jaw reached her toes at the same time—or so it felt. "Are you saying . . . someone took out the *toilets?* Why?"

"You tell me," he said, really angry now. "I arrived this morning, ready to move forward, expecting you to keep your word, half believing you'd had nothing to do with the vandalism after all. But stupid me, I found out I'd been fooled by the best of them—by a well-trained, pretty, pampered, Southern belle."

Them were fighting words, especially since she was suffering from the advanced stages of sleep deprivation—all because of him.

"I did nothin' to those toilets. I went home and tried to sleep. First you accused my dog of murderous intent, and now you accuse me of toilet cannibalism. And all I have is your flimsy word that you didn't do it. From where I'm sittin', you're the one with obvious criminal intent. You're out to con Miss Louella."

He winced, paled. Then he set his shoulders. "My word is all I have to give as a man and as a Christian. I do not lie. God is my witness at all times, Maggie. I said I didn't do it, and I meant it."

She faltered, then felt surprisingly defensive. "Well, *I* sure didn't sneak back into the house. Besides, I could never lift a toilet. It's too heavy."

"No, but you could harness Buford to one. Piece of cake for him. And you'd happily waltz off with a good chunk of change in your pocket. If you haven't heard of it, it's called bribery, Maggie, and it's against the law."

"Bribery? Who'd be bribing me? And why?"

The muscle in his jaw twitched. "Anyone with a reason to want me out of there, or out of business."

"You're crazy—no one's bribing me."

Clay ran a hand through his hair in the gesture Maggie knew meant frustration. Then his shoulders sagged, and his voice lost its edge. "I can't cover the cost of these repairs. I have to pay the subs."

She raised her hands in helplessness. "I can't give you any more money."

They'd reached a stalemate, and for some strange reason, Maggie felt pain in the vicinity of her heart. She didn't want Clay to be guilty. She wanted to believe his earnest voice, that invocation of his God, his insistence on his innocence.

But that belief would be irrational, since every time she came close to giving him the benefit of the doubt, calamity raised its ugly head. Right now Maggie was the fish about to drown in troubled waters, while Clay seemed intent on borrowing more of that trouble by the day.

Her office door slammed shut, causing both to jump. "Might I ask what this shoutin' match is about?" Mr. H queried. "Or do I already know by what I overheard?"

Every bit of blood drained from Maggie. She felt cornered, finished. The jig was up, and she could just about hear the fat sizzling on the fire. She'd lost the job she'd fought so hard to keep.

"I don't know how much Maggie has said about the trouble we've had at the mansion," Clay said, his words clipped. "Vandals have been hitting us since we began work. Fixing the damage has set us back, even though I've covered a good chunk of it. Maggie said from day one the budget for the Ashworth project was fixed, but I can't afford to pay any more from my own pocket, nor can I draw from my non-existent profit. And the destruction continues."

At least he hadn't accused her to her boss. "It's under control," Maggie said, her voice faint, carrying no conviction even to her own ears.

"Of course it ain't, Magnolia," countered Mr. H, as her stomach lurched. To make matters worse, he asked, "What do the police have to say?"

Clay turned away from the bank's president. Maggie stared out the window. Finally, steeling herself for the inevitable outcome, she said quietly, "They don't know."

Mitchell Hollings wasn't a man prone to explosions. Instead, he indulged in icy, silent rages. "Why not?"

"Because we decided against negative publicity," answered Maggie.

"That was downright stupid, Magnolia," he said, his voice well modulated, the words slick with frost. "Call them straight-away, and have them meet us at the site. This has to stop. There ain't no more money. If the mansion can't be restored on the original loan, it ain't gettin' restored. And call the insurance agent, and get him out here."

With a nod, she did as ordered. After gathering her pocketbook and telling Ruby where she'd be, Maggie drove to the house, feeling like a sheep on its way to becoming next week's broiled chop dinner.

❧

"Insurance," Clay muttered, swinging the hammer with unnecessary force. "I can't believe after all these years, I didn't even think to have Maggie file a claim."

Bam! Another blow with the hammer, another nail driven into one of the torn floorboards in the bathroom. "How could I forget something so basic?"

"As what, son?" asked Hobey from behind Clay.

Startled, Clay dropped the hammer. "How'd a man as big as you slip in here so quietly?"

Mountainous shoulders shrugged. "I wasn't quiet. You were just too busy fixin' to smack the daylights right outta that board. What's wrong?"

"You name it, it's gone wrong."

"More trouble with Maggie?"

"I'll say."

"So why doncha? Say what the trouble is."

Clay put down his hammer and sat back against the bathroom wall. "See this?"

"Yeah, an' I'm havin' a time figgerin' why you'd tear up a perfectly good toilet."

"That's the problem. I didn't do it."

"Ah. Reckon 'em vandals hit again."

"You reckon right. I'm not sure it isn't Maggie herself doing the damage."

Hobey sat on the heat register and crossed massive arms over his chest. "Nah. She's got her knickers too twisted over that job o' hers to do somethin' so dumb."

"I think she's taken a bribe."

"Come again?"

"You heard me."

"How so?"

Clay told Hobey of finding the letter from Hal on Maggie's desk, which led to a recounting of his checkered encounters with the unethical restorer. Then he summed it up by glossing over the confrontation in Maggie's office and Mr. Hollings's appearance, finally admitting that neither he nor Maggie had thought of filing an insurance claim for the damage. Miss Louella had been covered all along.

Hobey took off his Cincinnati Reds cap, rubbed his shiny dome, and gave Clay a shrewd perusal. "Tell me, son," he drawled, "are you good an' shut of your prison term?"

"What do you mean?" Clay said, startled.

"Well, you seem to think 'bout those months behind 'em bars every time you make a choice or take a step. 'Pears to me you're in jail just as much now as you were back then," Hobey said gently.

"That's not true!" Clay replied in shock. "I'm just cautious. I don't want to go back to where I don't belong."

"That's fair, and I don't want you back there, neither. But I don't see you livin' by what's real and under your nose, ya know? I see you livin' by what don't exist no more. You're believin' a lie. Counterfeit's what the Bible calls it."

"What lie?"

"That you're headed for jail again someday. That the only way to protect yourself is to hide your past an' fight off everyone what says somethin' wrong. Like Maggie."

"I'm not sure what you mean," Clay said thoughtfully. He didn't wear his past on his sleeve, but he didn't think he had to. Did he?

"'Member that King David? The one what got himself in such a stew? Well, in Psalm 32 he says them the Lord has cleared of sin, who live in total honesty, have his joy. An' I cain't say I seen a lot o' joy in you."

Clay was silent, since Hobey's remarks were hitting him hard.

"Well, King David also confessed his sins to God an' stopped tryin' to hide 'em. Looks to this old bricklayer like you're still hidin' a whole mess of stuff—an' it keeps you busy defendin' yourself instead of livin'. Have you forgiven them what put you there—and yourself for not stayin' outta there? How 'bout bitterness?"

Clay couldn't counter that one. He recognized the bitterness for what it truly was—a spirit of unforgiveness.

"'Member, son, it ain't a matter between you an' them what hurt you. It's a matter between you an' God. You gotta face the hurt an' hate, an' confess. Otherwise, you're rebellin' against God."

"No way! I love the Lord—"

"Never said you didn't. But I wonder if you don't still blame God for what-all happened to you."

Clay hated the thoughts milling in his mind.

"Were you walkin' with the Lord back then?"

"No, but I didn't do anything to land in jail."

"But you weren't submittin' to the Lord, neither. You were goin' your own way, tryin' to defend yourself."

"Yes."

"Well, ya see? Now you know better, but you're still fightin' that same battle. You gotta submit to him. All the way."

Later, Clay thought. He'd examine what Hobey said later. But right now, he couldn't stand another of Hobey's questions, for they'd cut too close. "I will, Hobey. Later on. Now, I'd better get back to this—"

"I ain't done, son."

Clay groaned inwardly. *Lord, do I really need to hear all this now?*

Then it struck him. He did. Hobey was merely God's instrument at that moment. After all, Clay's recent record didn't look too good. He'd committed to watching his words, and he'd turned around and blasted Maggie at least twice after that. What was wrong with him?

"How's your pride doin'?" asked the burly mason.

"Just fine, thank you very much."

"I'll say! Don't reckon you've given this mess to the Father, not without takin' it back, fixin' to help him here an' there. That's pride, Clay, an' that's sinful. The book of James says we need to confess our sins to one another so's we may be healed. So, son, I'm gonna do my part. I'm gonna pray for you. Then you have to do your part. If you need an ear for confessin', mine's right down the road. When King David confessed his rebellion, God forgave him—an' all his guilt was gone!"

Stunned and convicted, Clay said humbly, "I have a world of thinking to do."

"An' prayin'."

"Looks that way." Clay stood and stuck his hand out toward Hobey, who stood and took it in a warm, double-handed clasp. "I may have to change how I see things."

With a friendly slug to Clay's right shoulder, the mason said, "See 'em the way God sees 'em, son. You cain't go wrong then."

"Amen."

"An' amen."

FOURTEEN

"Insurance," Maggie said under her breath as she walked down the corridor toward her apartment. "I can't believe I didn't remember that."

Since the police and Mr. H had agreed it would do no good to publicize the vandalism and alert the perpetrators, they weren't going public with the information. As an agent of the bank—the payee on the policy—Maggie could file the claim directly; Miss Louella didn't have to know. Maggie was glad. She wouldn't want her elderly friend to be frightened.

To her relief—brief though it might prove to be—her boss hadn't said a word about her job. "I'll call the adjuster first thing in the morning, and Clay can go on as planned—"

"Talking to yourself these days, sis?"

Maggie stopped short at the words. "What are you doing here? there?" she asked, pointing to where Lark had set up shop on the floor in front of Maggie's apartment door.

"Waiting for you." Lark crammed a fistful of paper into her gaping, forest green backpack, lumpy with an alarming array of folders and printouts, pens and pencils, then scrambled up from her cross-legged position.

Maggie jingled the keys. "Well, I'm here now. What do you want?"

Her sister blocked access to the lock. "To ask some questions."

"That's getting old, since it's all you ever do: stick your nose where it doesn't belong."

The pugnacious look the eight-year-old Lark had worn every time she objected to whatever the six-year-old Maggie said made its return. "It belongs where I care enough to stick it. And I care about you."

"Couldn't prove it by me," Maggie fired back, annoyed at the interruption.

"Take my word for it," Lark said briskly. "And while you're at it, tell me why the cops and Mr. H met you and that Marlowe guy at the mansion today."

Maggie tapped a toe on the floor, hoping to convey impatience rather than the fear she felt. "Really, Lark, I can't discuss bank business with you. You're not a party to the matter."

Her efforts gained her nothing. Lark, the reporter, bristled with interest. "What'd they trash now? It must have been big to call in the cops."

Maggie waved the question away. "If you're so curious, ask the police. I can't speak on this to the press."

"I'm not asking as a member of the press. I'm asking as your sister—and I want to know what you're hiding."

Maggie tipped up her chin. "Nothing. Now, put an end to your third degree, and let me in. My dog needs me."

As if on cue, Buford yowled from inside. He had every reason to do so. He'd just spent eight-plus hours in his crate, and no doubt needed to heed the call of nature. Not to mention fill his tummy. His howls could cause him to be considered a nuisance, which would put an end to his tenancy—by contractual agreement.

Lark didn't move. "When you tell me what's happened and what kind of trouble you're in."

"I'm not in any trouble."

"With Mr. H, the cops, the vandals, and a stranger working on Miss Louella's house? I want to help. Give me details, so I can do what I do best," Lark said, reaching for a notebook and pen.

With a frustrated sigh, Maggie inched closer to the door, brandishing her key. "Stay out of it, Lark. This is *my* job, *my* career."

"But, Mag, I can help you investigate. I have experience following trails, checking out people. For example, what *do* you know about Marlowe?"

I know he kisses like a dream. The thought flew through Maggie's mind uninvited, and it terrified her.

"I-I know e-enough," she stammered. "I checked him out before I offered him the contract."

"Did you look at his credit history? How about the Better Business Bureau? And police records. Did you look into those?"

"I ran a thorough check on the man," Maggie answered defensively as her sister echoed Mr. H's earlier questions. "I called every one of his references. They gave me other names to contact as well, which I did."

Lark's green eyes bored into hers. "Did you check his credit record? What do you know about his financial dealings?"

"Everyone I spoke to said he charged fairly for his work, and he pays his bills on time."

"But is he solvent right now?"

"I wouldn't know."

"You should."

"I don't see why."

"Because it might give him the motive to steal you and Miss Louella blind."

"I don't think he'd do that," Maggie argued, even though Lark was voicing her own suspicions.

"How? What do you know about his character? You didn't look into a criminal record, did you?"

My word is all I have to give as a man and as a Christian. God is my witness at all times. Clay's words rang through Maggie's heart with the song of sincerity. But she doubted Lark would give them any more weight than she herself had.

Still, there was something about a man who called God his witness. Would a man like that commit the crimes at the mansion?

"That's what I mean, Mag," Lark said, pursuing her point. "You didn't think of those kinds of things because you aren't wired to go for the business jugular, while this Marlowe guy—"

"Clay, all right? His name is Clayton Marlowe."

Lark's auburn brows shot up to hide behind her red bangs. "Clay, is it? Oh, Maggie, have you gone and fallen for a con man?"

"Absolutely not! I have *not* fallen for Mr. Marlowe, and I haven't been conned."

As if to punctuate her point, Buford gave a masterful *"AWWWROOOOOF,"* keeping Maggie from blubbering herself into further humiliation.

Lark began pacing the empty hall. "I was right all along. You *can't* handle the mess you got yourself into, and I need to help you fix it."

"Enough, Lark," Maggie said, feeling beaten. "You've said more than enough. Now leave me be. Let me take my dog for a walk. I can handle *that* without too much trouble."

Lark blew out her breath in clear frustration. "Mag, I just worry about you."

Maggie's inner starch wilted; she couldn't fight anymore. In a low voice she said, "Don't. Whatever happens, happens. I can handle it." But her words lacked conviction, and both sisters knew it.

The key finally went in, and Maggie glanced over her shoulder. With a shrug but no more words, Lark swooped down and hitched her pack onto one shoulder. She started down the hallway, then paused. Her back to Maggie, she said, "I . . . I care, Mag. I really do." Then she made her way to the elevator.

Maggie's world turned dark. She'd failed at her job, failed at sisterhood. She'd just proven all the skeptics—like Lark— right. She *was* incompetent.

"I care," Lark had said. But to Maggie, it didn't feel that way.

Did *anyone* care? Did anyone love her, incompetence and all? Did she have worth in anyone's eyes? Did she matter at all?

After dinner, hours after the conversation—or inquisition, as it had felt like—with Hobey, Clay remained on his knees by his bed, his Bible open to the first chapter of James.

Hobey's questions had dredged up memories Clay would rather have left forgotten. But it seemed they'd festered inside him long enough, fouling up a heart that belonged to God.

Dismayed, he'd cried out, "Open my eyes, God. Show me what you want gone from me. I-I want you and your will and nothing more."

The first thing that came up was his loss of control over his tongue. He'd committed to speaking words of life to Maggie. But he'd failed—miserably.

Now here in James he'd reread the injunction for Christian·

to be quick to listen, slow to speak, and slow to get angry. It said anger never made things right in God's eyes. Clay knew he'd just lived out the truth of that.

His treatment of Maggie certainly hadn't been right. He'd accused her, virtually called her a liar, refused to accept her word, and demanded that she drop her accusations against him and accept his words as true.

While Clay wasn't convinced of her blamelessness, his response to her claim of innocence had been rotten. It had come from fear, as Hobey had pointed out—the fear of what she might do to him.

The worst indictment came in verse 26 of the first chapter of James: "If you claim to be religious but don't control your tongue, you are just fooling yourself, and your religion is worthless."

Maybe to some degree Hobey had been right. Clay had been deceiving himself with a counterfeit. He claimed to have faith, but he hadn't controlled his tongue very well. James called that kind of religion—faith—"worthless."

Pain tore at his heart. His actions shamed him. A lump of guilt solidified in his throat. His eyes dampened.

He'd again stumbled, sinned against God.

Through the remorse, he remembered Hobey saying, "You gotta confess."

Oh, yeah, he did. "Father God, I've sinned against you. You call your children to maintain self-control, but I keep blowing it over and over again. Every time I think I might wind up in jail again for someone else's crime, I lose it."

Flipping through the pages of his well-read Bible to Romans 8:31, he found Paul's question to the Romans and read it out loud: "'If God is for us, who can ever be against us?'"

Clay ached at the memory of his part in those exchanges with Maggie. No wonder she saw him in such a negative light and didn't trust him.

He scanned a few more verses, then stopped at verses 33 and 34, jolted by his conscience. For the benefit of his ears, his heart, he read out loud again: "'Who dares accuse us whom God has chosen for his own? Will God? No! He is the one who has given us right standing with himself. Who then will condemn us? Will Christ Jesus? No, for he is the one who died for us and was raised to life for us.'"

That was it. God would never accuse him. Man's charges didn't—shouldn't—mean a thing to a man who cared first and last about Christ. Clay had let human reproach assume a power greater than it deserved. When seen that way, being unjustly found guilty of embezzlement, a jail term, even Maggie's stupid suspicions, lost their sting. He should never have lashed out.

Clay groaned. He had to go to her—again.

He had to confess his sin—again.

Ask her forgiveness—again.

She wasn't a Christian.

Yet.

Maybe his repeated submission to God's will would chip away at the hardness in her heart, break through to her, lead her to questions that might give him a chance to tell her more about God.

But dare he? When he'd only begun to face the evil inside himself? Did he have the right to speak of God, of righteous living, of the walk of faith? when he himself was only tottering down that path?

The words of a hymn he'd sung during worship services in prison came to Clay with stunning force. "Trust and obey . . ."

All God asked of him was to trust and obey.

"Okay, Lord," Clay said, certain only of the One he followed, "I'll trust your leading and obey your Word. I have to face her, and if you want me to speak, then I trust you'll give me the words."

A measure of comfort soothed his sore heart, and the lump in his throat began to subside. Clay closed his Bible and turned off the bedside lamp. But as he opened the door to the second-floor landing, he realized turmoil still roiled inside him.

There was more he had to deal with. And probably all of it more painful than a bad temper and a tongue out of control.

He wavered, his hand holding the doorknob in a death grip. Should he go and face Maggie? Should he stay and face his sins?

As if the Lord himself had voiced the words, Clay felt them resonate through every fiber of his being: *In my time.*

He swallowed. "All right, Lord, in your time."

Closing the door behind him, Clay headed across town, taking the first step in his closer walk with God.

When Maggie answered the door, Clay zeroed in on her wet lashes and red-rimmed eyes. "You're crying!"

Her lips twisted. "No foolin'. What did you want?" she asked, her voice none too friendly.

"What's wrong?" he asked, ignoring her question, clasping her shoulders. "Is Buford . . . ?"

Maggie hiccuped in what must have been an effort at a laugh. "He's fine. And it's nothin'. Just a weak, feminine flaw, I guess."

"Weak? You? Try again, Magnolia Blossom. You're of the steel variety."

Her eyes widened in apparent surprise. "You're kiddin', right?"

"What about?"

"The steel stuff."

"You're a tough lady, Maggie Bellamy," he said, tipping her

chin up with a finger, making her meet his gaze. "But you're also human. Something's hurt or upset you, and I'd like to help. May I come in?"

She stepped back, waving him in. "Thanks, but you can't do a thing. I-I just had a disagreement with my sister."

"The redhead, right?"

"That's the one."

"Want to talk about it? I'm not a bad listener."

"It's old stuff. From when we were kids."

He studied her. She'd pulled her curls up and away from her face with a plastic thing that reminded him of the shark's teeth in the movie *Jaws*. Her tears had washed away what little makeup she'd worn during the day. Her eyes were puffy, her nose bright pink. And instead of her typical feminine suits, she wore a faded black-and-orange Orioles T-shirt and jeans with the knees all frayed.

She looked gorgeous. Soft. In need of comfort.

"So," she said, plopping down on a Victorian settee covered in cabbage-rose tapestry, "what brings you here?"

"Ah, yes," he said, not relishing what he had to do next. "My reason for coming."

"Is . . . ?"

"Well, I . . . ah . . . let my temper get the best of me. Again." Pointing to a plum velvet overstuffed armchair he asked, "May I?"

She nodded. "I've noticed your temper—couldn't miss it even if I was blinder'n a bat. On more than one occasion."

Since Maggie wasn't about to help him, he plunged in. "I hurt you by venting my anger on you. I'm sorry."

Surprise took over her expression. "That's okay," she said softly.

Clay leaned forward in the comfortable chair, pushed by the need for her to understand. "No, it's not. Not yet. I confessed to Christ and asked his forgiveness. I know he's given it, but it's not all I need. I need yours, too. Please forgive me."

Maggie's cheeks went pink. "Okay, I forgive you."

"Do you really?"

"Does it matter?"

"To me, a lot."

Clay felt the urge to squirm under the scrutiny of her pretty blue eyes, but Maggie was entitled to weigh his contrition, which was sincere.

Apparently she realized that. "I do forgive you, Clay. Honestly."

"Thanks."

After a period of silence and just as Clay was about to stand and say good-bye, Maggie leaned forward. "This is the second time you've asked my forgiveness—right away. Why?"

Is this the opening I asked for, Lord? "Well, I've recently been learning a powerful lesson—that there's a lot of sinful junk that sometimes sits and rots away inside you. If you don't deal with it right away, it can turn a good person into an evil one. And that's the last thing I want. So I want to make sure I do what the Bible tells me to: confess, ask forgiveness, and make restitution whenever I can."

"Your faith seems too simple, yet you cling to it."

"Yes," he answered, asking God for the right words, "but the walk of faith is anything but simple. To those who believe in him, God reveals mysteries in his own time. But those lessons and the waiting are often hard."

Frowning, she said, "How can it matter when you can't even see God? touch him?"

"Because he's there, by me, every step of the way. He's the one who picks me up when I stumble on that walk. And I love him for who he is, what he has done for me."

Maggie shook her head, a curl tumbling to her forehead.

She brushed it away from her face, then said, "I still can't see it. How can you say he's always with you?"

The words of another song slipped into Clay's thoughts. *Open my eyes, Lord, I want to see Jesus.* "Do you want to see how?"

She hesitated. "I honestly don't know."

"Then I'll pray that you'll come to know what you want." *And for God to open your eyes so you may see Jesus,* he prayed fervently.

"If you want."

"I do." With those words he stood and started to walk toward the door. "I'd better get home. . . . Oh, hey! Where's my buddy, Buford?"

"A neighbor down the hall has a teenage son who likes to walk my baby. I didn't feel up to takin' him out tonight, so I called Skeets."

Clay donned mock alarm. "You trusted your puppy to a kid named Skeets?" he asked in a teasing voice.

"If you ever see them together, you'll know we need to worry more about trustin' Buford with Skeets."

"Now why doesn't that surprise me?"

"Because you've met my darlin'," she answered, an unexpected giggle following her words.

"A meeting where I didn't come off looking my best."

"True." She chewed on her bottom lip, then asked, "Clay? Did you mean it when you said you'd make restitution when you could?"

"Of course. Is there something I can do?"

"Maybe," she replied, looking so needy that Clay longed to wrap his arms around her. But he knew that would be inappropriate. Suddenly she straightened. "I think there is. I can't afford to lose my job, and it's on the line. If you aren't trashin' the mansion, and I know *I'm* not, then someone else is. He has to be stopped before Mr. H goes half-cocked off the deep end, decides I'm as useful as hen's teeth, and adds insult to injury by firin' me. Would you be willin' to help Buford and me patrol the place nights?"

Clay blinked. "You want me to guard the mansion? With you and Buford?"

"That's what I said. Two heads are better than one, and since we also have a dog . . . well, you get the picture."

He did. Besides, just in case she was trying to pull another stunt, she wouldn't be able to enter the mansion without his knowledge. Plus if they spent more time together, maybe they could continue to talk of deeper, eternal matters. Maybe then they could get to know each other better than merely as contractor and banker. Yankee and Rebel. Accuser and accused.

And then the thought jumped, unbidden, into his head and startled him: *Maybe we could get around to the kiss we missed.*

FIFTEEN

"I'M NOT ONE TO SAY I TOLD YOU SO, LOUELLA," ANNOUNCED Myrna Stafford at the meeting of Bellamy's Garden Club, her voice brimming with satisfaction.

Hoots of skepticism—and laughter—filled the room.

Myrna glowered from turquoise-lidded eyes, then donned an expression of extreme dignity. "From the minute you told us about your great-grandaddy Asa's journal and his note about the Confederate treasure, I thought the whole treasure hunt was a stupid idea."

"It's not stupid at all," countered the president of the group. "And if you don't want to participate in our historic effort, that's fine. Just don't go gloomin' over our commitment to the Confederacy."

Discussion broke out. Someone said, "That's right!"

"You can't trust one who's never joined the Daughters of the Confederacy," another commented.

"Myrna's always set on spitin' someone."

". . . troublemaker . . ."

Louella smacked her gavel on the podium, hoping to keep the rabble from rising.

"Louella?" Philadelphia's pigeon-murmur voice broke the ensuing silence.

Louella nodded. "The Chair recognizes Philadelphia Philpott."

Rising, Philadelphia tugged on the sleeves of the sweatshirt covering her Peter Pan–collared blouse, smoothed down the skirt revealing an eyelet slip, then crossed a shawl over her waist. "Have you heard all the rumors about what's goin' on at the Ashworth Mansion?" the frail woman whispered. "After all, the police and Mr. H went to the house yesterday."

Louella waved expansively. "I asked Magnolia about it, and she said they'd come to do one of the regular inspections required by law. Someone had to do it, and you all know Woody Saunders hasn't yet taken over his new post as buildin' inspector, even though Herm Cavanaugh's body's cold in his grave three weeks now since he went home to be with the Lord."

Another burst of chatter sputtered to life, this time with comments like "Was he a Christian?"

"Lovely eulogy Pastor Richards gave."

"Did you stay for the supper after the funeral?"

"Elberta's tomato aspic didn't jell quite right this time. I don't think she uses enough—"

Louella banged for silence again. "Ladies, ladies. Let's not get sidetracked, shall we? As I was fixin' to say, I think there's a romance bloomin' in Bellamy. Magnolia and Clay Marlowe are busy circlin' each other, fightin' the electricity between them—and my, my, girls, is it *ever* hot! They're probably not even payin' attention to anythin' going on at the mansion."

Myrna rose, sniffed, then walked to the door. "If you believe *that*, Louella Ashworth, then I'm headin' home to fetch the deed to the Brooklyn Bridge. You're too gullible by half. I'm no one's fool, like some others I might name, so I'm gettin' while the gettin's still good."

Hairy purple sausages bobbing on her head, Myrna slammed the door to the room on her way out. After a moment of stunned silence, the room erupted for a third time.

"Well, good riddance to her rubbish . . ."

"Temper, temper."

"Prayer meetin' after the motion to dismiss, warriors."

Louella brought her gavel down again, this time with enough force to jar her shoulder. The babble continued, so she repeated her effort. To her shock, the mallet's handle broke off in her hand. The hammer fell on the floor and rolled within inches of Savannah Hollings's alligator pumps.

After retrieving the chunk of wood, the bank president's wife stood and said in a conversational tone, "Ladies, if I may?"

The room quieted instantly. "Thank you," she added with a smile. "I think I should discreetly inquire of Mitch what took him to the mansion. Otherwise, we have no way of knowing what happened."

"Excellent idea!" Louella cried, relief flooding her. "With that taken care of, we must consider the next step of our mission. . . ."

Once done with the business at hand, everyone exchanged good-byes, and the Prayer Partners set off for Ellamae's Dinner Diner, committed to praying for Myrna's attitude.

During their prayers, however, Sophie Hardesty, a hopeless romantic, brought up Clay's and Maggie's names. The gathered saints agreed that those two could stand some interceding on their behalf. Louella smiled as each woman took her turn. The petitions were for the blind in question to open their hearts and see the treasure the Lord had bestowed upon them.

❧

Standing outside the mansion at midnight on the second evening of Clay and Maggie's guard duty, Maggie found herself anticipating their meeting. She'd been unable to forget his fervent words in her apartment the night before—or the pleasant if tiring hours they'd spent guarding the Ashworth afterward.

When they'd met at the mansion a few hours after Clay's confession and plea for forgiveness, their easy cooperation during the first night of joint patrolling had surprised Maggie. Clay suggested that instead of cocooning up in the kitchen, they make use of the reduced light of the waning moon and circle the house every hour. His plan offered each sentinel the chance to nap as they alternated watches.

She'd found nothing objectionable in his strategy. Her presence and Buford's would keep Clay honest—or so she hoped. Besides, if Clay thought he could enter the mansion, trash a room without her knowledge while she slept, then play innocent, he had another think coming.

The night had gone well. There was no sign of entry at the mansion, and although she hadn't slept during her off time, Maggie hadn't felt the fear of the previous nights.

They'd talked quite a bit as they exchanged watches. She'd found Clay intelligent and well read. He loved the classics and also confessed a passion for art, as did she. But where he favored Remington's earthy sculpture, she preferred Monet's luminous paintings.

Surprisingly—or maybe not so surprisingly—he shared her appreciation for the work of the art-glass masters and even owned one original Louis Tiffany piece. Now Maggie was dying to learn what other interests they might share.

True, they differed on the matter of faith. But the depth of his belief inspired her admiration; his humility garnered her respect. And even, as much as she hated to admit it, her love.

She groaned. There it was again, the *L* word. Although she was fairly satisfied with their guard bargain, she couldn't help wondering if she hadn't made an error in judgment. They'd be spending hours and hours together, and now that they'd found common ground . . .

She groaned again.

Buford whimpered a response. "It's nothing, baby. Mama's just losing her mind." *And her heart.*

Then the animal stiffened, his head cocked, his nose twitched. Without warning, he barked loudly and charged off into the dark, pulling out the full twenty-one-foot length of his retractable leash.

"Buford," Maggie cried, yanking on the leash with all her strength, "you're telling the whole world we're here! Hush now. We can't patrol if you make a ruckus fit to raise the roof and bring down the curtain on our show!"

"Hey, there, buddy. It's just me," said the object of her ruminations, his voice low but rich in the quiet night.

Irritating man even sounds good! she thought as he reached down to scratch behind Buford's left ear. The massive dog began a goofy dance, prancing for Clay, gazing at him with doggy adoration and yipping his welcome.

"Buford," she called, but her baby had evidently forgotten her. A pang of pain crossed her heart, but she told herself she was being ridiculous. Buford loved her. He knew who his master—*mistress*—was.

"Hi, Maggie." Clay's voice again swirled around her, bringing her more pleasure than it should have.

Telling her heart to stop its absurd flutters, she said, "Ready for another night of rounds?"

He patted his pocket. "Plenty of treats for my pal."

At that, Buford resumed his minuet, alternating between

nuzzling Clay's Levi's and rearing up to plant platterlike paws on the man's broad shoulders. Generous licks were bestowed on his face as well.

Making herself focus on the matter at hand, Maggie asked, "Did the police have anything important to say?"

Clay shook his head, then sat with his back against the much-repaired chimney. "They know what we know. But they did get on my case about destroying evidence by repairing the damage."

"They warned me about concealing evidence, too."

"It wasn't the smartest thing to keep it to ourselves."

"Can't say it was."

"Did you contact the insurance company?"

"Mm-hmm, and the adjuster called after you'd left for the day. I met him here, and we walked through the house. The check will be in the mail no later than tomorrow."

"That's a relief."

"Only if there's no more trouble."

Clay nodded.

In spite of her every effort, Maggie found herself confessing, "I'm scared."

He turned to her in surprise. "Of what?"

She felt her cheeks warm and was glad of the dark. "Of all this . . . of what might happen."

"Your job, right?"

"Mm-hmm."

When he didn't answer, she grew uneasy. Maybe she shouldn't have spoken. But she'd carried her fear, her worry, her lack of confidence inside for so long that she felt the need to talk. Because he'd opened up to her in her apartment last night, she'd thought he might be able to tell her how he managed to go on with such confidence, despite the evidence against him. Surely he must be afraid, too.

"I'm sorry. I shouldn't have said a thing," she said quickly.

"I'm sure you don't understand. After all, you are hardly the type to get scared."

He laughed without humor. "Guess what? I live in constant fear myself."

"No way!"

"Yes, way."

"What can you be scared of? You're your own boss. And according to your references, you're the best. That's why I hired you."

"It doesn't mean much, when compared to other things."

"What things?"

He turned to her and sighed. When Buford scooted onto his lap, Clay extracted a thick chunk of rawhide chew from his pocket.

The puppy slid back onto the grass at the man's side and, with a blissful snuffle, began to gnaw.

Even though she resented her pet's easy acceptance of Clay, Maggie wasn't going to let Buford steal her chance to know Clay better. "What are you scared of?"

He sighed again, this time sounding as if the breath came from the very center of his being. "I guess it's time you knew."

"Knew what?" she asked, ready to shake out his words.

"About my past." Straightening his left leg and bending the right close to his chest, he tore a blooming dandelion from the earth and twirled its stem between his fingers. "There's something I haven't told you, and I should have. From the start."

Uh-oh. This didn't sound good.

His gaze on the weed, he continued, "Something happened my second year in college. Something that changed my life. I . . . went to jail."

His words knocked the breath right out of her. She hadn't known what to expect, but it hadn't been *that*. "Jail?" She managed a weak whisper. "For what?"

Again averting his face even though it was dark, he answered, "Embezzlement."

"I knew it!" she exclaimed, leaping up. "I knew you couldn't be trusted, Yankee. I can't believe I did this. It *was* my fault after all. What am I going to do now? And what am I going to say to Mr. H? Miss Louella? Lark?" He *had* been out to fleece them. "How dare you tell me you were innocent! You're nothing but a crook. A-a con!"

"Sit and hold your tongue, Maggie," he ordered. "I'm not finished yet. Since you asked, you owe me the courtesy of listening for a few more minutes."

Remembering Clay's willingness to apologize, his repentance of sins, his avowals of faith in God, she bit down on the offending bit of flesh. She plopped down on the grass, keeping a sizable distance between them. Gathering up Buford's leash, she gave it a firm tug. But the dog refused to leave his new hero's side. It figured! Even her dog had been bought by devious means—by a pro. "So go on," she said, madder by the minute.

"I didn't do it."

"Of course not," she scoffed. "Not even the guys on death row are guilty."

"Maggie, I was framed, and now I'm being framed again."

She didn't dare let his honest-Abe voice get to her again. "Your declaration of innocence underwhelms me."

"Do you think I would have stuck around if I'd been guilty?" he asked. "After the cops came into the picture? What have I gained from all this?"

She shrugged.

"Just hear me out. I was treasurer of a club at the school where I'd been offered substantial financial aid. My dad had died when I was fourteen, and Mom followed him right after my graduation from high school."

He turned toward her. "When I volunteered at a local

Historical Society, I worked with their treasurer. So when money disappeared, everyone knew I'd had access."

Grasping her shoulders, he insisted, "I never took a penny, Maggie, but no one believed me."

For a moment there was a break in the clouds and Maggie saw the anguish in his eyes in the moonlight. She felt his pain in the depths of her heart, but the words *embezzlement* and *jail* still rang in her ears. She steeled herself against his grief. "If you'd been innocent, it would have come out at the trial."

He dropped his hands. "Hah! The public defender assigned to me didn't care whether I lived or died, much less went to jail. He was getting paid the same either way. So I wound up behind bars, paying for someone else's crime."

Despite her efforts to harden her heart, Maggie felt the agony in his voice. Something told her he was telling the truth—at least about his past.

"If you were innocent, why didn't you appeal?"

"I told you, I had no money." Sitting back against the chimney, he brought both knees to his chest. Dropping his forearms onto them, he proceeded to rip the dandelion to shreds. "None. I couldn't hire a decent attorney, and the guy who sold me out wouldn't have done better on appeal."

"Couldn't you ask the court for another lawyer?"

"I did. *He* said he couldn't get me off. That an appeal would only keep me in jail longer."

"Oh, Clay." Her heart ached for him, hearing the harshness in his voice, feeling the muscled rage in the tense arm she touched. "How'd you survive?"

"I had no choice. I couldn't let a lie win."

"Was it as awful as one reads? You know, the fights, the drugs, the violence?"

"Worse."

That single word brought tears to her eyes. "How?" she choked out. "How'd you do it?"

He swiveled his head toward her. "You really want to know?"

"Please." The word rang like a cry through the night.

Taking a shuddering breath, he said, "I met Christ in jail, Maggie. It's through his grace, and only that, that I'm here today. . . . A guy named Isaac Dills had the cell next to mine. He was in for life. Rape and murder."

Maggie gasped.

"I couldn't believe he'd done something so inhuman because the man I met was gentle and kind. He helped me learn the ropes. He pointed out which guards I should watch out for, the inmates who'd do anything to get their next hit, and those who trolled new convicts in search of victims to satisfy their sick lusts."

Maggie moaned.

Clay didn't react, lost in the memory of horrors lived. "Thanks to Isaac, I was ready when a fight broke out. While I went for cover, Isaac went to break it up. He got a knife in the throat. I thought for sure he'd die. Somehow he recovered, but he lost his voice—he'd been a singer. The raspy words he spoke afterward taught me more about Jesus than I ever learned from his songs. That's when I knew I wanted what Isaac had."

"Just because a rapist spoke of God, you decided God was real?" Maggie asked, disbelieving.

Clay smiled into the night. "No, Maggie. I came to know Jesus through his love, his sacrifice, his saving grace. I was led to him by a man who'd sinned, then come to faith after repenting in jail."

"How can you say you *know* him? God? Jesus? You haven't seen or touched or heard him. I *still* don't understand—at least not beyond the Sunday-school-lesson level back when I was a child." Now that she knew about Clay's survival,

Maggie needed to know how to survive her troubles—even though by comparison to Clay's they seemed petty and vain.

"Do you *want* to understand?"

Shyly, Maggie nodded. "I realize now I do."

Clay's smile changed, became dazzling. He covered the hand with which she gripped his arm as if he were a lifeline— which she now felt him to be. "First thing you have to do," he said, "is tell God you want to see him, to know him."

"I can do that?" she asked. "He'll listen?"

"Of course. It's what I did."

"That's it?"

He chuckled. "Well, the prayer has to be a little longer. You need to confess that you're a sinner."

Maggie recoiled. She wasn't *that* bad. "I haven't killed anyone, stolen anything, or broken any of those other commandments, I'll have you know."

"There's more to sin than breaking one of the Ten Commandments," Clay explained. "There's Adam and Eve's original sin when they tried to make themselves like God by eating forbidden fruit. Then there's the sin of pride—saying you can handle everything on your own. Plus there's rebellion—choosing your own way instead of God's. Sin covers a whole lot of things that come naturally to us as humans."

Maggie's spirits deflated when she realized she didn't come out looking good. "If that's the case, then why would God want to know me?"

"He already does. He knows where your heart is; he knows everything about you—and still loves you. The Bible says that he loved the world so much—and you're part of the world— that he gave up his only Son, Jesus, so that everyone who believes in him will have eternal life with him. God wants you to know him, to recognize his love for you, and to accept his forgiveness."

"How can he forgive me if I'm so full of sin?"

"He already did."

"Who? Me?"

"That's why Jesus became a human like us—to take our sins upon himself and die on the cross. He did it for you and for me, so we could have a relationship with God."

The concept was so huge that Maggie could only grasp the edges. "I knew the Sunday school lessons said he was killed because the Jews didn't recognize him as the Messiah, but he cared that much? He did all that? For me?"

"He did it for you, me, everyone who accepts him."

"Is that why *you* accepted him?"

"Yes," he answered. "I was guilty of rebellion, of pride, and a bunch of stuff like every other unsaved person."

"So forgiveness of sins is what salvation is about."

"Exactly."

Maggie's heart began a strange growling, as though it needed food. Suddenly her questions, springing from her childhood loss, demanded answers. "How can you know he's there if you can't see him or feel him or hear him?"

"You can, Maggie. You can know him the way I do, without any doubt. You can see him with the eyes of faith, feel him with the touch of trust, hear him with the ears of hope, and know his voice through reading the Bible."

The conviction Maggie heard in Clay's voice turned her inner hunger into a gnaw. "You're sure I can know him, too?"

"Absolutely. Do you *want* to know him?"

The gnaw burst into a ravenous urge as Maggie acknowledged her need for someone to care for her enough to die for her. She knew she needed saving, since she floundered through life, stumbling, falling, drowning. She needed faith to go on day by day, despite the doubts of those around her. She needed to trust, to know hope. She needed guidance from God through his words—holy words that had seen a man through prison when he shouldn't have been there at all.

"I do," she whispered, tears spilling down her cheeks. "I want to know Jesus."

Rising to his knees, Clay gestured for Maggie to follow his lead. "Hold my hands," he said, offering the warm clasp she'd come to cherish. "Let's pray."

In a shaft of moonlight, Maggie saw moisture in Clay's eyes, joy in his smile. She took his hands and yielded her heart to a loving, waiting God.

SIXTEEN

As exhausted as he was from lack of sleep, the only thing Clay could focus on as he walked to work the next day was the truth ringing in his heart. Maggie Bellamy was now a Christian, and he knew without a doubt that he was falling in love with her.

That gave him pause. He'd thought they'd struck a good bargain, but he wondered now if he hadn't made a mistake, too. As they continued to guard the mansion, he and Maggie would spend hours and hours together. Last night, they'd found common ground, but he still didn't know for sure if she was innocent.

Yet he treasured the honor God had granted him in letting him lead her to Jesus. In that patch of moonlight last night Maggie's prayer had given birth to a bond between them he knew would never be broken. They belonged to God's family now and forever.

But did they belong together? As man and woman?

The question played at him, teasing him, leading him to hazy daydreams—and would lead, if he didn't watch himself, to smashed thumbs. He had better pay attention to what he was doing today, or the mansion and his hands would suffer.

Approaching the house, excitement surged through him. It wasn't the prospect of work but the chance to see Maggie again—talk to her, learn how she was this morning, her first as a sinner saved by grace—that drew him.

Clay's gaze rose, as always, to the leaded-glass window on the second floor. The soaring dove called him to rise above what bound him to earth.

That thought reminded him of his conversation with Hobey the other night. Maybe the canny old bear had been right about more than one thing. Hobey had reminded Clay that confession and honesty freed King David. And, after baring his soul to Maggie last night, Clay felt lighter than he had in a very long time. He'd cast off the chains of secrecy that had bound him for years. He felt free, if still earthbound.

With a glance heavenward, Clay said gratefully, "Thank you, Father, for Hobey's questions. They didn't feel good when he asked them, and talking with Maggie was one of the hardest things I've ever done, but he was right—your *Word* is always right. I needed to confess, to quit hiding, living behind bars. Thanks for your guidance, and for the chance to talk with Maggie. If my prison term is what it took to save her, then I see the purpose to those months. Now. In your time. Even though I still don't know why—"

"Talkin' to yourself?" Maggie asked, startling Clay.

He smiled, taking in her golden curls, sparkling eyes, and slim figure enhanced by a blue linen suit and a cream lace-trimmed blouse.

"Praying," he answered, anxious for her reaction.

"I did too—before I left home. Even though I'm not sure I did it the right way. I figure it's bound to take me some time to learn the ropes, if you know what I mean."

He clasped her elbow and guided her up the porch steps.

"There are no ropes to learn, Maggie. You talk to God like you talk to anyone else—me, for instance. Tell him what's in your heart, the good stuff and the bad. He's always listening."

"How do you know all this?"

"I've learned it over the years by reading his Word. Every day, a little at a time. Thinking about him, his thoughts, his actions, his love. Do you have a Bible?"

"I had a little white one for Sunday school, but I don't know where it is. And the only other one I know about is the big family one, and that's at my parents' home. Lark lives there now."

"You want to ask her for it?"

She grimaced. "Not particularly."

"Fine. We'll go shopping for one after work tonight. That is, if you'd like."

A brilliant smile dawned on her face. "I'd like that very much."

"Then let's get work out of the way. We'll have something to look forward to afterward."

"Sounds good."

As she stepped to the door, Clay placed a hand on her shoulder. "But, Maggie?"

She turned, dislodging his hand. "Yes?"

Help me, Father. "You have to take the problems with Lark to the Lord. Something's terribly wrong between you."

Her smile vanished. "There's always been problems. The Bellamy Blossoms have never gotten on well."

"Pray about it, will you? Ask the Lord to guide you, to show you how to work through the mess."

She nodded. "I'll pray, but I'm not sure there's a solution. People need to respect one another to work a problem through. No one respects me."

The reappearance of self-doubt bothered Clay, especially since he didn't think she was right. "I wouldn't say that. I respect you. Miss Louella does, too. Hobey speaks well of you, Mr. H has you in a responsible job, and I'm sure others think highly of you, too."

She snorted and turned the key in the lock. "Nobody thinks I'm worth more'n dirt."

"Well, do *you?*" Clay asked, his eyes probing hers thoughtfully.

She reacted as if an unseen blow had knocked her back a step. "Ah . . . well . . ." She snapped her spine straight, thrust her chin forward. "I know I can do my job."

"That's not what I asked."

She averted her gaze. "Well, I'm worth every bit as much as any other Blossom, that I do know."

"Listen to me. Remember last night when I told you God loved you enough to let Jesus die on the cross for you?"

Her features softened, her stance eased. "Of course."

"Do you think he would have done that if you weren't worth a lot?"

"Oh!"

"Yes, oh! Jesus is God's beloved Son. And God wouldn't have given up his Son for a woman without worth."

Wonder bloomed on her face. "He gave up his Son for me. . . ."

"That's how much God loves you. You matter to him and right now, you're worth that much to him, just as you are. You don't have to prove yourself to him."

"What a wonderful God he is!" Maggie said in a reverent voice. A moment later, twin tears gleamed in her eyes. "Knowin' that is so humblin'."

Thickness clogged Clay's throat. "Everyone who meets the Almighty can't help but recognize his majesty and his truth."

"If that's the case," Maggie said, straightening again, this time not with defiance but with a confidence he'd never seen her wear before, "Lark, Mr. H, and everyone else is wrong about me. I'm not a delicate, worthless Southern belle!"

Clay laughed. "Oh, you're a Southern belle with a delicate beauty, all right. But you're also a child of the King, precious in his sight."

"Not hardly a worthless excuse for a woman."

He choked. If she only knew how well she succeeded as a woman . . . in a man's eyes . . . *this* man's eyes. "No, believe me, you're *not.*"

Hearing the tone of his words, her cheeks flushed. He drew closer, his gaze never leaving hers. As he placed his hands on her shoulders and felt a tremor run through her, he paused, waiting for a rebuff that never came.

Thank you, Lord!

Then he kissed her. His lips came down on hers and pressed against them, telling her with his mouth how much she mattered to him.

When Clay ended the caress, she sighed, eyes closed, lips parted. Maggie Bellamy was the most beautiful woman he'd ever seen—and not in the perfect lines of her features, the exquisite mass of her golden hair, but in her discovery of her faith, her true self. She was quite a woman, his Maggie was.

He gave her another soft, brief kiss and, for the sake of his sanity, pulled away. "Let's—" he croaked, then cleared his throat—"let's inspect the place and get to work. We'll talk again later, okay?"

She nodded, looking dazed, amazed, and well kissed. Clay couldn't help the satisfaction thrumming through him.

Then they entered the hallway. Like droopy streamers the morning after a party, the wallpaper dripped off the wall, leaving some areas bare and others partly ravaged. Spots marred the just-finished floors, where the aged wall covering had puddled, and an acrid smell suggested the use of some form of stripper.

"How on earth . . . ?" he cried.

"Who could have done it?" Maggie demanded.

"When—" she started.

"When—" he asked simultaneously.

As both took in the ridiculous scene, they wondered exactly who they were dealing with. They knew neither of them had done it—they'd stayed within sight of each other the whole night through. Well, they *had* taken turns. Questions, unwanted ones, rose again.

Clay sighed. "At least it was paper we were going to cover, and I have plenty of finish for the floor. But it'll take more time. . . ."

"No serious damage done, then?"

"Doesn't look that way. Just more busywork for me."

"Do we call the police?"

"I don't dare not."

"Neither do I."

"Let's go."

"Mm-hmm."

Taking her hand in his, Clay led Maggie to the kitchen counter, where an ancient black dial phone held court. Alarm, bewilderment, and dismay still swirled in him, but this time, the soft fingers holding his soothed the bite of fear, the ache of loneliness.

He hoped his presence did the same for her.

❧

Although discovering the torn wallpaper had marred the morning, today had been Maggie's best day for longer than she cared to count. Clay's words about God's love—for her, *her*—had lit a spark of joy in her heart. His offer to take her shopping for her own Bible had warmed her soul, and their kisses had brought to life a feminine longing she'd never known before.

Touching her lips, Maggie marveled at the sensations she still remembered. Clay's caring touch had thrilled her, made her feel more womanly than she had thought possible. She'd secretly wanted the caress to go on and on and on, and she'd walked around in a daze for hours, unable to forget a single second of their kiss.

Something in Clay's gaze had told her it wouldn't be the last they'd share.

It was now nearly midnight, and she'd come to the mansion early. She hadn't wanted to be late, to miss any of their time together.

"You traitor," she told Buford, crouching down to scrub the dog's neck and earning ecstatic grunts for her efforts. "You've lost your heart to that handsome Yankee scalawag, haven't you?"

A slurp of the puppy's raspy tongue bathed her face with love.

"I think he's still pretty crazy about you," Clay said.

She fell back on her rear, having heard nothing of his approach. "Great guard I make," she said, laughing. "The vandals could have come, stolen me blind, and walked off with the whole kit and caboodle for all's I'd have heard."

"I don't think so," Clay answered, then dropped down next to her, tugging at her hand.

Maggie pointed at her dog and said, "I should have just named him Benedict. Look at him."

Buford had jumped on Clay's lap, looking ridiculous as he pretended to be the lapdog he wasn't. His tail whipped back and forth, slapping a muscular thigh without eliciting a complaint.

With a wriggle, the bullmastiff dropped his head and nuzzled Clay's jeans pocket. "He's just opportunistic," Clay said, pulling a roasted pig ear from its hiding place. "He knows I come bearing gifts."

"What about these?" Maggie held up her bag of freeze-dried liver chunks.

"He's hungry for pork?" Clay asked with a loopy grin.

They both laughed, and the pup chomped. Night sounds surrounded them—the chirp of a cricket to their right, the hoot of an owl to their left. A just-bloomed early rose scented the air, as Clay scooted closer to Maggie.

When he dropped an arm around her shoulders, she sighed with pleasure. "How was your day?" he asked.

"Well, starting with the wallpaper, then the police interviews, you were there for most of it, so you should know."

"Then it was pretty great."

"Awfully sure of yourself, aren't you?"

"Hmmm . . . how about if I say of us?"

Maggie's heart skipped a beat. "O—kay."

"Do you like your new Bible?"

"It's beautiful," she said on a sigh. "Even though you didn't have to buy it for me."

"I wanted to give it to you."

Reaching into her canvas tote, she withdrew a thick cardboard box. She stroked it, remembering the care Clay had taken to make certain she found the exact binding she wanted. "I couldn't leave it behind."

"Great! How about I read some of my favorite passages out loud?"

"Would you?" she asked, thrilled by his offer.

"For you, anything."

Maggie's breath caught in her throat. She looked up and met his amber gaze in the moonlight. As if his eyes were vats of sweet, thick caramel, they enticed her with their sweetness and warmth. Time stopped; her heartbeat slowed.

Clay came closer, tightening his hold around her shoulders,

his lips curving in a slight smile. She placed her hands on his chest and leaned into him.

"Maggie . . ." he whispered, as his lips met hers.

Again.

Then, reluctantly, he pulled away, asking God for the power to focus on his written Word.

He was in love. Clay no longer held any doubt about the state of his heart.

He loved Maggie Bellamy. And he was glad, very glad, he hadn't spent his adult life playing at romance, fooling himself about love. He wanted to share the real thing with this delicate, feisty lady who'd somehow managed to steal his heart against his will.

But it wasn't against his will anymore. All he wanted now was to spend every free minute with Maggie—laugh with her, talk to her, kiss her, and hold her close.

Clay also wanted to grow in faith with Maggie at his side. Last night had been like the best dream he'd never had. After another earth-moving kiss, they'd sat back, Maggie curled at his side, and he'd read Scripture—mostly the psalms—by flashlight to her.

Clay had hoped—prayed—she'd grow bold enough to read to him. And when she did, his heart had felt huge and full, as if his world was, for the first time in a long time, right.

"What a wonderful, wonderful, wonderful Lord we serve . . ." he sang softly to himself, seeing his happiness reflected in the azaleas bursting red, orange, purple, and white across the lawns on either side of the sidewalk. Redbuds sported their purple-red blossoms, and the grass everywhere had borrowed the color of emeralds for its daily garb.

Bellamy preened on a day like today. Clay decided he'd

better look into selling his home in Gettysburg. He couldn't imagine Maggie ever leaving Bellamy, and he couldn't imagine ever leaving Maggie.

Man, he had it bad. He had it good!

In fact, so good that he'd had Hobey's wife, Ellamae, pack a picnic lunch at the diner for him and Maggie. He was now on his way to steal her from her office for a half hour under the shade of a willow tree on the banks of Langhorn Creek.

Half of him felt ridiculous; the other half of him felt like breaking into a Gene Kelly dance. Someone would be sending out an army of little men in white jackets to round him up soon if he didn't watch himself.

He grinned from ear to ear. "What a wonderful, wonderful, wonderful Lord we serve. . . ."

At Bellamy Fiduciary Trust he paused to greet Ruby and ask, "Is Miss Bellamy busy right now?"

"Yes, but I don't think she'll be much longer. Won't you take a seat?"

Today he'd agree to anything. Well, anything reasonable. Waiting for Maggie to finish whatever business she had at hand felt eminently reasonable, even wise.

He picked up the latest copy of *Architectural Digest* and whistled his song again. As he flipped through the pages, noting very little in his love-fogged state, Maggie's door opened.

A man's voice rang out. The blood in Clay's veins froze. "Pleasure doing business with you, Maggie," said Hal Hinkley in his cultured baritone.

"All ours, Mr. Hinkley," she responded.

"You'll get the check in the mail before the week's out," Hal added, backing into the doorway, blocking Clay's view of Maggie.

"No hurry."

"You won't regret doing business with Hinkley Home

Renovations, Miss Bellamy. I guarantee it. And you can't discount that kind of money, either."

Enough! Bile clawed at Clay's throat as he rushed from the bank, blinded by a haze of repugnance. Rage roared in his ears; fear stole his every thought. The ache in his heart made breathing a struggle.

Maggie had been dealing with Hal all along, just as he'd suspected. Her prayers and kisses had meant nothing to her—other than a means to lull him into docile compliance.

He'd been a fool to buy her act. He'd *wanted* to believe her. Even when common sense had warned him—time and again—that she couldn't be trusted.

Hurting worse than he'd hurt since prison bars had closed him in, Clay returned to the mansion, bitterness burning his gut. He gave the picnic lunch to the electrician's men, who thanked him for his generosity, but who—wisely—after one look at his face, refrained from asking why.

Clay, however, did nothing but demand answers from God, who suddenly felt too far away to touch, to see, to hear.

SEVENTEEN

AFTER WORK THAT UNREAL DAY, WHEN ONLY DETERMINATION had kept him going, Clay hurried to Cammie Sprague's home, his refuge in town.

His landlady greeted him, but Clay only managed a bland hi in response. His heart was broken, his mind tormented by a sick mix of remembered atrocities and visions of a future looming with more of the same.

He held no illusions about Hinkley's motives. The guy hated him; his jealousy of Clay's success had colored all their conversations, meetings, differences. Besides, Hal had shown his hand at the very start of the current mess. "I'm going to show those dumb hillbillies they made a mistake by not hiring me," he'd said.

It looked as though Hinkley figured it was time to make good on his threat. He'd apparently come to Bellamy with Maggie's blessing—or at least her foreknowledge.

The only losers in Hal's ugly game would be Miss Louella Ashworth and Clay himself.

The vandalism at the mansion ran along the lines of

Hinkley's tactics, yet Clay had let himself be lulled by the man's absence from the town. He'd wondered if Maggie had been helping his nemesis, but because of his growing feelings for her, he hadn't wanted to believe the evidence.

He could no longer deceive himself.

Maggie was the one—in every respect. The one who'd stolen his heart, his present, and more than likely would steal his future as well. Although he could accept living with shattered personal dreams, Clay couldn't let her and Hal send him back to prison so easily.

"Lord," he cried out from his prone sprawl across the bed, "I can accept, as hard as it is, that Maggie's not the woman for me. But I can't imagine what good it'll do to let me take the fall for Hal. Or for Maggie, since taking bribes is against the law."

Clay closed his eyes against the sting of defeat. He couldn't believe he was fighting for his life again, just as he had years ago.

"I have to trust your Word. Otherwise, there's nothing left. I have no reason to live. You said you'd never leave me or abandon me, and even though I've never felt this alone, I *will* believe your promise. I *will* claim what you offer: your peace, your love, your comfort. Even when I can't see or feel it."

As he voiced those last words, Clay realized how much he sounded like Maggie. But unlike her, he'd known God's blessings in his life. He had proof of the Almighty's unending love in their many-years-long relationship. He didn't have to do it alone.

Anxious for prayer and Christian fellowship, Clay picked up the phone and punched out Hobey's number. It rang once, twice, three times, and then an answering machine picked up. "This is Horace Hobey. If it's after 5:30 on a weekday night, I ain't available. For a masonry emergency, dial 555-1314.

Otherwise, leave a message, an' I'll catch you back soon. God bless you."

Discouragement threatened, but Clay refused to let it take root. He prayed again, this time straight out of God's Word. "'Even when I walk through the dark valley of death,'" he read, focusing on the familiar words of Psalm 23, "'I will not be afraid, for you are close beside me.'"

He repeated the verse, seeking to steep his whole being in its comfort. Then he remembered Cammie. Should he . . . ?

Even though he felt awkward about asking, he knew Cammie, his sister in Christ, would join him in prayer. Then maybe he wouldn't feel so alone, and the cold dread in his gut wouldn't spread and freeze him altogether.

His energy renewed, Clay left his room and went downstairs, but as he neared the kitchen, he heard sobbing, followed by Cammie's soothing voice. He paused in the doorway, stopped by the scene before him. Cammie's support was already in use.

Suze McEntire, the young boarder who'd stayed in Bellamy to graduate with her high school class after her parents were transferred out of state, sported a red nose, swollen eyes, and a devastated expression. She sat staring at Cammie with love and a pleading expression. At the girl's side, their landlady wrapped an arm around shoulders heaving with sobs.

Evidently the teen needed mothering. Clay was a full-grown man, and he could face his trouble on his own—with God's help.

How he wished things had been different! That *Maggie* had been different. Then he could go on and face whatever came at him with her warm hand in his, lending him the encouragement and support he craved. He wished he could go to her for prayer.

Yesterday he would have. But no more. Irony nipped him. If Maggie had been different, he wouldn't be facing . . . Clay refused to voice his fears. If she'd been different, fear and memories and visions of trouble to come wouldn't be swamping him. He wouldn't have fallen for a Judas in the guise of a beautiful woman.

The woman who'd sold him out for a handful of dollars.

Father God, help me.

"Hi," Maggie called out when Clay arrived at the mansion later that night.

Instead of the smile—and kiss—she'd been hoping for, all she got in response was a cold, "Hello, Maggie."

Stunned by the sudden change in the man she was coming to love, Maggie fought her disappointment. It didn't look as though the new Bible in her bag would be put to use tonight. Something was troubling Clay. "Are you all right?" she asked, concerned.

His response was icy. "Just fine. Like you."

What was that all about?

His crossed arms and aggressive stance invited no questions, however, so she forced herself to turn to the matter at hand. "How do you want to work the patrol tonight?"

At that moment Buford's patience apparently expired, and he launched himself at Clay. To Maggie's amazement, the taciturn man grinned, letting himself be thrown down onto the grass. In a jumble of arms, legs, paws, tail, and slurping tongue, the two rolled and tumbled across the yard, Buford yipping his pleasure, Clay laughing heartily.

If it hadn't been for the curt exchange, Maggie would have sworn things between her tiny family of woman, pup, plus possible future member, were doing great. Now she couldn't help wondering if she'd been building castles out of thin air and asking for that skinny little ol' Roquefort moon to boot.

As she watched, Clay wrestled her massive pet—who'd clearly transferred his allegiance to the bigger, more fun human—pinning him to the ground. The puppy panted and yelped, thrilled by the rough play Maggie was physically unable to give him since Buford weighed in at one hundred pounds, and Maggie at only ten more. As Clay rubbed the dog's exposed belly, she wondered if she'd made a mistake adopting such a large hound.

Then she remembered her pre-Buford loneliness, her need for security, and admitted that a smaller breed wouldn't have offered both. She didn't want to lose her dog's love, too.

"Enough!" Clay cried a moment later. From his back pocket he took out a hefty, liver-flavored Nylabone chew. Buford accepted the proffered gift with typical enthusiasm.

Clay then stood, tall and strong, limned by moonlight, watching the pup gnaw.

Stepping closer so she could see his face, Maggie studied the play of expressions in the dim light. Before long, the joy Clay had shown during his rambunctious game with Buford disappeared. In its place came a harshness she hadn't seen there in a number of days.

"I'll do the rounds tonight," he said curtly. "You and Buford can keep watch right where you are. If you see or hear anything—" the derision in his voice hit her like an open-handed slap—"I'm sure you'll let me know."

Tears welled in her eyes. Something was very wrong, but Maggie had no idea what. "What's the matter . . . ?"

She let her words die off when his humorless eyes sliced at her, the leashed emotion in them striking at the burgeoning feelings in her heart.

With a short nod, she turned to her dog, reaching for him and rubbing his neck. "Fine. We'll let you know."

As Clay strode off, a tear slid down Maggie's cheek. What had gone wrong? Last night had been special—magical—like a dream come true. Only she'd never in her living days had such a wonderful dream. Now . . .

Hesitantly, she appealed to God. "I don't know what I might have done to turn Clay against me again. Did I somehow show myself to be lacking? Has he lost faith in me? I only know I love him. So if it's okay with you, could you please fix this mess? I want things back as they were."

But Maggie knew things could never go back to the way they'd been when she, Lark, Cammie, her mom and dad had been a family. Things had never been the same after her parents died, no matter how much the eight-year-old Maggie had cried out to the God her mother had prayed to, to the God Maggie had first believed in. In her teen years she had grown to question and eventually doubt God.

But she couldn't afford to doubt God this time.

This time, just thinking that Clay had misled her in her newfound faith, thinking that what she'd read in her Bible might not be real, was more than Maggie could bear. She'd be left desolate. She'd have nothing . . . no hope. She'd be completely alone.

Buford groaned in doggy happiness.

She was alone except for a dog whose loyalty and love could be bought by an artificially flavored treat.

"Help me, Jesus," she pleaded, clinging to her fragile faith as she dried the evidence of her pain.

🌿

"Looks like trouble's a-bloomin' in paradise," Louella Ashworth commented to her companion, the wildly successful girdle entrepreneur, Mariah Desmond, as they watched Maggie and Clay leave their posts at the mansion at five o'clock the next morning.

"It surely looks that way," answered Mariah, sighing. Then

she brightened. "But the coast is clear. We'd better get to work. Oooh, this is such fun! I never imagined we ladies of the Garden Club could find such excitement. First my girdles, now the Ashworth Treasure. Isn't it good that God keeps us growin' and useful no matter how many wrinkles and gray hairs we sprout?"

"Hush now, Mariah," Louella chided. "I'll have you know I succumb to neither scourge."

Mariah giggled. "Only your hairdresser knows, dear. But does your plastic surgeon?"

"I don't have a plastic surgeon!"

"Then what's your secret?"

"It's a secret."

"Oh, pooh! I didn't think you'd be that selfish. But since I haven't noticed many lines on *my* face yet, and I *am* fifteen years younger than you, I'll let you keep your secrets awhile longer."

Louella scowled. "I'm not fifteen years older."

"Of course you are, but that's not important. The Ashworth Treasure's what matters. I'm itchin' to find it, and we only have an hour and a half for tonight's mission."

The two black-leotard-clad ladies slipped out from behind the forsythia bushes on the periphery of the Ashworth property and hurried up the back steps of Louella's ancestral home.

"I really thought the wallpaper stripper would do the job," Louella commented, locking the door once they stood in the kitchen.

Mariah clucked in sympathy. "I did too, when I bought it. But then I read the directions. After that, I had my doubts."

"I should have listened to you, dear," Louella conceded with grace—even though Mariah's fifteen-year comment still smarted. "You were right. Now we have to spend more time strippin' the paper in the pantry, the hall, even the bedrooms. We can't rightly know just where Great-Granddaddy Asa hid his treasure without thoroughly lookin' for it. We'll have to keep on keepin' on as best we can."

Mariah nodded as she walked to the pantry. "The iron should do the trick. It melts old dried-out glue fine."

"Let's not waste any more time then."

Mariah plugged the cord into the wall to heat the iron up, and the two women turned their attention back to the apparent souring of Maggie and Clay's relationship.

"I'm fixin' to despair, Mariah," Louella commented. "I haven't seen two more stubborn cusses in all my born days. Why, anybody with eyes in her head can see they're meant for each other."

Looking thoughtful, Mariah leaned against the wall. "Maybe. Maybe not."

"What do you mean?"

Mariah paused, and her expression grew sad. "Maggie's not walkin' with Christ now. That speaks of deliberate, stubborn blindness. If she carries on with that choice, why then, they may be better off apart."

"Humph!" Louella snorted, determined to see her old friend's granddaughter happily paired with the man God had sent to her. "We just have to pray harder and longer on that girl's behalf so God will bring her back home."

"I won't argue with that." Mariah licked her index finger and tested the iron. It sizzled. "We're fixed to go, Lou. What would you rather do? Heat the paper or scrape the stuff once the glue melts?"

"I don't care, do you?"

Mariah shook her head, then handed Louella the hot iron. "Let's take turns. Goodness knows, there's plenty of paper to strip."

Louella pressed the iron against the paper they'd scored during their last mission to the mansion. "So," she asked her friend, "how's the world of comfortable girdles these days?"

"Lucrative, dear, very lucrative."

"We're plumb prouder'n punch of you, Mariah."

"Well, I'm thankful the Lord's blessed my efforts. I wanted women—me!—to have a foundation that wouldn't stop our breathin' or eatin' while keepin' everythin' in its proper place."

"You've done it!" Louella snapped her waist with her free hand to indicate the girdle that snugged her beneath her leotards. "Very well, indeed."

"Why, thank you—"

A sudden hiss, followed by a crackle and ending in a curl of smoke, cut off her words. The wall covering turned black as the edge of burning red flew up and out along the lines the women had earlier cut.

"Help me!" Louella cried, batting the paper.

"How?" gasped Mariah, blowing on the voracious scarlet line.

The fiery boundary of the paper changed as the aged stuff gave in to the hunger of the budding blaze.

Slapping the flames with her bare hands, Louella cried, *"Ouch!* Use the phone! *Ouch, ouch, ouch!* Call the police, the fire department. *Ow!* Oh, this isn't workin'. Tell 'em to hurry! Just don't let on who you are."

"I'm goin'. Use water to try to douse it while I talk."

Louella ran to the sink, picked up in her reddened hands the empty coffee mug someone had left behind, filled it, and ran back to the wall. "This wasn't supposed to happen. Why, we're just strippin' wallpaper. Any old fool can handle that without torchin' down her house. For cryin' out loud, why can't we find that treasure?"

In the scant seconds it had taken her to fetch the water, the fire had devoured an alarming spread of century-plus old paper, now dry and perfect as kindling. By now tongues of fire licked the ceiling, and Louella's cup of water did nothing to stop their growth.

Mariah popped her head back around the corner. "I'll bet dear Detective Marvin Pinkney never had to worry about this kind of thing," she said, waving toward the now-blazing wall.

Then it hit Louella. Dear, sweet Lord Jesus, what had she done? In her desire to find the Ashworth Treasure, she'd gone about her search in entirely the wrong way. Because she loved Marvin Pinkney books so much, she'd turned to those instead of God's Word for guidance.

Would Scripture have led her to such surreptitious actions? Would it have encouraged the destruction that now spread before her eyes? No. Never. God's Word always taught truth and light and Christlike actions. What she and the Garden Club were doing certainly didn't fall between those parameters.

Oh, dear, the Garden Club. In her misguided enthusiasm for Marvin Pinkney's detective work, she'd unwittingly led her friends astray. As president, she had a great opportunity to show godly behavior; instead, she'd fallen well below God's standard. And she was even on the prayer committee!

O, Father, forgive my sin, she prayed. *I took my eyes off you and turned foolishly to human guidance instead of your perfect truth.*

As Louella helplessly watched the flames increase, she knew true remorse, real repentance. Still, due to the consequences of her sin, her ancestral home's existence now stood in jeopardy. Could it be saved, or would her foolishness destroy what was so important to her?

The devastation she'd unwittingly caused appalled her. "Tell them to hurry!" she cried to Mariah. "I can't lose the house. It's all I have left."

"I did, dearie, I did," Mariah answered, her forehead furrowed. "They're on their way. Now, honey, unless you want to explain what we're doin', I'd advise us to run. And pray!"

Tears in her eyes and misery in her heart, Louella took a

few halting steps toward the door. Her heart urged her to fight the fire, but common sense told her she didn't have the means with which to do it. She wouldn't gain anything by getting caught, either.

Casting a final glance at the ruination they were leaving in their wake, she did as Mariah had urged. "Lord, I didn't mean for our treasure hunt to come to this. So please save the house. Whatever you can."

The two friends left, stealing through the beginning daybreak so that no one was the wiser to their presence in the besieged home.

From the depths of heavy slumber, Maggie heard a persistent ringing. She moaned. It was already time to get up, and she'd just dropped onto her bed for a nap after the wretched night.

"All right, all right," she grumbled, sitting up and smacking the button on the clock.

Buford snuffled from his plaid bed in the corner, but the ringing didn't stop. Then Maggie realized it hadn't been her clock ringing.

"Hello," she mumbled into the phone. Seconds later, she screamed, "Fire? At the Ashworth Mansion? B-but it's not possible!"

When the volunteer fire chief asked her why not, she mumbled an inane response, unwilling to confess she'd just spent the night outside the burning building. "I'll be there as soon as I put on some clothes."

Now she knew why Clay had acted as he had. He'd been planning to torch the place after she left.

Fury blazing in her, Maggie threw on her old jeans and an Orioles sweatshirt, locked a disgusted Buford into his crate, and ran out.

This time no number of earthmoving kisses was going to save that scheming, good-for-nothing, lying, cheating, Yankee crook. Not only had he harmed Louella's property, but he'd also tried to destroy a Confederate treasure.

Maggie, as a loyal member of the Daughters of the Confederacy, would never let his crime go unpunished.

Nor would she forget Clay's felonious larceny. After all, he'd stolen her heart.

※

As Clay fought the demons in his mind, hoping to steal a wink or two of sleep, the telephone rang. Muttering under his breath, he picked it up. "Yeah?"

"Clay?" asked Hobey.

"Sorry. I'm not asleep, but I'm also not awake."

"Didn't expect you to be, son. It's mighty early yet."

"It's early, all right." And Clay wasn't going to get *any* sleep now. "So this must be important. Right?"

"I'll say. I'm a volunteer fireman here in town, an' I just been called to a fire at the Ashworth. Just thought you'd want to know."

Lead congealed in Clay's gut. "A fire," he said, not asked. "In the mansion."

"That's what I said."

The urge to slug the wall pushed Clay forward, but he forced himself to wait, think, pray. "I'll be right there."

"You sure you want to?"

"No. But I know I'd better go."

"I was a-feared of that. Just remember, you ain't alone. The Lord's with you, an' I'm there, too."

"Thanks, Hobey. See you in five."

Struggling against the rage that roared in his ears, Clay tugged on the clothes he'd removed an hour ago. Now he knew what Hal had been doing in Maggie's office. All that remained to be seen was what the future held for him. Something in his gut told him he wasn't going to like it.

But no one had ever called him a coward. With another silent plea for strength, Clay ran to the Ashworth Mansion. As he approached, he counted three police cars—Bellamy's entire force—an aged fire engine, hoses, a group of men in pajamas and other leisure garb, and a clot of neighbors watching the excitement from across the street.

Then he saw her.

Eyes wider than he'd ever seen them, Maggie met his gaze. For a moment, he thought he read a plea there, that needy something he'd often noticed. She took a step toward him.

From inside the mansion, a man called out, "More hose!"

She turned to the house, stared at the glow visible through the first-floor windows. Then she shook herself and drew herself up as tall as her diminutive height allowed. With a final glance at him, she spoke to the uniformed man at her side.

The man nudged the officer at his other side. Both faced Clay.

Nausea churned in him. He'd seen the expression both these officers wore once before on other officers. As they strode toward him, Clay gazed straight at them. He had nothing to hide; he was innocent.

Nevertheless, the first one to reach him said, "Clayton Marlowe?"

"Yes," he answered, head held high, a wordless prayer in his heart.

"You're under arrest. You have the right to remain silent. . . ."

EIGHTEEN

THE FOLLOWING HOUR CRAWLED BY WITH AGONIZING
clarity. Clay had known what was coming before it actually
came. The humiliation and debasement of being handcuffed,
searched, fingerprinted, and interrogated, thrust him back
into the nightmare of eight years ago.

Only this time, it was worse. This time he'd been betrayed
by the woman he'd come to love.

When he asked on what grounds the police had based their
arrest, he learned that Maggie, as an officer of the bank, had
pressed the charges and revealed his past. The local authorities
had electronically checked with those in Pennsylvania, and his
record had come up.

Apparently they'd failed to notice or had ignored the later
notation clearing him of all charges; the exculpatory evidence
had surfaced well after he'd served his term, and the two references were probably not listed together.

The cops had focused on the statement that branded him:
Clayton Marlowe, guilty of embezzlement.

Embezzlement was a fancy name for theft. Maggie had

accused him of vandalism in a scheme to swindle funds from Miss Louella Ashworth and the Bellamy Fiduciary Trust.

She'd presented her evidence well. She'd told of the night he entered the mansion through the window, revealing his working knowledge of locks. She listed the damage the mansion had sustained, pointing out that none of it had been enough to ruin the house, only sufficient to excuse requests for further funds. In her opinion, no one but an expert in construction could have carried out such a careful scheme. Clay had the knowledge and expertise needed—and the prior conviction.

Finally, Maggie had accused him of trying to romance her in order to gain access to the house. She'd even tainted his fondness for Buford with the brush of evil design.

When Clay had asked how the vandals had entered the mansion, the interrogating officer had said they'd found no evidence of forced entry. Clay had pressed the point, reminding the policeman that he'd gone in that one time through a window with a faulty lock—a lock that had since been replaced by a solid dead bolt.

The officer hadn't commented, but continued his endless questioning.

Then, from somewhere in the glutinous mass his brain had become, Clay remembered his Miranda rights. "I need to call my lawyer."

He was led to a telephone, where he dialed the familiar number, and proceeded to endure Grant Smith's thorough chewing out. His friend, however, ended by promising to be there in a couple of hours. His grilling halted until Grant could reach Bellamy, the officer in charge, Petrie, as his nametag read, said, "Let's get you to your cell."

Clay nodded, then paused. He closed his eyes, suffered another stab of disillusionment, then offered a wordless utterance to God before speaking. "I need to press charges myself, Officer Petrie."

Surprise widened the man's brown eyes. "Against who?"

Again, pain struck him, but Clay knew what he had to do. "Against Magnolia Bellamy and Hal Hinkley."

"For what?"

"For conspiracy to defraud Miss Louella Ashworth and the Bellamy Fiduciary Trust, for petty vandalism, and for defamation of character—mine."

Officer Petrie rubbed his fresh-shaven chin. "Look, Marlowe, just 'cause you're steamed 'cause you got caught, don't mean you can go accusin' others of your crime."

"In this country," Clay said, keeping his voice even, his words temperate, "a man is innocent until proven guilty. I'm not lashing out in revenge. I have evidence that points to them."

As Petrie stared at Clay, he scratched the hard ball of a belly that bulged out over his too-tight belt. Clay's expression must have conveyed the sincerity of his accusation because the cop finally said, "Okay, buddy. Let's go over what you got."

Clay enumerated the facts. Hal had threatened to "show those hillbillies" their mistake in hiring Clay—a comment that didn't please the officer. Maggie had been in contact with Hal, the man who'd often tried to blacken Clay's reputation in an effort to win more business for himself. Hal's visit could be corroborated by Ruby Fulkes, Maggie's secretary, as could the conversation Clay had overheard, a conversation where a transfer of money from Hal to Maggie had been discussed. Then he listed the correspondence between Maggie and Hal, correspondence he'd seen, which could probably be verified by checking her office files.

Clay referred to what he'd seen as Maggie's automatic assumption of ulterior motives on Clay's part even before she'd met him. Now her early accusations seemed more an effort to set him up and to sour Miss Louella against him, preparing the owner of the mansion for the final chapter in the plot.

Finally, he related Maggie's insistence on keeping the only key to the mansion in her possession at all times. *She,* not him, was the only person who'd had unimpeded access to the mansion. And she'd spent many nights in the house allegedly alone but for her dog. Who knew? Maybe Hal had been with her all along.

"So you see, Officer Petrie," Clay said, winding down, "there's enough evidence to arrest them. If nothing else, to detain them for questioning."

A reluctant nod came his way. "I've wrote it down, Marlowe. I'll follow up with the chief. Now we got to get you where you belong."

Clay ground his teeth. "I belong at home. I did nothing to that house but work to restore it. And I'm going to prove it." With God's help and Grant's legal acumen.

As he walked down the cell-lined hall of the Loudon County Jail, Clay couldn't suppress the shudder that wracked him. The sight of steel bars, the dead expressions on the faces staring out at him, the reek of institutional death, were all too familiar.

His spirits sank lower with each step. When Petrie took out his massive key ring, the clinking of keys ripped a hole in Clay's heart. He remembered that sound.

After opening an empty cell, Petrie stood aside. "Make yourself comfortable, Marlowe. Looks like you'll be here for a while."

To Clay's surprise, he heard no derision or taunt in the officer's words. He glanced at his jailer and saw compassion in his dark eyes. With a nod, he stepped inside the cubicle and strode to the bunk built into the wall, noting the thinness of the mattress and blanket—all too familiar to him.

Then the bars clanged shut. The sound thundered through Clay, echoing in his bones, stealing his strength, his breath. His legs gave way. His senses swam. Bile churned in his gut, rose to his throat. Dizziness overtook him, and he collapsed on the bed.

It had happened—again. Just as he'd feared. He was back behind bars for someone else's crime.

The blackness in Clay's head frightened him. Utter and complete nothingness surrounded him. Was this what death was like?

For him, it might as well be. What did he have to live for?

This time, nothing would save his career, his name. It was all gone.

Maggie . . . he felt as though he'd lost his only chance at love, happiness, and a future when he'd lost her. But had he ever had her? It didn't look that way.

Her betrayal hurt worse because of her lie. She'd pretended to come to Christ. She'd feigned devotion to God.

Then she'd sold him out.

But God was all-powerful, wasn't he? He could get Clay out of this mess, couldn't he?

Old questions returned, their lack of resolution making them a greater torture than they originally had been. Why hadn't God protected him the first time? Why was Clay sitting in jail again? When he'd done nothing. He was inno-cent, yet bearing the punishment for another's sins. "Why?" he uttered in agony.

What good would come of his imprisonment? He no longer felt Maggie's conversion had given purpose to his first time behind bars. What good could come of a repeat term?

It would do *him* no good. It would devastate his life. What life he'd managed to restore for himself in the years since his last imprisonment.

He'd never had an easy life. It had been full of loss from early on.

His father? Dead when Clay turned fourteen.

His mother? Dead when Clay turned eighteen.

His college career? Dead when he turned nineteen.

His dreams of being an architect? Dead at nineteen, too.

His hope of love? Dead at Maggie's hand just weeks before he turned twenty-eight.

He'd fought hard to rebuild his life after his release from prison. He'd worked more hours than anyone else, made sure nothing he did was questionable. He'd kept his reputation above reproach, building block by block a new life from the ashes of the old.

Just as he now strove to restore old homes from the wrecks they'd become, giving them a future, as he'd hoped to do for himself. The Ashworth Mansion had come to represent his life, his commitment, his efforts. Its future was his.

Yet his future was dead at Maggie's pretty hand.

"But God, I'm innocent!" he cried. "Why me?"

In his heart Clay felt a response. *So was my Son.*

He stilled. The darkness in his head eased; the knot in his throat tightened. What had he heard? Was he going mad? Hearing voices? Hallucinating from grief and pain?

Or had he just imagined it?

My Son went to the cross for others' crimes.

This time Clay knew he hadn't conjured the words. He knew that voice. He'd heard it before, deep in his spirit.

He bore your sins when he had none. He paid for you.

Clay froze. The truth of the gospel came down on him, clear and ringing. Jesus had borne his—Clay's—sins so that he might find forgiveness and have new life. God's Son hadn't fought against the sacrifice.

"But, Father, good came from Christ's death. What good can come from mine?"

How can you know what's in my will? my plan? How do you know your response to adversity won't lead a soul to me?

Clay quaked in shame. He, who for so long had said he wanted God's will more than his own, had spent years resisting that will. It wasn't because he believed God had sent him to jail but because he'd lacked the faith to believe God could redeem his time behind bars.

Until Maggie. For a brief time, he'd believed. Then she'd betrayed him, and he'd been arrested.

Still, Christ had gone to Calvary for him. God had allowed his Son to die that Clay might live. That awesome truth slashed the turmoil in his mind, cutting through the darkness like a sword of light, revealing his weakness and flaws with blinding clarity, finally bringing Clay to his knees.

Tears rolling down his face, Clay let his old self die in that prison cell, understanding at last the fullness of his rebirth in Christ. He'd thought he'd died to self years ago, in another cell. But he'd lived a lie, a counterfeit. He'd clung to pride, to the secrets he hid, to the lie. He *had* been in bondage all those years.

He'd never been innocent. Innocent perhaps of theft, but not of other sins. On his knees Clay finally understood what Hobey had tried to tell him. Clay had thought he'd been striving against a system that had unfairly judged him a thief. He'd actually been battling a greater foe.

Scripture laid it out bluntly. Clay had let himself be deceived, despite the many times he'd read that clear and unequivocal passage. Paul had warned the Ephesians; perhaps they'd heard those words better than he did.

Put on all of God's armor, Paul had urged in chapter 6, *so that you will be able to stand firm against all strategies and tricks of the Devil. For we are not fighting against people made of flesh and blood, but against the evil rulers and authorities of the unseen world, against those mighty powers of darkness who rule this world, and against wicked spirits in the heavenly realms.*

The Great Deceiver had deceived Clay. His own human pride had brought him down to a pit lower than the one circumscribed by prison walls.

Clay sobbed, repentance in his wounded soul, regret in his heart for the pain Christ had borne for him. "Forgive me, Father, even though I don't deserve your mercy. Jesus, I added to your suffering, and you didn't complain as I have time and time again.

"O, God, you call us to be Christlike, and I failed. I blamed you for what happened, for not saving me from the hell of jail. But you didn't keep your Son from dying on that cross, did you? You used his death for a blessing—the greatest blessing of all. So if you have some use for me—*any* use for me— here, then I accept my fate. Your will—" the words came out in a strangled burst—"not mine. Even when I don't understand. I'm yours, Father, really yours this time. Forgive me for taking so long to see."

The words of that favorite song ran through his mind again. As acid tears of regret, repentance, and renewal flooded his face, he choked out, "Open my eyes, Lord, I want to see Jesus, to reach out and touch him. . . ."

Hours after the fire department brought the blaze under control, Maggie struggled to explain to Cecil Wiggon and his sidekick, Scott Petrie, why she came to have the key to the mansion, why she'd been in contact with Hal Hinkley, why she'd spent night after night sleeping in the house with only Buford by her side.

To no avail.

They clapped handcuffs on her wrists—which promptly

fell off, since they'd been made to restrain large men, not diminutive women—and hauled her into Loudon County Jail. When she arrived in the bustling, depressing building, she saw Hal Hinkley, similarly braceleted, being led away by a cop she didn't know.

Scott and Wiggon led her into an interrogation room, then proceeded to pepper her with question after question, demanding to know what seemed to her the most inconsequential minutiae. Of greatest interest to them was the substantial check Hal had written in her name to benefit the future Ashworth Historical Foundation.

Since she hadn't gotten around to establishing the foundation yet, as she'd hoped to do during the restoration of the mansion, the two cops refused to believe it was an innocent misunderstanding.

And of course, she didn't need a lawyer. Why, she was as innocent as a newborn babe in the woods, pure as the driven snow, with clean hands to show for her efforts, even though someone—a certain Yankee someone—was busy trying to give her a black eye just because he got caught holding the bag now that Maggie had let the cat out.

Nevertheless, they'd hauled her off to a dreary cell. So here she sat, more alone than she'd ever been.

Clay, the man she'd fallen in love with, had put her here. What a fool she'd been.

Her fears had all come true. She was alone—totally and completely alone.

Her parents had died.

Granny Iris was gone, as well.

Her sisters . . . well, she'd never had them.

Her career? Shot.

Her credibility? Maggie snorted. She'd never had that anymore than she'd had her sisters.

Her heart? Stolen and torn to shreds by a good-looking carpetbagger.

Her future? Who knew? She didn't. If she was to believe her Bible, God knew. But she didn't know where he was—not when she was still sitting here. Surely he knew she didn't belong in this little box, in this awful company. Once she got out of here, Maggie was going to volunteer to help those women she'd seen as Wiggon had led her to her cell. Now that she knew what jail was like, her compassion for them knew no bounds.

The only boundaries Maggie knew were those drawn by the walls of her cell. She was locked in, bound by steel bars.

She needed to get out. She needed to be free, before this dismal hole stifled all the life out of her.

But . . . what life? What did she have to live for? The hope she'd known only hours before was gone, stolen by the man who'd already taken her heart. All she had was a dog. And an animal's affections could easily be bought—as Clay had shown her. Maggie had nothing left. No family, no career, no friends, no dog. No love.

For God so loved the world that he gave his only Son, so that everyone who believes in him will not perish but have eternal life.

Maggie jerked upright. Who said that? She'd read the words in her Bible—Clay had told her to read the Gospel of John first—but she knew she hadn't spoken them out loud. She doubted any of the other prisoners had either. Did any of them know God? about him? about his Son? about Jesus' death on the cross? For her . . . for them?

My love, said that voice again.

"What?" Maggie asked, looking but finding no one in her cell but herself. "Who said that?"

I have loved you even as the Father has loved me. Remain in my love. When you obey me, you remain in my love, just as I obey my Father and remain in his love.

It hadn't been an audible voice, Maggie now realized. She'd heard the words in her heart, where they'd lodged after reading them with Clay in the moonlight. They'd meant so much to Maggie, who in her loneliness craved love more than the air she breathed.

God had spoken to her through his Word. He'd come to comfort her in her hour of darkness. Surely he'd see her through even this.

Footsteps and voices rang out from the entry to the cell block. Keys clinked as the voices approached. Maggie winced. She recognized the voices. All of them.

Not only was Scott Petrie approaching, but he came bearing blossoms. Bellamy's Blossoms.

"I swear," Lark was saying to Cammie, "I don't know what you and Maggie did all those years I was gone from town. Cammie, you're too sweet, too trusting, and too young to know what you're doing. Not to mention too pregnant, widowed, and hormonally challenged at the moment."

"Lark," Cammie answered, her voice soft as always, but this time somewhat strained, "I did what I had to do. As a Christian, God calls me to honesty and compassion. I couldn't let that man rot in here when I knew he hadn't done a thing. Anyway, that's not what matters now. Now we need to get Maggie out of this horrid place. She needs a bath, a meal, and a bed. In that order."

"You have company," Scott announced, standing outside Maggie's cell.

Resigned to her fate, Maggie rose. "What tidings of questionable joy do you two bear?" she asked her sisters.

Jabbing the key into the lock, Scott opened the bars and gestured for Maggie to come out. "What?" she asked him. "You've changed your mind about me? So soon?"

"Your sisters posted bail. You can go home now. Only don't

go guardin' the mansion again. You or Marlowe. We'll haul you back if you try. The PD's takin' *our job* back."

Dismay and, yes, bitterness, swelled in Maggie's middle as she glared at her sisters. "You two couldn't bear the embarrassment of Maggie's latest mess-up, could you? Even though I'm innocent of all these stupid charges."

Lark sighed. "Mag, I have no idea what you've gotten yourself into since you refuse to talk to me about it. I just couldn't see leaving you in this place—" she waved, her mouth a twist of disgust—"until things became clear."

"So you think I'm guilty."

"I didn't say that."

"But you don't think I'm innocent either."

Lark didn't respond.

"Thanks, *sis,*" Maggie said, disdain dripping from her last word, betrayal burning in her throat, "for that rock-solid vote of confidence."

"Enough, you two," said Cammie, concern on her face. "Maggie, you look awful. When's the last time you had a decent night's sleep?"

Maggie shrugged.

"Sleep deprivation is nothin' to laugh at. Let's get you home. Maybe you can think better after you get some rest. We'll help you clear up this mess. We'll do everythin' we can to get you acquitted, you know. Not just post bail for you."

"And how'd you do that?" Maggie asked, knowing the state of her sisters' finances.

"Never you mind that now," Cammie answered, averting her gaze.

"Yeah, Mag. Let's get out of here," added Lark.

Maggie was too exhausted to ask more questions. They waited as Scott opened the steel cell-block door, then headed for the discharge desk. She moved slowly, her feet feeling as though they'd been dipped in concrete, her head throbbing like a kettledrum, her muscles rigid, unwilling to obey her commands.

Through her misery, she heard masculine voices. Then a single voice with the power to steal her breath away spoke. "Cammie," Clay said, walking toward the sisters.

Maggie stared in dismay, his face still evoking an emotional rush in her.

"Are you all right?" asked Cammie.

"Thanks to you," he answered, gratitude in his tired grin. "You can't know what it means that you vouched for me."

"Well, I couldn't just keep quiet since I heard you come in the house at ten after five this mornin'. I knew you hadn't left after that, either, at least not until after the phone rang. I'd gone to the kitchen to start breakfast at a quarter past five."

Maggie stared at her sister. "You know him?"

"He's boardin' with me."

She gasped. "You mean . . . he's been living at your house, and now you're the one who set him loose? The man who did all this to Miss Louella, *plus* had me locked up?"

Cammie's eyes begged for understanding; Maggie found none.

"Clay was in my house this mornin'," the youngest Blossom said. "If, as you told the police, you were with him guardin' the mansion all night and he was in my home after that, then he couldn't have set the fire. I had to speak up, just as I had to get you out of here."

"Er . . . you two know each other?" Clay asked, his gaze bouncing from Maggie to Cammie and back to Maggie again.

"Of course," Cammie answered. "Maggie's my sister."

"That explains the eyebrow!" Clay exclaimed—inexplicably, Maggie thought.

Then Maggie glared at Cammie. "Some sister. One who betrays her sister for the sake of a crook."

"I didn't betray you!" Cammie's voice broke.

"No, but you've never been on my side either."

"Give her a break, Mag," demanded Lark.

Maggie spun. "You're a good one to talk. You always talk *at* me, but you don't listen to what I have to say. You've never given me the credit you give a gnat."

Lark had the grace to blush. "I'm just worried about you. I said you weren't tough enough for this job, and I warned you you'd wind up in jail. Well, here we are."

"Now wait just one minute," Clay interjected.

Bellamy's Blossoms glared at his intrusion.

Maggie turned back to Lark. "What gives you the right to decide what's good for me? That you were birthed two years before me? Your superior attitude?"

"Just a dose of common sense, and yes, maturity."

"Lark, I don't think you're right on that," Cammie offered.

Maggie whirled to face her other sibling. "You! You're too naive to know what's what. Tell me about the bail money. Where did it come from? Did you do what I said with your annuities?"

Cammie waved the question away. "I had other things to worry about. I'll get around to it. Soon."

"See? You're not mature enough to know what's good for you, much less me," Maggie said.

"Maggie has a point," Lark said, stunning Maggie. "But we do, too."

Cammie's glistening eyes shamed Maggie's heart.

So her life had come to this: public admittance on the part of her sisters of Maggie's lack of worth; public accusations and insults on her part; more distance between the three surviving Bellamys.

"Magnolia!" she heard Skeets call from the entrance to the jail. Maggie looked up, and a glimmer of pleasure pierced her misery as she saw the boy holding Buford's leash. Tears welled in her eyes. A great big, slurpy, doggy kiss wouldn't set her world to rights, but it would sure go a long way toward salving her wounds.

Buford trotted in, his tongue lolling happily to one side. "Oh, baby," Maggie said, dropping to her knees, her arms open wide to receive her dog's affection. He hurried his pace, gave a wag of his tail. Suddenly he yipped in joy, panted, ran, giving a loud *"AWWWROOOOOF!"* in greeting. Then . . . he ran right past her and launched himself at Clay.

Maggie's world came crashing down around her in the lobby of a jail.

Even her dog had betrayed her.

NINETEEN

HOLDING THE TELEPHONE RECEIVER A PROTECTIVE FOOT from her ear, Maggie said, "I heard you the first time, Mr. Hotshot Officer Cecil Wiggon. You told me I run the risk of landing back at the Hotel Steel Bars if I get caught guarding the Ashworth Mansion again. Do *you* think I'm stupid, too?"

A lot of hemming and hawing on the phone made Maggie's stomach sink. "You can stop your jawing whenever you're ready, Wiggon. I got the idea." She sighed. Things were bleak indeed. "Tell me something. Did you boys tell that slippery Yankee to stay away from the property, too?"

"How could we, Maggie?" asked her now-former friend. "The guy's got a contract to fix the place. We can't keep him from workin', especially since we know he couldn't have done a thing to the mansion."

That hurt. She, who'd been concerned about this kind of disaster from the start, wound up charged with all sorts of crimes she didn't commit, while the man who'd started the trouble got off scot-free. Thanks to her ever-loving little sister.

"I see," she murmured. "I won't even step foot on the

Ashworth's sidewalk again. I promise. Now, I'm in desperate need of a nap. If you'll excuse me . . . ?"

They hung up, and Maggie collapsed on her bed. From his cushion in the corner of her room, Buford rose, then clambered up and lay at her side. He nuzzled her hand, whining when the rub didn't materialize.

"I can't see my way clear to babying you right now, Buford. Not after you shamelessly abandoned me for that scalawag at the jail."

The dog crawled higher up on the bed, then slurped her face with his big tongue. For once she didn't giggle. His actions made her feel worse.

How? Maggie didn't know. She'd already felt awful, what with all those horrible thoughts and images she couldn't stop.

Well, there sure wouldn't be any more moonlit walks around the mansion with Clay. No more whispered confidences, no more comforting, no more shared Bible reading or prayers.

She had to quit thinking like that. The stuff churning in her head was making her loopier than a loon. She needed sleep—to block out the thoughts, to give her the rest she'd missed, to help her gain perspective now that her world had flipped upside down.

Tugging the pale blue summer-weight cotton blanket up under her chin, Maggie tucked her left arm under the pillow and closed her eyes. The warmth of imminent slumber crept over her, relaxing tight muscles, soothing her aching head.

She slept.

Later—she didn't know how much later—her ringing phone woke her up. As she reached for the receiver, she realized she'd come to a decision. She knew what she had to do next.

"Hello," she said, her voice slumber thick.

"Magnolia?" asked Mr. Hollings.

"Of course." Maggie had known this was coming. She just hadn't expected it so soon.

"I'm sorry to have to do this," the president of the Bellamy Fiduciary Trust said, "but I'm sure you can understand my position. Whilst these charges hang over you, I'm forced to think of the bank first. Your services are no longer needed. You needn't come in for your belongin's, either. Ruby is packin' everythin', and she'll fetch it to you after work this afternoon."

Even though she'd expected it, even though she understood the bank's position, facing the reality of her dismissal was devastating. "I understand, Mr. Hollings. And I'll look forward to seeing Ruby later this afternoon."

But Mr. H wasn't quite done. "The board has agreed on a generous severance package," he continued. "Especially seein' the accusations against you. We hope this shows none of us think you guilty of anythin' but carelessness and poor judgment. We don't for a moment think you were fixin' to swindle the bank or Miss Louella. You just ain't cut out to handle complex business matters. You'll be better off in a less-demandin' job."

He paused, obviously waiting for her response. Maggie thought better of giving it to him, since it wouldn't be particularly pleasant right then.

After a moment, he cleared his throat and went on. "You're a delicate li'l lady," he said. "Reckoned so from the start. But out of respect for Iris's memory—dear woman—I gave you a chance at the bank. It ain't your fault you're not the business type. You're a lady, you know, teas and pleasant company. It's best you know now and find somethin' more genteel to suit you. We wish you the best."

After a mumbled farewell, Maggie hung up. She thanked God for the rest he'd given her, for the lucidity that was returning to her mind. Otherwise she would have mouthed off something she'd later regret.

Mr. H had said such hateful things.

Yes, Maggie knew what she had to do next. She had to go

to Leesburg, invest that severance package Mr. H mentioned in a good lawyer, and clear her name. Once she accomplished that, she would go apartment and job hunting. In Leesburg. Far from the town that, even in its name, held nothing but trouble and turmoil for her.

She was leaving Bellamy for good.

❧

Hours after the debacle at the jail, Clay woke up to another gorgeous, early summer Virginia afternoon. He heard birds chirping in the vast maple outside his window, children playing in the yard next door. He smelled the fragrance of freshly mowed lawn, felt the warmth of the sunshine pouring in his window.

Too bad it didn't reach inside his aching heart.

He hurt—for both himself and Maggie. He'd seen the agony in her face when Buford had run past her and greeted him instead. He knew what that dog meant to her. He knew she believed herself alone, unloved.

But she wasn't. God loved her. He did, too.

But they didn't belong together. She didn't believe in him, and he wasn't sure what he believed about her. He was going to miss their patrols of the mansion. There wouldn't be any more Scripture read by moonlight, no more wonderful talks, no more games with her lovable dog.

Even though he questioned the sincerity of Maggie's conversion, Clay hoped God's love had made an impression on her. The Lord could comfort her, no matter how bleak things seemed. Clay couldn't stand to imagine how lonely Maggie probably felt right now. Hinkley didn't count as support, company, comfort. The guy was out for himself. Now that the authorities knew she was guilty, too, Hal wouldn't do Maggie any good.

Clay couldn't see how she wouldn't be guilty, no matter

what she'd said. She'd had everything: motive—money; access—the key; expertise—Hal at her side. And yet, impossible as they were, his feelings for her remained.

He dropped to his knees and prayed. "Father, I'm heartbroken. I knew better than to get involved with a woman who didn't know you, but I let my interest in Maggie convince me it was your will for me to lead her to you.

"It doesn't look that way anymore, and I ask your forgiveness for taking my eyes off you. I know you forgive me, but I also know I'm suffering the consequences of my actions. Give me the strength to stamp out my feelings for Maggie, too, if that's your will. Help me finish my job to the best of my ability and to remember to choose your will, not mine, when I face more trouble."

After donning his terry bathrobe and grabbing clean clothes, Clay headed for the shower. Since the authorities, propelled by Miss Louella, had turned the key to the mansion over to him—after confiscating it from Maggie—he wanted to check out the extent of the fire damage. He wanted to know just how much longer he'd have to stay in Bellamy.

Although he'd played with the idea of moving here after he'd finished with the mansion, the events of the last twenty-four hours had proven that idea his most misguided yet. He wanted out.

Clay was leaving Bellamy the minute he could.

※

As Maggie approached the Ashworth Mansion—on the sidewalk *across* the street, keeping her promise to Wiggon—she noticed the open front door. Clay was probably inside assessing the fire damage.

She hadn't been able to stay away, no matter what kind of warning Wiggon came up with. The house meant too much to her. It grounded her in her heritage as a Southerner, a Confederate, one who would fight until the bitter end. She couldn't—wouldn't—betray those men and women who'd given up everything for the South. Those folks had made her who she was. They'd given her the legacy she meant to carry on: strength, triumph, and success. Even though she could no longer have a part in restoring it.

She hurried along, her gaze refusing to turn from the house. *Lord?* she asked silently. *You know I didn't do anythin' wrong—other than maybe fall for the wrong guy—so why is everyone against me?*

From the darkest corner of her memories—and dark it was—a phrase came to her. She remembered Granny Iris repeating it as Maggie had cried herself to sleep the day they'd buried her parents. "Our heavenly Father said," her grandmother had whispered, "he would be with us as he was with Moses. He would never fail us or abandon us. You have the best Father of all, Maggie-girl. He's in heaven, watchin' over you."

Granny Iris had said it so many times that finally Maggie asked her not to do so again. That Father had been too far away to feel. When her beloved grandmother died, Maggie's seventeen-year-old heart had hardened more against the God who'd taken all from her. All but long-forgotten words. It seemed the words had burrowed into her, surfacing only when she felt as abandoned as she had then.

Now the resurgence of those words surprised her. Where had they come from? Was God answering her question? Was he the one who wouldn't turn against her? the one who would love her, no matter what?

She stopped, closing her eyes. A tear rolled down her cheek. "O Lord," she whispered, "I need your loving arms around me now. I feel so cold, so empty. I'm scared of leavin' town. You know I never left because I didn't think anyone out there would give me a fair shake on account of my looks, just as they don't here. I'm terrified of startin' over again. If they don't lock me up, that is."

I will never fail you or abandon you.

Maggie caught her breath. "Really?"

I have loved you, my people, with an everlasting love. With unfailing love, I have drawn you to myself.

Then Maggie remembered. Clay had read that Scripture from the book of Jeremiah when they'd guarded the mansion. He'd assured her the Lord meant it for her as much as for the Israelites he'd originally said it to.

With unfailing love, I have drawn you to myself.

Yes, God had drawn her to him, and he loved her.

I will never fail you or abandon you.

When everyone else had, God still spoke to her. He was at her side, even out in the middle of the sidewalk!

I have loved you . . . with an everlasting love.

A ray of inner sunshine, deep in her secret self, pierced the darkness of her mood. She wasn't alone; God was with her. If he was with her, who else did she need?

A smile made its way onto her lips. Maggie opened her damp eyes. She looked around her and for the first time noticed how glorious the day was. She'd been released from that awful jail, she'd slept, and God had just spoken to her. What more could she want?

Out of the corner of her eye, she caught a movement in the doorway of the mansion. Clay.

She froze.

He froze.

From either side of the vacant street, they stared at each other, separated by events neither could discount, kept apart by harsh words, doubts, fears. Although Maggie couldn't see his eyes, she felt his stare on her, as avid as hers on him.

She ran her gaze from his dark waving hair down past his

shadowed face to his broad shoulders and strong arms. She noticed his fisted hands, his long legs, his wide stance. She wanted to run to him, to curl up beside him as she had the night they'd read Scripture. She wanted to talk about God with him, pray with him, hold him close to her heart, to know he loved her as much as she . . . loved him.

She took a step toward him.

He came forward a matching pace.

Her heart beat faster. Her breath caught in her throat. She reached out a hand. . . .

No, it wasn't possible. She pulled back, stuck her hand into her trousers pocket, and turned back toward town.

But she couldn't take another step. She glanced over her shoulder. Clay still stood there, as if cast from stone, watching her, studying her every move. For what? To use it against her?

Clay couldn't be trusted, no matter what exonerating evidence Cammie had come up with. Maggie had trusted him, and he'd turned against her, knowing how much restoring the mansion meant to her. He had to know, somewhere in his heart, that she was innocent. Yet he'd charged her with a crime.

As you did him, said her conscience.

But he's a Yankee!

You're a Rebel.

Unlike her, though, he'd been convicted once before.

Had he been guilty then?

She faced him again, willing the answer to her question to float from him to her. He'd insisted he was innocent. Didn't all crooks say that, though?

She remembered telling him so the night he'd led her to salvation. She also remembered his speaking words that had moved her, touched her heart. Words that again made her wonder if she hadn't misjudged him from the start.

Speaking of God, Clay had said, "You can know him the

way I do, without any doubt. You can see him with the eyes of faith, feel him with the touch of trust, hear him with the ears of hope, and know his voice through reading the Bible."

Could the sincerity she'd heard in his voice then have been real? If so, could a man who knew God that well possibly be a thief?

She took a step toward Clay.

Could a man who held a woman as tenderly as he had held her, one who led her to Christ, who gave her a Bible, who kissed her as Clay had kissed her, do it all for the sake of a scam?

Another step.

And Buford. Would a scheming conniver intent on a swindle take the time to befriend a dog? Dogs were supposed to read people well. Would a dog fall for a sham?

She stepped closer a third time.

He moved forward, his gaze on her.

Her heart skipped a beat. What would happen next? *Lord!* she cried in her heart. *Should I go to him? Or should I just go?*

An earsplitting *whaah-aah, whaah-aah, whaah-aah* blared close, ripping the air.

A police siren! What now?

Maggie turned and saw the patrol car careen around the corner. It roared up to her and screeched to a halt. The howling stopped. Wiggon leaped out. In a more decorous manner, Miss Louella exited from the passenger side.

"Maggie!" her erstwhile schoolmate Wiggon cried. "I'm so glad we found you."

Dear God, what now?

"Yes, Maggie, dear. It's a blessin'. No need for you to worry unnecessarily."

"What . . . ?"

"What's the matter?" Clay asked as Maggie's voice gave out. He came to stand at her side, his expression concerned.

"Nothin'!" Miss Louella exclaimed. "And isn't that splen-did?"

Maggie shot a questioning look at Clay, only to meet the matching one he sent her way.

"Look, Miss Louella," Wiggon said, blushing to the roots of his white blonde buzz cut, "I think I'd better do the explainin' here. It's my job, you know."

"Why, yes, dear. Of course it is. And you do it so well. Doesn't he, Maggie?"

Maggie nodded, her heart pounding, her wrists tingling from the memory of those too-large handcuffs falling off.

"It's like this," Wiggon said. "You know you were booked on conspiracy to embezzle an' criminal vandalism, right?"

She glared. "I could hardly forget, Wiggon."

His cheeks blazed. "It seems," he hurried to say, "Miss Louella an' Mrs. Desmond were out for their mornin' aerobic, an' they both saw you go home at five o'clock."

Maggie shot a glance at her elderly friend, who nodded, beaming. She turned back to the cop. "And . . . ?"

Doffing his regulation hat, Wiggon wiped his damp fore-head. "An' Lucius Noddley swears he seen you go into your buildin' from his post at the guardhouse an' not come out until *after* the fire engine's siren started up."

The implications of Wiggon's words sank in. "If that's the case . . ."

"Yep!" Relief fueled Wiggon's exclamation. "You're pretty much off the hook. Ain't no reason to doubt all three witnesses, so we're droppin' the charges. Only . . . don't be leavin' town anytime soon."

When she frowned, he added, "Just in case we need you to testify against whoever did it, that is."

"You know I know perfectly well what you mean, Cecil Wiggon. I wasn't born yesterday. You sure as anything are no balm in Gilead, so don't try to sell me this new bill of goods.

You want me in town just in case Miss Louella, Mrs. Desmond, *and* Lucius are somehow all wrong."

Wiggon blushed again but didn't argue.

Miss Louella cleared her throat. "Ah . . . Wiggon? I *know* Magnolia didn't do it."

Three pairs of eyes shot queries her way. Miss Louella blanched, took a step backward, then blushed. "I just *know* . . ."

Maggie humphed. "I'll wait, only don't let the grass grow under those longboats of yours before getting down to brass tacks and seeing eye to eye with me. I didn't do it, and you know it."

Wiggon raised his hands in surrender. "Fine, Maggie, I'll head back to the PD." He rounded the car and slipped behind the wheel. "Just quit messin' with stuff you can't handle, willya?"

Maggie sniffed loud enough for everyone to hear, but her heart had begun to sing loud enough to drown out Wiggon's verbal slap. *Thank you, Lord.*

"Cecil, dear," Miss Louella called as Wiggon turned on the ignition, "don't go forgettin' me, now. I need a ride home."

"C'mon, then, ma'am. I'm due back to the station pronto."

As the two harbingers of good tidings pulled away, this time minus siren, the moment grew awkward between Maggie and Clay. She wanted to ask him if he'd really meant everything he'd told her that other, wonderful night. She also wanted to yell, "I told you so!" at the top of her lungs.

Stealing a glance at him, Maggie found him frowning. "What are you thinking?"

Distaste curled his lips. "What about Hal?"

"What do you mean, what about Hal?"

"Are the police going to let you go even with all the connections to him? Let him go, period?"

"What connections? The guy turned in a bid; I turned him

down. He followed up with interest in the future Ashworth Historical Foundation and then came once to my office to discuss supporting our efforts on behalf of the Confederacy. That's it."

At Clay's skeptical look, Maggie held her ground. "What do you want the police to do? Charge me with vaporizing so I can walk through walls? All those folks saw me go home. I didn't do a thing. Maybe Mr. Hinkley's the one. The police still have him, I think."

Clay crossed his arms. "Your innocence remains to be seen. Even your sisters have their doubts about you. It looks to me as if you've been in Hinkley's pocket all along. I doubt you'll find life on the ugly side of prison bars to your ladylike, Southern-belle tastes."

Maggie's heart dropped. Clay was right. Charges against her had been dropped because she'd been alibied, but she hadn't been cleared.

Then again . . . "What about you? You have the key now."

His jaw tensed. "I'd be stupid to do anything but fix the house."

She tipped up her nose. "Just as I'd have been dumber'n a fence post to trash anything while I had the key. Besides, you can't believe a word my sisters say about me. They don't know me. They don't even think I can think."

They stared at each other, recognizing they'd reached another impasse.

To her surprise, Clay's expression softened. "You know, Maggie, I told you once before that you needed to take this trouble with your sisters to the Lord. I meant it. There's a lot of hurt, anger, and bitterness between you three."

She couldn't deny the truth. "It's always been that way, as far as I can remember."

"Looks that way." He closed his eyes.

He's praying, she thought. *Is he really—*

"A wise man recently told me," he said before she could finish her thought, "that I was in bondage to my past. At first I didn't believe him, but God showed me he was right. It seems you're in the same situation, bound by what's happened in your family for years. I think that stuff's just stuck inside you, rotten and hurtful and ruining your relationship with your sisters."

"Bondage?" Maggie asked, shocked by the hideous word, and even more by the concept.

"Yes. Tied down by the troubles of the past. As long as you're bound like that to the anger, the fear, the sadness, then you're fighting a spiritual battle. My friend reminded me of a passage that tells us we're not fighting against flesh and blood, but against the evil of the unseen world, against the powers of darkness who rule this world."

His words rang with truth, and Maggie nodded. "It does seem that the trouble between Cammie, Lark, and me is greater than we are."

Clay stepped toward her, placing his hand lightly on her arm. Again the warmth of his touch went deep, moving her. "God doesn't want you in that mess. Scripture says that before Christ came, we were slaves to the spiritual powers of this world. But God sent his Son to buy freedom for us, and because we became his children through Jesus, we're no longer slaves but God's sons and daughters."

"But how do I break away?" she asked.

Clay smiled ruefully. "That's the tough part. You start by living a life of faith, walking daily with God. You renew your mind by reading his Word. Then you're able to get a better hold on your emotions and clean up the pain of the past. Find freedom at last. Real freedom."

"Freedom . . ." she said softly. Freedom from the sadness, the loneliness, the anger, the pain, the tears, the fear. "Funny you should say that right now, right here."

"Why's that?"

For a moment, she hesitated. Again, she was about to reveal something private, something she'd never told anyone else. *Should I, Father?*

"Maggie?" Clay asked, interest in his eyes.

She swallowed hard. "Well, I've always envied the freedom of the dove in the window up there—oh, no!"

At the same time, Clay let loose a wordless bellow.

"Come on," he said, grabbing her hand and dragging her across the street. "I can't believe it. The cops posted a guard out here. How could someone have gotten in? And why did they have to take out the window? *That* window?"

Maggie, running to keep up, asked, "What . . . do you . . . mean, that . . . window?"

"It's special," he growled, his long legs eating up the steps to the porch in one leap.

Maggie scrambled up, trying to match his pace—without success. "Of course . . . it's special . . . that dove's . . . so . . . free!"

"Exactly!" Clay answered, lunging up the curved mahogany staircase. He paused and looked down at her. "It's God's Holy Spirit, rising above the sin and evil on earth. Why would someone even touch that window?"

Maggie shook her head, huffing and puffing after running up the stairs in his wake. "I . . . don't know! And . . . I like . . . your . . . interpretation. God's Spirit . . . freedom."

After studying her for a moment, Clay turned and ran up the rest of the stairs. Wondering at the meaning behind his intent gaze, Maggie quickly followed.

They hurried into the bathroom and came to a standstill, Maggie slamming into Clay's back. "Sorry!" she said, then stared at the hole in the wall.

"Just look at that!" Clay yelled.

"I'm looking. I see it."

"No. Not the hole. Look at the floor."

He stepped aside, and Maggie saw what he meant. Below the circular gap in the wall, the stained-glass panel lay on the often-refinished floor of the bathroom. The curved bits of frame that had held it in place for more than a hundred years surrounded it neatly. The dove hadn't been broken, just grounded. It needed help to soar again, just as Maggie needed help to get beyond her pain.

The plaster on the wall, however, told another story. Chunks had been ripped out, and not just from around the dove's former spot. The baseboards had been removed, stacked inside the cast-iron tub, and the plaster behind them had been gouged out in the same way.

It didn't make sense.

The cops had kept watch.

Maggie looked up at Clay and found him studying her. "You know what this means, don't you?" she asked.

"Of course."

"We're in hot water again, even though we're both clean as hounds' teeth. If we beat around the bush instead of stirring up a hornet's nest to find us an ace in the hole and make them eat humble pie, why then, we're going to have a tough row to hoe in the prison salt mines."

He chuckled. "Good to see you haven't let all this trouble change you one bit, Maggie."

"Oh, but you're wrong," she said earnestly. "I have changed. I've been born again in Christ. And with him, I'll get through this. I'm not alone anymore."

A strange expression crossed his face. Then he said, "You never were alone, even though you thought so. I've never been against you. It was hard to do what I believed I had to do. Can you forgive me? For pressing charges against you?"

Maggie's jaw dropped. She shut her mouth and said honestly, "That's asking a lot."

Clay's chin jabbed out again. "No more than you're going to ask of me. Or what God asks of all of us."

Maggie ran her gaze over his face, his hair, his sturdy build, then back to his honest golden brown eyes. Could she forgive him?

"I'm going to have to pray about it," she finally said.

"I'll do the same. *After* we report this latest mess."

In agreement, they closed up the house and headed back toward town. As they approached City Hall, which housed the tiny, three-man Bellamy PD, Clay paused. "You know, Maggie, the first step to freedom is forgiveness. For those who've wronged us and for ourselves, too. Watching you, seeing the pain and fear you feel, I've recognized my own. I need to clean house again, go back eight years and once and for all forgive those who did me wrong. That's where I have to start. You have to examine your heart and find forgiveness, too."

"I said I'd try." The intense light in his eyes unnerved her. "And I'll pray about it. But I can't give you more than that right now."

He didn't answer right away. He studied her face, making her uncomfortable. Then he said, "It's not for me I ask," he said. "It's for you and your sisters. To break those chains that bind you to the past, you're going to have to forgive them."

His words hit Maggie harder than the sound of the closing cell door had.

TWENTY

"IF YOU FORGIVE THOSE WHO SIN AGAINST YOU, YOUR heavenly Father will forgive you. But if you refuse to forgive others, your Father will not forgive your sins."

Maggie read the words from the book of Matthew aloud for the ninth time. After she and Clay had reported the latest episode of vandalism and been subjected to another grueling interrogation, he'd encouraged her to look up the verse.

She did and had been shocked by Scripture's bluntness. God expected from her what he extended to his children—to her. If she understood what she'd read, she had to forgive in order to receive forgiveness.

Could she forgive Clay?

She honestly didn't know. He'd pressed charges against her even though she'd declared her innocence over and over again.

Had circumstantial evidence made it that difficult for him to believe her? Even after they'd spent time together, after she'd opened up to him? Had he been misled by a . . . what had he called it? A counterfeit?

On the other hand, she'd pressed charges against him, too.

He'd insisted from the start he had none but the best inten-
tions toward Maggie, Miss Louella, and the mansion. But the
evidence against him had been compelling; he'd *looked* guilty.

So had she, and she'd been innocent.

Had Clay been innocent too, despite the evidence against
him?

Yes, it now looked as though he had. And yet, she'd turned
against him, despite her growing feelings for him.

She'd obviously hurt him. Maggie now understood Clay's
coldness the night before the fire. He'd believed she'd been
plotting against him with Hal Hinkley—a man Clay insisted
wanted nothing more than to put him out of business from
sheer jealousy and greed.

Her behavior around Clay had been questionable, even
uncharacteristic. Why, she'd acted like a bold . . . Northerner.
Was Yankeeness contagious?

If her actions had pushed Clay away, had his tenderness
been real? Had it spoken of growing feelings for her?

Mutual claims of criminal intent lay between them. Until
they cleaned the slate, the love she once thought was growing
between them would go nowhere.

So could she forgive him?

"Lord?"

*If you forgive those who sin against you, I will forgive you. But
if you refuse to forgive others, I will not forgive your sins.*

Something inside her stood and yelled silently, *But I don't
feel like forgiving him. He hurt me!*

If you forgive those who sin against you, I will forgive you.

There was no question. God spoke clearly. She had to
forgive Clay, no matter what she felt. "Okay, Father, I don't
know how I'm going to do it, but you've told me to forgive
him, so I . . ."

Reluctance rose again, but she stated, "I need your forgiveness for all my sins, Lord, so I *will* forgive Clay. But you're

going to have to help me. Maybe with some of that renewing of the mind and controlling of emotions Clay spoke of. I can't do it on my own, but you're so powerful, so mighty and strong, I'm sure you can change even my feelings and thoughts. . . . So here goes. I . . . forgive . . . Clay."

As soon as she spoke the words, she remembered Clay's saying she had to ask forgiveness for something else, too. *"It's not for me I ask,"* he'd said. *"It's for you and your sisters. To break those chains that bind you to the past, you're going to have to forgive them."*

Everything in Maggie recoiled. "Lord, you don't really mean that, do you?"

If you forgive those who sin against you, your heavenly Father will forgive you. But if you refuse to forgive others, your Father will not forgive your sins.

As of its own will, her gaze turned to the Bible on her lap. The verse in Matthew leapt out at her, no less glaring than if it had been written in neon pink.

Lark and Cammie had hurt her since as far back as she could remember. Even though Cammie was two years younger, she'd always joined Lark in designating Maggie as the princess in the tower who couldn't rescue herself, the dumb cluck who didn't have the sense to do the right thing. Maggie'd been on the receiving end of their blonde jokes more often than she cared to count. They'd even defied Granny Iris's warnings to not pick on Maggie; as a result, they'd racked up regular doses of her discipline.

As the three women had grown up, Maggie's sisters had assured her she wasn't college material. But not for the same reason as Cammie, who'd simply wanted a husband, a home, and kids. The younger and older Bellamy Blossoms had insisted Maggie would do better in Bellamy, where everyone accepted her ineptitude. Everyone knew pretty, delicate, useless Magnolia, lovely to look at, but if touched, likely to wilt and crumble. Well, when life touched, it battered, and Maggie had crumbled—just as her sisters had expected. And they'd informed her—and the whole town—of that fact in jail.

Their lack of respect for Maggie had always made her doubt herself, which in turn had made her fight all the harder to prove herself worthy . . . of their love.

How could she forgive them?

They'd made her life a vast expanse of loneliness. They'd stuck her on a pedestal for ornaments too fragile for use and made sure she stayed there. So she'd fought by toughening herself far beyond what had felt natural, and she'd set out to prove herself.

She'd always wished she could reach her goals without having to demonstrate again and again she wasn't the delicate magnolia blossom for which she'd been named. Maggie had believed she had more—steel, Clay had called it—in her spine.

Now she could admit it—she'd been jealous of her sisters. Lark's career success and Cammie's contentment had sharpened Maggie's sense of inadequacy. And, even though she'd tried, she'd failed to hold on to her simple job at the bank.

She'd based her efforts on what she carried in her, the legacy of heroic Southern ancestors. Like them, she fought to the finish, stood strong—even when she'd feared she'd end up like the Confederacy, beaten by a more powerful foe.

How could she forgive her sisters?

If you refuse to forgive others, your Father will not forgive your sins.

How could she not?

She would.

Her stomach churned. "But I can't!" she cried.

The doorbell rang. Maggie *harrumphed* when Buford charged forward with an enthusiastic *"AWWWROOOOOF."* She couldn't just pretend she wasn't home. It was nearly midnight, and the pup's howling couldn't be missed. She couldn't say she'd been out walking the dog.

If she didn't open the door, whoever stood there might decide she was at the mansion tearing up something new. Old. Whatever.

Setting her Bible aside, Maggie stood. She'd get through this. She was no longer alone; God was with her.

The sight that greeted her on the other side of the door resembled nothing she'd ever seen before. Or imagined.

"Maggie, dear!" a blackfaced, leotard-and-tights-clad female exclaimed in Miss Louella's voice. "You won't believe what's happened."

Without warning, the lady charged into Maggie's living room. Although the voice sounded like Louella Ashworth's, the specter before Maggie looked nothing like the heiress she knew and loved. "Miss Louella?"

"Yes, dear?"

"Why are you dressed like—" Maggie waved, unable to find an apt description for what she saw—"that?"

"Oh, honey-girl." Miss Louella threw herself onto Maggie's couch as she chattered on. "I've just had myself the most thrillin' night of my life. I found the treasure."

Had the woman lost her normally sharp mind? "Treasure? What treasure?"

"Don't you remember givin' me my great-grandaddy Asa's journal?" Miss Louella queried. "Well, inside those pages he talked about a Confederate treasure!"

"Well, what is it?" Maggie asked.

"I don't know yet," Miss Louella answered with more verve than Maggie thought a woman her age could muster. "But that's why I'm here. The Garden Club decided that seein' as you worked so hard to restore the mansion and you've suffered so much from those false accusations, we owe you the honor of retrievin' the treasure from its hidin' place. Come along, now. The girls are all waitin' on you."

"Girls?"

"Yes! The members of Bellamy's Garden Club—save Myrna Stafford, of course. She's home sulkin' since no one took kindly to her pooh-poohin' our efforts."

"You're sure there's a treasure?" Maggie asked, skeptical.

Miss Louella's face wore an obstinate cast as she went to the door. "Of course, Magnolia. Great-Granddaddy Asa wrote it in his journal, and my very own eyes read it. We just had us a time figurin' out the clues, is all."

"What clues?"

"Why, he had everythin' mapped out in that black book of his. We couldn't figure it out for the longest time. He states clear as day that he hid a treasure of our beloved Confederacy in the mansion."

This Maggie had to see to believe. "Well," she said, "since I am a loyal member of the Daughters of the Confederacy, I'm always happy to learn of another piece of our past comin' to light."

Miss Louella stopped just shy of turning the knob. "Ah . . . Maggie, dear. You have a teensy-tiny problem."

Uh-oh. "You want me to wear leotards and goop for this?" she asked, feeling not quite that patriotic.

"It's about your membership in the Daughters of the Confederacy," Miss Louella said, head down.

"What about it? I always keep it current," Maggie said, stumped.

"Yes . . ." Miss Louella responded reluctantly. "That's the problem. You see . . . you don't qualify."

"What do you mean, I don't qualify? I turned in my geneal-ogy years ago. Everything was approved."

"I know, dear." The older woman wrapped an arm around Maggie's shoulders. "But new information has turned up."

"What new information? And where?"

"In Great-Granddaddy Asa's journal is where. He wrote of his sadness upon learnin' from none other than Stonewall Jackson of Rupert Bellamy's defection to the North."

"Impossible!"

"I don't reckon so, dear. Rupert, as you know, was with Stonewall up until Chancellorsville. But accordin' to the journal, he'd been troubled by the divided nation and worried about emancipation. He had himself a long talk with Stonewall, and the general tried his best to talk sense into Rupert. Old Jack thought he'd made progress, but the next day, your great-great-great-granddaddy was gone."

Maggie sighed with relief. "Well, of course he was. Everyone knows that's when he died."

"No, dear. That's what the general let on, on account of his friendship with Rupert. What really happened is that Rupert defected. And Old Jack told Asa, who didn't believe a word of it. Until he met up with Rupert after the war. Learned his tale then."

Maggie felt the world shift beneath her feet. Rupert Bellamy . . . a defector? Then that meant she didn't share in the legacy of the Confederacy. She didn't descend from that proud line of people who'd fought for their right to govern their state as they saw fit. She wasn't who she'd always thought she was.

Everything she'd believed was a . . . lie. A counterfeit.

So who was she, if not a Confederate?

What did she have to stand on, since her personal worth had never been much?

As she struggled to make sense of what Miss Louella had just told her, Clay's voice rang in the back of her mind. The day after she'd met Jesus he'd said, *"Oh, you're a Southern belle with a delicate beauty, all right. But you're also a child of the King, precious in his sight."*

So she wasn't a Daughter of the Confederacy. But Clay had called her a child of the King.

Up until now, she'd been able to verify everything Clay said in God's Word.

You're a child of the King.

Her eyes opened wide. *Ooo-eee!* Maybe being a princess wasn't half bad; if what Clay had said was true, she was a child of the Almighty.

Clay had also said something else. He'd told her that God so loved the world—and that she was part of that world—that he gave his only Son—Jesus, who'd come to life as a man to die at Calvary—so that everyone who believed in him would not perish but have eternal life.

That was a pretty solid statement. Something true, firm. Something she could stand on. Something no fickle ancestral loyalties could ever change.

God loved her, and she didn't have to prove herself to him.

Maggie's heart began to beat faster. For so long she'd wanted proof of God's existence. She'd needed to see him, touch him, hear him. Now she had.

She'd met the Lord—just as Clay had said he had years before. When she'd been brought low and locked up in jail, she'd felt God comfort her with the touch of trust. On the sidewalk across the mansion, she'd heard him with the ears of hope, and she'd recognized his voice through his words. Now she was seeing him with the eyes of faith, standing on his promises, on which she would build the rest of her life.

Jesus was the one who would hold her through the lonesome nights, bind her wounds, cheer her successes, dry her tears. He was the More she'd hungered for. And he'd given it to her at great cost to himself.

"Miss Louella," she said softly, "it's all right. I don't mind not being a Daughter of the Confederacy after all."

"You don't?" Miss Louella said, taken aback.

Maggie shook her head. "I belong to a better group—a family that matters more than a historical blip. I'm a daughter of the King, a child of God. No genealogy can ever take that away from me."

"Oh, child . . ."

Maggie smiled, her joy lighting up her heart, sending her spirit soaring, flying high . . . like the dove in the stained-glass window. "Don't you be crying, now. It's wonderful news. I'm a princess in God's kingdom, and so are you. We're sisters in Christ, and we've a treasure to find. Let's not keep the others waiting any longer. They'll be more worked up than a bevy of beavers, fit to be tied, and coming at us like gangbusters."

Miss Louella hiccuped a chuckle. "Maggie, honey, we have to do somethin' about the way you butcher the king's English."

"I beg your pardon!" Maggie objected, drawing herself up to her full height—but coming up short next to Miss Louella's five-foot-nine frame. "I do no such thing. I just have a way with words."

The chuckle turned to laughter. "One no one else can follow. But you're right. Let's get back to the mansion."

"And the treasure."

The two women hurried to Maggie's Miata, tucked themselves into the small import, and roared down deserted streets. Although she stopped for every stop sign and resisted the urge to run red lights, Maggie proceeded at her usual speed. She hoped Wiggon was home in bed and not prowling around, ticket pad in hand.

Arriving at the mansion in record time without incurring another fine, Maggie pulled up to the curb. Both women jumped out and flew up the porch steps, Miss Louella leading the way. She flung open the massive teak doors and called out, "She's here!"

To Maggie's amazement, a gaggle of gardeners met her, all

garbed in funereal exercise clothes—some looking better than others—their faces uniformly smeared black.

"What took you so long?" Mariah Desmond asked.

"Gabbin', honey," Sophie Hardesty answered. "Louella and Magnolia are great friends, and both can talk the feathers off a chicken."

"And here we've all just been coolin' our heels, fixin' to sneak a peek at that treasure," scolded Florinda. Then excitement sparkled in her gaze. "But seein' as I'm taller than her, I'll be able to look over Maggie's shoulder. I'll be the first to see!"

"Louella, I should get a front spot," argued Sarah Langhorn. "I'm a bookseller, and the treasure's likely to be another journal. Maybe even . . . Stonewall's own."

A sigh sibilated through the room. Then someone said, "But I want to see, too!"

Another piped in, "I've worked my nails plumb to ruin lookin' for that treasure. I've earned a front-row seat."

"Me too!"

"And me!"

As Maggie watched in dismay, shoulders nudged necks, elbows jabbed bellies, and hips bopped thighs. Each member of the Bellamy Garden Club challenged another for prime viewing space. A couple of *ouches* and *ows* rang out.

Miss Louella rolled her eyes. "They're hopeless," she said to Maggie. Turning to her friends, she called, "Ladies, ladies! Let's have some order, shall we? We're all civilized here, and we must show Southern breedin' and propriety."

Maggie nearly roared with laughter. A flock of elderly flower growers, wearing leotards and theater greasepaint, gathered in a century-old wreck of a house and squabbling for position didn't exactly conjure up visions of ladylike teas and cotillions.

Although the noise abated somewhat at their leader's

262

behest, some of the ladies still strove to gain advantage over others. So the mansion's heiress had to push her way to the front of the group clustered at the door to the pantry. "Poor Magnolia can't even get in here," she said, "much less bring the Ashworth Treasure out of its hidin' spot."

Dozens of elderly eyes turned to Maggie.

Forcing a serious expression onto her face, Maggie stepped forward. As she joined Miss Louella, a respectful hush descended on Ashworth Mansion. Maggie turned to the club president. "Miss Louella, if you'll show me where the treasure is, I'll satisfy everyone's curiosity."

Stepping aside, Miss Louella pointed to the charred remains of a pantry cupboard. "It had a false back. And here we'd been concentratin' our efforts on the bathroom!"

Comprehension finally dawned on Maggie. "The bathroom . . ." she echoed weakly. "You mean—"

"You were the ones who tore up the bathroom?" Clay demanded, his footsteps heavy in the quiet house. "Three times, no less?"

Maggie spun toward the front door in time to see Hobey, the mason, join Clay. Both men wore outrage on their tired faces.

"My chimney!" hollered Hobey. "You crazy women ruined a whole week's work. An' you're after sayin' you were lookin' for a false back? Clear as mud, Louella Ashworth."

Maggie faced her elderly friend again, who now looked ashamed. If Miss Louella's cheeks hadn't been smeared with black, she'd have sported red circles.

"We didn't really ruin anythin'," the misguided treasure hunter said, but her voice lacked its usual starch. "We made sure what we did was fixable." At the darkening male scowls, she hurried on. "And you did a splendid job fixin' everythin', gentlemen. I'm right pleased with the work you've done on my house."

Clay stepped forward, not mollified. "Are you 'right pleased' that you sent Maggie and me to jail?"

Sincere distress made the paint on Miss Louella's face ludicrous. "Oh, dear me, no, Clayton. I wouldn't ever do anythin' to harm anyone or the mansion either. That's why I was so troubled after the fire. I couldn't sleep. I wasn't rightly sure what to do next. Dear Mariah went for a walk with me, and we tried to figure some way out of the mess we'd made. Although we didn't realize it at the time, God made sure we saw Maggie and Buford return home, so we were able to testify truthfully on her behalf. We're so thankful Camellia vouched for you, because we'd never have kept our efforts a secret at your expense. And when I found out you'd both been arrested—I felt terrible. I'm so very sorry we put you through that. You simply *must* believe me."

Clay shook his head in helpless disbelief. Maggie watched to see how he would respond to the totally sincere—if misguided—elderly woman. "All that work . . . those holes in the mahogany walls . . . the parquet . . . the delft tiles. That poor bathroom!" he moaned.

Mariah Desmond separated herself from the group of chastened women. "We're mighty sorry, Mr. Marlowe, we truly are. We felt we needed to find the treasure, so we'd hurry over and do our lookin' after you left in the mornin'."

Maggie laughed. She had to. Otherwise she would have cried. To think they'd suffered so much for so little. "Why didn't you just tell us you were looking for something?" she asked. "It's your home, Miss Louella. Why did you feel you had to skulk around and hide your identity?"

"I'll tell you why!" exclaimed a newcomer.

Maggie turned and beheld yet another astounding sight. Purple hair rolls anchored by a hairnet, Myrna Stafford stomped into the already crowded pantry. Thick white cream glistened on her face and frilly pink lace peeked over the tightly crossed lapels of her orange bathrobe. Tall rabbit ears waggled on plush-furred slippers as she approached.

"Louella's fixated on that Marvin Pinknut fool," she said, her voice acid enough to cut through paint. "She's so fuzzy-headed she's convinced he's real, so she figured she was up to matchin' his antics. Woman can't tell the difference between fiction—bad fiction—and real life."

"That's not so, Myrna," argued the maligned lady. "Only fuzz that's here is that stuff on your feet. I can too tell the difference. You're just full of sour grapes because no one wanted to do as you said and give up our patriotic search."

"Just remember," Myrna continued, looking, if possible, even more absurd in her getup than the treasure hunters, "there's no worse fool than an old fool. I'm here fixin' to tell you, you've made a fool of yourself this time."

Miss Louella paused, then said, "Myrna, I've apologized. And I do ask Maggie's and Clay's forgiveness. I caused them more trouble than I ever dreamed I would."

"So where is this treasure?" Myrna asked, sniffing.

Miss Louella pointed to the rear of the charred cupboard. "There, and we want Maggie to bring it out."

"May we stay and watch?" Clay asked.

Louella smiled again, looking almost like herself—save for the black gunk on her face. "Of course, Clayton, dear. You and Hobey are always welcome in my home. Any time at all. You too, Myrna. Join us for this glorious moment in the history of the Confederacy."

As Maggie stepped to Miss Louella's side, the room hushed. In spite of the revelations about who had been behind the damage at the mansion spinning in her head, Maggie felt a spurt of excitement. What had Miss Louella's ancestor hidden in the wall of his home?

She slipped her hands into the large gap in the ruined

plaster and wood—obviously pried apart with the crowbar on the floor.

"To your right, Maggie, dear," urged Miss Louella.

Maggie moved, and her hands met something solid: a shelf, and on the shelf, a stiff bundle. She bit her bottom lip, concentrating on withdrawing the parcel from the niche without knocking more plaster from the wall. A moment later, she brought it out.

In the light she saw a rectangle wrapped in age-damaged, dried-out leather, the corners cracked and peeling. The package measured about twenty-four inches by eighteen inches by three inches. Years must have passed since it had last seen the light of day. As always, Maggie couldn't suppress the thrill of touching something that had endured so long. She ran a respectful hand over the brittle hide, then gently blew the dust away.

"Well," Myrna said impatiently, "aren't you goin' to open it?"

"Of course," Maggie said. "Miss Louella, would you do the honors?"

"The honors belong to you, dear. Remember, it's our way of apologizin' for the hurt we caused you."

"There's no need for more apologies. I do forgive you—all of you." She glanced at the man standing not ten feet away and saw the spark her words brought to his eyes. She smiled and caught her breath when he smiled back. A ripple of anticipation ran through her.

"Go ahead, Maggie," he said, his voice deep and rich. "Show us the treasure you found."

TWENTY-ONE

MAGGIE TURNED THE ASHWORTH TREASURE OVER IN HER hands and began prying apart the stiff ends of the leather covering. As the hide cracked more, chunks fell off in her fingers.

Dismayed, she looked at Miss Louella, the rightful owner of the bundle, who nodded in encouragement. Maggie hated harming any of the ruined wrapper.

Finally she lifted the leather and revealed a yellowed piece of paper covered in spidery writing. The page lay on top of what appeared to be a gray garment of some sort.

"Miss Louella," she said, "I think you should take this from here."

"If you insist," agreed her friend, unable to mask her excitement.

Maggie handed over the treasure, then stepped aside, affording Miss Louella the greatest amount of light. With shaking hands, the older woman took the parcel in her left hand and picked up the aged sheet with her right.

"It's a letter!" she exclaimed. "Shall I read it?"

For once all the members of the Garden Club agreed. Maggie stepped further aside, letting the women come close to Miss Louella. Not watching where she was going, she bumped into a solid wall of warm human bulk. "Oops—sorry."

"I'm not," Clay whispered in her ear, clasping her shoulders.

Maggie turned her head, a shiver running straight from where he held her to her middle. Blue eyes met brown, and something private and tender was exchanged. Both smiled.

"Later."

"Later."

"Here goes," said Miss Louella, her voice quivering with emotion. "'Dearest Hiram and Heloise'—those were dear Asa's children, you know. Hiram's my granddaddy.

"'As your mother has pestered me to do for years, I am improvin' her pantry. At the same time, I take the opportunity to preserve somethin' I have long treasured. The Great War of Northern Aggression has been over for almost ten years, but the principles for which I fought friends and foes still burn in my heart.

"'You have heard me speak of my commandin' officer. Your grandfather's esteemed friend, General Jackson, became my hero and leader when I joined his troops after his visit on my sixteenth birthday.

"'From that day thirteen years ago, I modeled my actions after those of that courageous man. While he often spoke of his desire to see the Republic preserved, Stonewall was a Virginian and believed the South had a just cause. He fought brilliantly, and we soldiers gave our all for our much-loved Old Jack.

"'One of the darkest moments of my life came the second of May of '63, when I witnessed one of our sentries mistake

Jackson and his escort for Union cavalry. He fired on the general, wounding him. He died of pneumonia soon after.

"'I'll never forget Old Jack's silent prayers while in the thick of battle, and I remember well the battered Bible he carried. Stonewall fought for what he believed and died servin' his God and his country. A man can wish no more.

"'It was with great joy that I found the garment here enclosed when I returned home from the war. It brought to mind the man whose courage, skill, and faith I'd admired.

"'In the years since, Yankee carpetbaggers have brought many changes to our beloved South, and I fear for my memento, so I'll hide it behind the pantry wall and leave you word of its whereabouts elsewhere. Treasure it and what it represents, as I have.

"'Your loving papa, Asa Ashworth.'"

The silence in the room was palpable. Not a dry eye remained. With shaking hands, Miss Louella passed the letter to Mariah Desmond, then turned her attention to the fabric long hidden in the wall. Carefully she grasped it, crying out when the cloth crumbled at her touch. "Oh, no! It's ruined. It didn't last."

Gasps of dismay rasped throughout the room. Then Sophie Hardesty cleared her throat. "What is it, Louella?"

"I believe it's . . . General Jackson's uniform coat. But I daren't look at it any closer, since what I touched fell to bits."

"Hmmmph!" snorted Myrna. "So you went to all that trouble for shreds of a rotted old coat. Figures you'd wind up with nothin'."

"No, Myrna," said Maggie, catching everyone's attention. "It wasn't for nothing. The letter's the true treasure Asa left behind. There are truths worth fighting for, those General Jackson took with him into battle. That Bible he carried was his comfort, his strength, and helped him stand for what he believed. As Asa Ashworth said, a man—or a woman—can wish for no more than to serve God."

As the hands on her shoulders squeezed in gentle support, Maggie pressed her fingers into Clay's. "I for one," she added, "will serve God."

At that, the gathering turned into a discussion that evolved into a celebration. Garden Club members gathered around Miss Louella, all wanting a glimpse of Stonewall Jackson's decayed coat.

Even Myrna pushed her way to the front, sniffing. As she shoved Philadelphia Philpott out of her way, Philadelphia stumbled on the long black cape wrapped around her frail frame, causing Myrna to trip over one of her rabbit ears and fall headlong into the precious parcel in Miss Louella's hands.

"Oh, no!" Mariah cried as the coat fell to the ground.

Miss Louella dropped to her knees. "Move back so I can see what I'm doin'."

Tears rolling down her black-mottled cheeks, Asa's great-granddaughter eased her hands beneath the cloth. As she tried to lift it, pieces fell, the fabric having turned into the dust of time. A tarnished brass button rolled off the decrepit coat and onto the kitchen floor.

Philadelphia scurried to pick it up, her cape billowing as she knelt. "Don't cry, Lou," she said in her papery voice. "You still have the buttons, and they won't rot."

"Neither will Asa's words," added Clay, turning Maggie toward him.

A ripple of agreement rustled among the ladies at her back. As Maggie stared up into Clay's strong face, her doubts fell away.

"Forgive me for hurting you," she whispered. "I should have known you were speaking the truth. For so long I'd been told I had no sense, that I just couldn't trust my judgment.

Fear for my job, of making a fool of myself over you, stole what sense I *do* have. I was wrong to accuse you."

He smiled crookedly. "You beat me to the punch. I'd planned to meet you first thing in the morning to ask *your* forgiveness. Then Hobey called me, saying he'd noticed activity at the mansion, so we came over together. I knew how much the mansion meant to you, and still I let my fear of going back to jail blind me to what sat right before my eyes. I'm sorry I pressed charges against you."

"I do forgive you."

"I forgive you, too."

All the while they'd spoken, Clay's arms had slipped around Maggie, his hands rubbing her back as she'd once wished they would. His touch was sure, gentle, soothing, yet exciting. She placed her hands on his chest, feeling the steady beat of his heart beneath her right palm.

He smiled.

She smiled.

He brought his mouth to hers and kissed her, his lips speaking more clearly than his words had. Maggie's heart soared, her joy multiplying with his caress.

She loved him, and she knew he couldn't kiss her like this without deep feelings on his part. Happy tears sprang to her eyes.

"Aha!" cried Wiggon, startling Maggie and Clay apart. "You're all under arrest. I caught you red-handed this time."

"What . . . ?" Maggie asked, stunned to see her friend in the hallway, gun drawn, aimed, and ready to shoot.

The members of the Garden Club sprang into action, seeming to bounce off each other and the walls like chattering gnomes, with their squeals and shrieks rising in pitch until the noise threatened to shatter eardrums.

In obvious self-defense, Wiggon pulled out his whistle and shrilled it. The women stopped, then turned on Wiggon, surrounding him in a dark cloud. The expressions on their painted faces matched the hue of the paint.

Wiggon backed up a step.

Clay chuckled, and in the momentary silence, said, "I'm not sure about that red-handed business. It looks like you're dealing with blackfaced bandits instead. They can explain everything. As for Maggie and me, we're off to find some peace and quiet. We have a lot of talking to do."

"Praise God!" cried Miss Louella.

"It's about time," cheered Sophie Hardesty, beaming beatifically.

"Just make sure you invite me to the weddin'!" said Florinda, winking.

Philadelphia laid a soft hand on Maggie's arm. "I'll be prayin' for God's blessin' on your union."

Mischief dancing in his eyes, Clay covered her wrinkled hand with his own. "Be careful when you use that word, ma'am. Magnolia Blossom's very sensitive about the Union and the Confederacy."

The smile died on Miss Louella's lips. "Uh-oh."

Maggie shook her head. The joy the women had expressed at the obvious reconciliation between her and Clay warmed her heart. Maybe she hadn't been as alone as she'd always felt. Maybe she'd been blinded by the turmoil of the past, in bondage to the pain, as Clay had said.

"It's all right," she said. "I want everyone to know. I'm done with secrets and hidden troubles." She turned to Clay. "Turns out, Yankee, I've no hereditary claim to the Confederacy."

Gasps of shock exploded among the gathered gardeners, most of whom were also members of the local chapter of the Daughters of the Confederacy.

"What do you mean?" Clay asked.

"I've a black sheep up my family tree. My great-great-great-grandfather, Rupert Bellamy, didn't die at Stonewall Jackson's side at Chancellorsville as we'd always thought. Asa Ashworth's diary revealed that just before the general led that rout of the Union, Rupert defected to the North."

The spark of scandal caught among the women. Whispers flew. Stares darted to and from Maggie.

"Why, I never . . ."

"That takes the cake . . ."

"With the town named after that Rupert . . ."

"And them Bellamys pillars of the community, and all . . ."

"Shame . . ."

"Iris Bellamy must be spinnin' in her grave. . . ."

At the resumption of the hubbub, Wiggon blew his whistle again. This time he only succeeded in lowering the volume. "Would somebody please tell *the law* what in tarnation is goin' on here?"

"Why, Cecil Wiggon," said Miss Louella, taking his arm and leading him to the pile of gray threads on the pantry floor. "Can't you see? We're after celebratin' the discovery of another treasure of our honored Confederacy."

Wiggon doffed his hat and scratched his head. "What is it?"

"Stonewall Jackson's uniform coat."

"Looks like a mess to me," Wiggon answered, demonstrating remarkable powers of observation.

"Don't worry," said Miss Louella, "there's more. And it gets better. Dear Great-Granddaddy Asa left the most marvelous letter." Miss Louella nodded toward Maggie and Clay. "But the treasure's not as wonderful as Magnolia's and Clayton's arrival at reason. Seems they've finally seen that God made them one for the other, if those arms wrapped around each other mean anythin' at all."

Wiggon glanced toward them. "Oh, yeah, Marlowe," he said. "Your lawyer called. He ain't comin' on account of his car got hit by a semi on his way south. He got burned and is recovering. You might could check with Percy Baker on Main Street if you're needin' legal help."

Dismay darkened Clay's expression. "So that's where he's been. I wondered." He winced. "And it happened on his way to help me."

"Well, wonder no more," said Wiggon. "And Maggie? That Hal fellow? Well, he's bad news. There's a fistful of warrants out for him in Pennsylvania. They take precedence over ours on account of him bein' a resident and them bein' older. So we're havin' to ship him north. Let them take first crack at him. Gives you time to prepare a good defense on this here swindle and vandalism case."

"Ah, Wiggon?" Miss Louella said.

"Yes, ma'am?"

"There's somethin' you should know."

"Like what?" Only then did he seem to notice the odd appearance of the crowd. "Hey! Who all's this, wearin' them weird things? And what all's that stuff on your face? their faces? And what are Maggie and Clay doin' here, in the middle of the night, wrapped like vines around each other, when both know they could land back in jail just like *that!*"

He snapped his fingers as Miss Louella dragged him outside. As they went, she said, "That's what I'm fixin' to tell you."

Maggie glanced at Clay, felt her cheeks warm at the revealing expression in his eyes, then hastily withdrew her hands from his chest. He grabbed her hands, placing them right back where they'd been. "Not so fast, you Southern Yankee, you. Put those arms around me and hold on tight. We have a future to plan."

"But there's so much I have to tell you yet."

"And we've years ahead of us in which to do the telling."

"Oh!"

Clay swooped down and picked her up. "Hang on!"

"I'm not letting go, Clayton Marlowe," she said, laughing, loving him. "Not when I've found the greatest treasure of all."

"And what would that be?"

"God's love and goodness. His forgiveness, his joy."

A look of mock injury spread on Clay's face as he carried her out the mansion's front door, holding her close to his heart. "What about me?"

"Oh, you're the ribbon on the birthday gift, the cherry on the sundae, the thirteenth doughnut in the baker's dozen. You're even the cat's meow!"

Clay's eyes twinkled. "You're the apple of my eye."

Maggie winked. "You're the only fish in my sea."

He nuzzled her temple. "You're all the eggs in my basket."

She rubbed her cheek against his. "You're the biggest frog in my small pond."

"Oh, Maggie . . ."

"Clay . . ."

They kissed in the moonlight, as they had once before. But this time as they caressed, their joy had a new fullness. Long, loving moments later, Clay whispered, "You're the best."

"You're my treasure."

"You're my love."

"And you're mine."

Dear Reader,

I'm so glad you decided to visit Magnolia and me in Bellamy. My time in this small, quaint Virginia town has been wonderful—filled with laughter and insights and thoroughly satisfying. I hope and pray the quirky residents, including the canine one, have stolen your heart as they have mine.

Because I'm blessed with a wonderful sister, I thought it would be fascinating to look at the relationship between sisters in a series of books. But three sisters who share a rich, loving relationship like mine and Lou's wouldn't have much to work on. So I thought of three women who don't know each other as well as they think they do. Thus, "Bellamy's Blossoms" were born.

Their troubles truly bothered me. Why do they see each other as they do? What pulls them apart, when it seems more logical for them to have grown closer after the death of their parents? Why has only one maintained a rich, loving relationship with God? And what will it take to bring them back to his loving arms . . . and to the sisterhood God meant for them all along?

I love Proverbs 17:17: "A friend is always loyal, and a brother is born to help in time of need." As an eldest sibling, and a writer, at that, I just had to discover the Blossoms' stories—to lend them a hand straightening out their problems, of course! And without making things too easy on them, either. So I included the lively ladies of the Bellamy Garden Club, a number of handsome, stalwart men, trouble of the mysterious as well as the romantic kind, and a pack of pooches for good measure—and fun. Always fun, since our Lord blesses us so richly. Not only does he offer us forgiveness, salvation, and eternal life at his side, but he also fills us with his joy.

Thank you for visiting us. Scripture says, "Taste and see that the Lord is good. Oh, the joys of those who trust in him!" I hope you will return to Bellamy to watch Lark and Camellia discover the abundant gifts our heavenly Father has for them as well. Until then, may the Lord richly bless you and fill you with joy.

Ginny Aiken

About the Author

A former newspaper reporter, Ginny Aiken lives in south-central Pennsylvania with her husband and four sons. Born in Havana, Cuba, and raised in Valencia and Caracas, Venezuela, she discovered books early on and wrote her first novel at age fifteen. (She burned it when she turned a "mature" sixteen!) That first effort was followed several years later by her winning entry in the Mid-America Romance Authors' Fiction from the Heartland contest for unpublished authors.

Ginny has certificates in French literature and culture from the University of Nancy, France, and a B.A. in Spanish and French literature from Allegheny College in Pennsylvania. Her first novel was published in 1993, and since then she has published numerous additional novels and novellas. One of her novels was a finalist for *Affaire de Coeur*'s Readers' Choice Award for Best American Historical of 1997, and her work has appeared on various best-seller lists. Ginny's novellas appear in the anthologies *With This Ring, A Victorian Christmas Quilt, A Bouquet of Love,* and *Dream Vacation.*

Magnolia is the first book in this delightful new series called Bellamy's Blossoms. Watch for *Lark,* the second book in the series, coming in Fall 2000.

When she isn't busy with the duties of being a soccer mom, Ginny can be found reading, writing, enjoying classical music, and preparing for her next Bible study.

Current HeartQuest Releases

- *A Bouquet of Love,* Ginny Aiken, Ranee McCollum, Jeri Odell, and Debra White Smith
- *Dream Vacation,* Ginny Aiken, Jeri Odell, and Elizabeth White
- *Faith,* Lori Copeland
- *Finders Keepers,* Catherine Palmer
- *Freedom's Promise,* Dianna Crawford
- *Hope,* Lori Copeland
- *June,* Lori Copeland
- *Magnolia,* Ginny Aiken
- *Prairie Fire,* Catherine Palmer
- *Prairie Rose,* Catherine Palmer
- *Prairie Storm,* Catherine Palmer
- *Reunited,* Judy Baer, Jeri Odell, Jan Duffy, and Peggy Stoks
- *The Treasure of Timbuktu,* Catherine Palmer
- *The Treasure of Zanzibar,* Catherine Palmer
- *A Victorian Christmas Cottage,* Catherine Palmer, Debra White Smith, Jeri Odell, and Peggy Stoks
- *A Victorian Christmas Quilt,* Catherine Palmer, Debra White Smith, Ginny Aiken, and Peggy Stoks
- *A Victorian Christmas Tea,* Catherine Palmer, Dianna Crawford, Peggy Stoks, and Katherine Chute
- *With This Ring,* Lori Copeland, Dianna Crawford, Ginny Aiken, and Catherine Palmer
- *Olivia's Touch,* Peggy Stoks— coming soon (May 2000)
- *Awakening Mercy,* Angela Benson—coming soon (Summer 2000)
- *Freedom's Hope,* Dianna Crawford—coming soon (Summer 2000)
- *Lark,* Ginny Aiken—coming soon (Fall 2000)
- *A Prairie Christmas,* Catherine Palmer, and others—coming soon (Fall 2000)

Other Great Tyndale House Fiction

- *As Sure As the Dawn*, Francine Rivers
- *Ashes and Lace*, B. J. Hoff
- *The Atonement Child*, Francine Rivers
- *The Captive Voice*, B. J. Hoff
- *Cloth of Heaven*, B. J. Hoff
- *Dark River Legacy*, B. J. Hoff
- *An Echo in the Darkness*, Francine Rivers
- *Embers of Hope*, Sally Laity & Dianna Crawford
- *The Fires of Freedom*, Sally Laity & Dianna Crawford
- *The Gathering Dawn*, Sally Laity & Dianna Crawford
- *Home Fires Burning*, Penelope J. Stokes
- *Jewels for a Crown*, Lawana Blackwell
- *The Last Sin Eater*, Francine Rivers
- *Leota's Garden*, Francine Rivers
- *Like a River Glorious*, Lawana Blackwell
- *Measures of Grace*, Lawana Blackwell
- *Remembering You*, Penelope J. Stokes
- *The Shoe Box*, Francine Rivers
- *Song of a Soul*, Lawana Blackwell
- *Storm at Daybreak*, B. J. Hoff
- *The Scarlet Thread*, Francine Rivers
- *The Tangled Web*, B. J. Hoff
- *The Tempering Blaze*, Sally Laity & Dianna Crawford
- *Till We Meet Again*, Penelope J. Stokes
- *The Torch of Triumph*, Sally Laity & Dianna Crawford
- *A Voice in the Wind*, Francine Rivers
- *Vow of Silence*, B. J. Hoff
- *Unveiled*, Francine Rivers—coming soon (Spring 2000)
- *Unspoken*, Catherine Palmer—coming soon (Summer 2000)

HeartQuest Books by Ginny Aiken

The Wrong Man—A feisty young woman makes one last-ditch effort to meet the right man—and it backfires in hilarious fashion. But as she seeks God's will, she learns that the "wrong man" may be just right for her. This novella by Ginny Aiken appears in the anthology *A Bouquet of Love*.

Log Cabin Patch—In a logging camp in turn-of-the-century Washington State, a Log Cabin patch quilt symbolizes the new hope awaiting a lonely young woman. This novella by Ginny Aiken appears in the anthology *A Victorian Christmas Quilt*.

Something Borrowed—Emma's prayers are answered when she inherits a ranch. More than land is at stake, however, when a former bounty hunter disputes her claim. This novella by Ginny Aiken appears in the anthology *With This Ring*.

Magnolia—Magnolia Bellamy is sick and tired of her reputation as one of "Bellamy's Blossoms." If only her parents hadn't been so poetic in naming their three daughters, Maggie wouldn't have to work so hard at proving herself. But prove herself she will! No matter what it takes, Maggie is determined to prevent modern-day carpetbagger Clay Marlowe from swindling both the bank she represents and her client and friend, the charming, elderly Miss Louella Ashworth.

Clay Marlowe, Yankee though he is, finds the prospect of restoring the once-glorious Ashworth Mansion irresistible. Trouble is, he may have to eat the extra cost to bring the project in on budget. And that's before a mysterious outburst of vandalism threatens to drive the costs even higher.

Maggie and Clay—as different as two people can be—clash on everything from money to music. But along the way, each grudgingly begins to admire the other's devotion to their common goal: leaving the past behind and pressing on toward God's plan for the future. But can their growing trust and love withstand a shocking revelation from Clay's past?

Book 1 in the Bellamy's Blossoms series.

Lark—Larkspur Bellamy is back in town, and everyone Richard Desmond meets feels compelled to tell him. As if he didn't already know. Eight months ago, Lark debuted a literary criticism magazine to great acclaim. Now she's gunning for Des Richter, a reclusive playwright, the darling of the literary world. Des Richter gives *no* interviews, but Lark is determined to ferret him out. Little does she know—or reckon with—the true identity of the mysterious writer: her old nemesis, Rich Desmond.

Book 2 in the delightful series Bellamy's Blossoms. Coming in Fall 2000.